MW00436713

ALTERED PLANS

A Novel

Barbara Wesley Hill

Barbara Wesley Hill

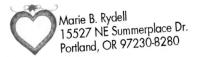

My dearest friend,
Marie —

You made it sound
as if you really liked
Barbara's first book.....
So....Happy Valentine's Day!

Lovingly,
Shari,
Cho and Chu

For two Evelyns

~Evelyn Wesley, my mother.
She passed her love of reading on
to her four daughters.

~Evelyn Hill, my mother by marriage.
She'd have assured
everyone knew about my novels.

~Always, Gene

Title ID: 9055378
ISBN-13: 978-1726132749
ISBN-10: 1726132749

BISAC Code:
Fiction/Christian/Historical/Romance/City & Town Life/
Alabama/Chicago IL/Evanston IL/Birmingham AL

Altered Plans: a novel / Barbara Wesley Hill

Scripture quotes are from the *Holy Bible*,
New International Version© .

Acknowledgements

As in everything, I thank God.

Deep appreciation to my editor, Alison Rouse
and my friend Charlena.
And to countless friends and family—your encouraging
words gave me the courage to continue writing.
I cannot thank you all enough.

Cover Design by Rachel Bostwick

Also, by Barbara Wesley Hill

Only a Breeze

http://www.amazon.com/dp/1546930248

Author Page:
https://www.amazon.com/author/bwhill

ALTERED PLANS

~~ 1 ~~

Chicago, Illinois

Nineteen Fifty-One

Before the ink dried on his diploma, Russell Townsend was hired by *H. H. & J. Architects*, one of the largest, most influential architectural firms in Chicago. He was hand-picked by Julian Hurt, a well-known architect throughout the Midwest.

Fascinated with each aspect of the work, Russell worked tirelessly twelve to fourteen hours a day, six or seven days a week, and loved every minute. He'd been working six months when Mr. Hurt sent for him. "Have a seat, Russell."

"Thank you, sir."

A man of energy, Mr. Hurt remained standing. Physically, he was overweight and rather unattractive, but at six-foot-four, he towered over most men and his booming voice came with authority. As he spoke today, he paced between Russell and the expansive window overlooking the city.

"Russell, I wanted time to see for myself whether you would live up to those glowing reports and predictions I received before hiring you. I rarely *glow*, but I believe in giving credit where it is due and I like what I've seen so far. You come close to matching my insistence on solid foundations for perfectly designed architecture, without cutting corners."

"Thank you, sir."

"You will go far, Russell, if you're consistent and don't get lazy or overly ambitious. Remember, the timing is all mine."

"I will always give my best for the firm."

Returning to his own office, Russell was flying high. Praise from *the* Julian Hurt. The office grapevine, which flourishes in every large corporation, often spoke of the fear this man could generate in anyone.

He likes me.

Any employee entering or exiting Julian Hurt's office was noticed. As Russell exited today, he was aware of nothing other than a deep sense of satisfaction. Others observed him with curiosity, and a number of female employees observed him for reasons other than his position.

"I thought him a Greek god my first day at work," Miss Sheridan was heard to comment. "He walked several feet ahead of me. The way he walked and carried himself was distinctive. Obviously, he doesn't meet Greek-god requirements, not tall enough, but when he turned... I suppose he'd remembered something... I hope I didn't swoon aloud when he began walking toward me. He wasn't what I expected... his nose is a bit too large," she twittered, "but, honey, those eyes got me—the darkest blue eyes I'd ever seen, and against tanned skin with nearly-black hair... my heart still jumps when I see him."

"Have you ever talked with him?"

"No," Miss Sheridan admitted, "only to speak. He's very polite. He'd only have to nod his head in my direction, though...."

Her companion commented, "He is a bit different, I suppose—slender, good build, well-toned but not muscular. He always seems to be at work. I wonder when he has time to exercise?"

"Just can't get those blue eyes against the dark skin out of my mind."

"Ladies, you are gossiping, and it's unattractive," interrupted Mrs. Camp, supervisor of the clerical department.

"Mrs. Camp... is he married?"

"Yes, I believe so, though he seems more committed to the firm than anything else. In addition, young Mr. Townsend is reportedly a nice guy.

"Yes, ladies," she winked, "all of the above and good looks, too, but apparently unavailable. And your break is over."

~ 2 ~

Nineteen Fifty-Three

Work at H. H. & J. Architects went smoothly and time passed quickly. Just after Russell's second anniversary with the firm, he was assigned to the planning team for an important upcoming project for the McGuire brothers—a unique building, to bear their name—hence, the *McGuire Project.*

Mr. Hurt hinted at the possibility of making him a member of the team to oversee the actual building. If appointed to the team to oversee such a significant project, it would be a show of confidence from Mr. Hurt and could likely give Russell the credentials needed to secure his career. Consequently, as Russell studied the blueprints, he was intent on creating precise, detailed figures and notes

A month into the planning, Russell jotted notes as he studied the electrical section of the blueprints.

Knock-knock.

"Come in."

A young man timidly opened the door.

"Well?"

"Yes, sir. I'm Alan Parker, a new courier. I am to pick up the original blueprints for the McGuire Project. The draftsman has realized a copy isn't in his safe. I am to return it to you before the end of the day."

He observed the young man, who was close to his own age. "The *original…* for Bill Trinney? I'm *working* with the blueprints—I have a deadline to meet."

"He needs the original to make a clear copy for his records, but I can come back later."

A bit unusual, negligent actually that Bill didn't make a copy for his own safekeeping. Often the draftsman keeps the original himself.

Bill Trinney had headed the planning team and drafted the final blueprint. Russell might now suggest minor changes, but his time was primarily spent re-figuring material costs and sources before the second contract was finalized with the McGuire brothers.

"Tell you what, Alan, I have a lunch meeting shortly, which should allow plenty of time for a copy. Come back in thirty minutes and pick it up. Just stay with it while Bill makes a copy. Bring it straight back and give it to no one but *me* before I leave tonight."

He'd barely changed position or moved more than a few feet from the work table when Alan returned. He rolled the blueprints and slid them into the leather cylinder.

"Return only to me, Alan. Clear?"

"Yes, sir."

Russell grabbed his jacket from the chair and locked his desk and office door as he left for the meeting. Returning two hours later, a secretary handed him several phone messages, all deemed urgent.

"There goes the rest of my day."

As expected, he was on the phone for hours. Alan came in at five-thirty with the blueprints, and quietly motioned to the drafting table with a questioning expression. Russell nodded and mouthed *thank you* as Alan exited.

Locking his office later, he thought again of the young man who called him *sir*. He gave himself a mental pat on the back for being in a position of respect. It was almost nine o'clock. He hadn't taken a day off in two weeks and was exhausted. Yet another night he would not be home before ten.

I miss time with family, but it's worth it. If not for planning and hard work, I could have been the courier this afternoon, rather than the architect. And this is only the beginning.

Each December, the firm held a grand Christmas party in the ballroom of the Lancer Hotel, one of the firm's best-known projects several years prior. All employees were invited, right down to the cleaning crew. No family members or guests were included, with the exception of wives of the board members. The food was gourmet, liquor flowed freely and a well-known band played. No one wanted to miss the event of the year.

"Good evening, Mr. Hurt… Mrs. Hurt. It's a lovely evening, as usual."

"Russell, you may call me Julian outside formal meetings."

"Thank you, sir." Russell beamed. He admired Mr. Hurt—his money, power, influence, knowledge—and wife. Mrs. Hurt was one of the most gorgeous women he'd ever seen, face and figure to match. He'd heard others remark that it was like meeting beauty and the beast. Julian Hurt had everything life could offer as far as Russell could see. And he liked *him*.

Other reasons to attend the firm's Christmas party were the elaborate gifts and bonuses dispensed, and important announcements made.

"Ladies and gentlemen," Mr. Hurt's voice boomed over the microphone.

The partners had gathered to express individual holiday greetings. Several announcements had been made about the coming years' projects, plans, and promotions. Mr. Hurt now had the platform. Having gained everyone's attention, he continued. "We have one more thing before we bid you good night. You have all heard of the upcoming McGuire Project, though details have been closely guarded. Construction will soon begin, and we have finalized the list of those appointed to the team to actually oversee the building from foundation to completion. They are Joel Herndon, Samuel Barton, Russell Townsend..."

Russell heard no more. He'd just opened the envelope containing his bonus check, which was significant, but this assignment meant much more. Mr. Hurt had made good on his word. This project would be one of the most exciting in the world of architecture, a unique office building expected to be the talk of Chicago, as the McGuire brothers had requested. He was enthusiastic about the assignment and the building itself, which would be magnificent. At the age of twenty-seven, he was a rising star in the world of architecture.

I cannot wait to tell Brenda. What a Christmas gift! He smiled at the thought—Brenda's sweetness always brought a wave of happiness.

At the same time, his heart swelled with pride. The words of a former teacher echoed in his mind, "You've chosen a good career and should expect to make a good living. Nevertheless, it would be in your best interest to put aside thoughts of getting into the top-tier firms. Without powerful connections, it does not happen."

He knew I had no connections. I'd worked my way through school. But I did get in, on my own. I'd like to see his face now... and I'm just beginning. Nineteen fifty-four will be a very good year.

Russell failed to remember a teaching from his youth.

Do not boast about tomorrow, for you do not know what a day may bring.

~ 3 ~

Nineteen Fifty-Four

In spite of the snow and ice, groundbreaking for the McGuire Building took place in early February. A faint hint of the unique design became visible in May, already gaining attention. The building team was pleased with the progress and took pleasure in sending weekly reports to the firm's partners.

Discussing wiring with the electrician at the job site one morning, Russell was interrupted.

"Mr. Townsend?"

"Yes."

"I'm from Mr. Hurt's office with a message. He'd like you to read it and give me your reply."

This was unusual, but Russell opened the sealed envelope and began reading.

"From the Desk of Julian Hurt
May 7, 1954

Russell,

I received disturbing news about a structure going up in St. Louis, Missouri, which looks quite similar to our McGuire project, though the St. Louis building is further along. I hope you can explain.

Report to the conference room adjacent to my office at two o'clock this afternoon. All partners will be present.

Julian Hurt"

Russell stared at the note, reading it once more. The courier cleared his throat. Russell glanced at him, then back at the note.

"Mr. Townsend? Shall I return to Mr. Hurt with a message?"

"Tell him I will be there promptly at two," he replied. It was only nine o'clock. His stomach churned. He had no explanation and no idea exactly what Julian meant. All partners would be present? He returned to the task at hand and worked until twelve. He would return to his office to freshen up, at least change shirts and put on another tie. Then he would have time to think about the situation. Perhaps he was imagining too much.

At five minutes before two, Russell presented himself to Julian's secretary. "Yes, Mr. Townsend, the board members are here, but Mr. Hurt asked that you wait until he calls for you."

The fifteen-minute wait seemed an hour. At ten past two, Mr. Hurt buzzed his secretary. "Send Mr. Townsend in, please."

Russell rose and smiled as she opened the conference room door for him. He sensed sympathy in her eyes, a look he'd never experienced.

As he entered the conference room, he was well aware of the presence of each board member. With the exception of Mr. Hurt, they sat around the enormous mahogany table observing him as a jury might view the accused. No one spoke or smiled. There was nothing to put him at ease. Mr. Hurt stood behind his chair at one end of the table.

"Have a seat, Mr. Townsend," Mr. Hurt instructed.

There was one vacant chair. He'd called him *Mr. Townsend*, removing any hint of friendship, or that he might relax a bit. As Russell sat, Mr. Hurt turned to the portable screen beside the table and nodded to an employee who started the projector. A clear picture of a building in progress appeared on the screen.

Russell gasped. It was the McGuire Building! There was no mistaking the outline, the distinct roofline and unique entrance. How could this be?

"Well, Mr. Townsend?" Mr. Hurt demanded, his voice filling the conference room. "Do you deny this being an exact duplicate of *our* building which was to be one-of-a-kind—the one all Chicago would discuss?"

Russell couldn't speak.

"Not to *mention* the exorbitant amount of money the McGuire brothers have paid our firm for a unique building! Mr. *Townsend*, can you explain?"

The room was totally silent. Not even the sound of breathing could be heard. Appropriate, he thought—it was as if he was attending his own funeral. He looked into each face and finally looked Mr. Hurt in the eye. He gripped the heavy table with sweaty hands to steady himself before standing.

"I have no explanation, Mr. Hurt... board members... I am as shocked as any of you." In desperation, he searched the board members' faces. "May I... respectfully... ask why I am the only member of the planning team called in?"

"The blueprints were given into *your* safekeeping," replied Mr. Stockton, a senior partner. "You have been asked for an explanation. Have you shared the blueprints with anyone, taken them home, or left them unattended even for a short time?"

"No, sir. Before construction began, I made notes as I studied them. When I left my office, the blueprints were locked inside a safe and my door locked. I was very careful."

"To your knowledge, they never left your office? You didn't show them to anyone outside our team?"

"Of course not."

Julian Hurt spoke again, looking only at Russell. "Do you know what this does to our credibility? Do you know this makes the McGuire Project almost totally useless, as well as our being a laughingstock? People are already talking behind our backs, saying we've tried to copy another's work and make a big splash as if no one would notice. We stand to lose our reputation as *well* as a fortune."

Russell's mind raced. "I assume you have discussed this with Bill Trinney, sir. As the originator, it seems he would be the first person to come to mind. How careful has *he* been?"

Incredulous, Mr. Hurt roared again, "Bill has been with us for ten years. He hopes to be a partner one day and it may happen soon. I trust him implicitly."

"Well..." Russell began hesitantly, "He *did* let the original go without having a copy in his possession. And he didn't realize his mistake for months."

Mr. Hurt was growing angrier, his face red. "On what *basis* do you make such an accusation?"

"The fact that he sent a courier to me before construction began, confessing his mistake. He needed the original from me to make a copy." Russell was aware of eyebrows rising all over the room.

"*Facts*, Mr. Townsend. When did this happen, did you comply, and, if so, how long were the blueprints out of your sight? Also, who *was* this courier?"

Sweat had formed on Russell's brow as he struggled... to think... to remember. Could he be blamed if there was cause to believe Bill Trinney, the person who originated the blueprints, had put the company in this position? Had Trinney sold them out?

"It was during the first week of August, Wednesday or Thursday... around noon, because I had to leave for a lunch meeting. The young man's name was Alan Parker. I remember because it was the same as a teacher I had in high school. He returned the blueprints about five-thirty the same evening. I was on the phone, but he put them on my drafting table and I checked them before locking them in the safe for the night."

No one spoke or moved. Mr. Hurt finally sat, looking around at the board members. "Russell." A glimmer of relief spread over Russell—he'd called him by his first name.

"Yes, sir?"

"Return to your office. Remain there until you hear from me. And speak with no one in the meantime."

"Yes, sir."

It was to be an excruciating hour and a half wait.

Knock, knock.

Russell rose quickly to open his office door.

Julian Hurt entered the office solemnly and sat in one of the large leather chairs. Without a word, he motioned for Russell to sit across from him.

"Russell, this is one of the worst days of my life. I trusted you and saw a bright future for you in our firm. Please don't interrupt or you will be fired without another word.

"I spoke with Bill Trinney in the presence of the board members. He denied each of your statements. He showed us the copy from his safe, dated on the date he originally completed it, months before the incident you mentioned… or dreamed. He knows nothing of a courier and never sent anyone for blueprints… at *any* time. In addition, I checked with our personnel office. We've never had an employee by the name Parker and no new couriers within the past year.

"Therefore, I do not know whether you fabricated your story or whether something was pulled over on you. You have, however, shown less intelligence than I expected, and have admitted to letting the blueprints go with a person unknown to you. You're to blame for the blueprints getting into other hands, causing irreparable damage to our company. It will cost us money, jobs, reputation, and probably astronomical court costs. You are *fired* as of this moment—dismissed from the firm without compensation.

"You may take nothing except the certificate on your wall, which, I promise, will be worth nothing. You will likely never work again as an architect. You actually owe me thanks for not pressing charges—you could have gone to prison."

"Sir…" Russell began.

"No. Get your coat and that thing off the wall… no, not the briefcase; it stays. The security guard is at the door to escort you out and collect your keys."

Russell walked slowly to the coat rack, removed his light jacket and heavier coat. He looked at his diploma a few feet away, beautifully framed and proudly hung. He removed it and held it under his arm as he turned to look at Julian… Mr. Hurt.

"I *am* sorry. I did not knowingly do anything wrong… Julian. Apparently, I took a young man at face value who claimed to be a courier for the firm. He lied, hurt people I care about and ruined me. I'd like to think the truth might come out in time, but it appears there is little chance. In any case, I made a huge mistake."

His eyes were brimming with tears. Not wanting to further humiliate himself, he exited quickly. On the way to the elevator, he located the key ring in his pocket. As he stepped into the elevator, he removed his car and apartment keys before handing the remainder to the guard. Getting off the elevator, he looked at no one. He had to get home before he collapsed.

I've lost everything… everything of any importance. It's all over. At twenty-eight years old, I'm a failure. How can a life crumble in less than eight hours? I was on my way to the top... I deserved to get there. Where did I go wrong?

He had one bright light left in his life. But how could he ever explain *this* to Brenda?

Still in shock, he walked in the direction of his apartment, his mind reeling.

Along his route, sidewalk planters had recently been filled with bright spring flowers and the few trees along the street had budded with the promise of new life and new beginnings. In the distance, colorful kites fluttered high above and boaters enjoyed the perfect May weather on Lake Michigan.

Russell was aware of none of it.

The most important project—my life—has been crumbling, unnoticed. As a house built from a perfect blueprint and the best materials on a poor foundation, it collapsed. But I thought my foundation solid!

His vision of becoming an architect began long before completion of junior high school. In his mind was a carefully-drawn blueprint and the realization that hard work was required every step of the way to bring it to fruition. And he did work hard. He made top grades throughout junior and senior high school in order to qualify for the best architectural school. Once accepted, he surpassed each requirement, graduating at the top of his class. His cornerstone was set.

The actual building began when he was hired by H. H. & J. Architects.

I followed the plan perfectly. Yet, everything important is gone.

I can't create an entirely new project now… from ground up without a blueprint, from materials and a rough plan not my own.

Numb with disbelief, he realized he'd reached his apartment.

He was right in his latest assessment—he could not successfully build a solid foundation, a life… *alone.*

Russell Townsend yet had much to learn.

~~ 4 ~~

Beacon, Alabama

September, Nineteen Fifty-Four

Dare Perry parked in the teachers' parking lot across from Beacon Elementary School to wait for her sister, Doreen, who taught third grade. She leaned back to relax, knowing the wait would be at least thirty minutes. Her sister had asked that she follow her to the new automotive shop across town, where she would leave her car. Dare would take her home from there.

How cute the children are as they end their school day, she thought. Many were in straight lines, happily walking to their assigned buses. Others were being instructed to be orderly as they waited in a separate area to be picked up by parents. A smaller group appeared more independent, apparently walking home. Her attention was drawn to two small girls holding hands, both blond and laughing. *Sweet, probably sisters.* Suddenly they saw someone.

"Pop!" they shouted.

The girls were evidently surprised and delighted to see their father waiting for them. They ran to him, vying to be first into his open arms. Such open, *mutual* joy between parent and child. Observing from her car, the scene somehow filled Dare with joy as well.

Witnessing their laughter and delight, one might assume they'd been apart a while. She knew this wasn't the case—it had been only a few days since her sister pointed the man out to her. His name was Russell Townsend, a widower with two daughters and new to the area. She wasn't acquainted with other young widowers, but she'd bet most did not embrace fatherhood with the exuberance she was witnessing. She was mesmerized by the scene... each girl took one of her father's hands and began walking down the sidewalk, continuing to laugh and talk.

Long after the trio disappeared, she continued to stare in the direction they'd walked. *How can I be so enthralled watching strangers?*

The girls *were* surprised and thrilled to see him waiting for them after school. It was a short walk. They arrived home before covering all the day's news.

Entering the house, they shouted, "We'll race you up the stairs."

He smiled, pretending exhaustion. "Might be I'll be too tired to play *Jacks*."

"No! We'll have them out when you get upstairs."

He looked around to see whether anyone stood in a doorway frowning at the noise. All was clear.

Russell thought about the day he'd registered them in their new school, the day after Labor Day. Their new landlady had reassured him, "You'll have no problem registering the first day of school."

He was thankful all had gone smoothly. Walking toward the school, he'd noticed the large windows in most classrooms raised in hopes of a rare breeze. He was not accustomed to such high temperatures in September,

The property and structures were impressive for a town the size of Beacon. The grounds were immaculately kept, as were the buildings, though old. The elementary school was separate from the high school on the same property. With no window screens, insects appeared to invade classrooms, though the high school boys didn't seem to mind as they sat on the wide windowsills shouting or whistling at the girls outside... until a teacher entered the room.

Russell, Rose and Ella Townsend were living temporarily at a boarding house a block from the school. On the first day, they left early to walk to their new school. The middle-class neighborhood was pleasant and well-kept. Russell observed children walking from many of the homes, which made him feel it safe for the girls to walk alone. And they had each other.

Entering the school, children and parents were milling around in the wide hallway. The office was just inside to his right. Inside the reception area, he noted the door to the office marked *Principal* was closed. The reception area was noisy and busy, with the phone ringing and several parents competing for the secretary's attention. The name plate on the counter read, "Miss Ginger Lee Cotton." She looked up as the bell on the door jangled.

She instructed pleasantly, "Sign in. I'm going as fast as I can."

He signed the book and the three of them sat to one side. He was happy for the opportunity to observe the secretary and a few locals as they interacted. All were friendly and relatively cooperative, though insistent with their requests. Miss Cotton appeared efficient and patient under the circumstances. She was young, mid-twenties, rather tall, probably five-foot-eight, brown hair to her shoulders, smooth skin, recently tanned from summer, with large, sparkling brown eyes. She wore a bright blue sundress and moved with energy and grace, as if she had worked here many years. Unlikely, at her age.

Surprisingly, the reception area cleared in less than fifteen minutes.

"Mr. Townsend?"

Their eyes met. He felt connected with her as she gave him her full, welcoming attention.

She's very observant and seems to care about people. She has a good figure, too... great, actually.

"Yes, Miss Cotton?"

She held her hand out as they shook hands. *I haven't held a woman's hand since Brenda.*

"Call me Ginger Lee. Not *Gingerly*—Ginger Lee," she laughed. "I *oughta* drop the Lee, but I'm used to it and so's everyone I know. You're new here. These your girls?"

He completed the required forms and returned them.

"Looks fine. The principal will finalize the enrollment and she's available," she informed, motioning them toward the closed door. With a quick tap on the door, she opened it and introduced them to the principal, Mrs. Greer, a pleasant-looking middle-aged woman.

Russell had the girl's birth certificates and most current medical records. "I'm sorry I don't have Rose's report card from first grade, but she did well and was promoted."

Scanning the paperwork, Mrs. Greer replied, "Perfectly all right, Mr. Townsend. I understand. Rose will be placed in a second-grade classroom, Ella in first. I trust you and your daughters will feel welcome to our school and our town. I believe you'll be happy with the school and they will enjoy being here. Our building is old, but we're proud of our teachers and high standards."

Though Mrs. Greer appeared to be in her fifties, her clothing and manner seemed better suited to one much older. Russell correctly guessed she'd had to work hard to gain the position of principal, but he was amused as she straightened her back to add, "Our standards are as high as any big-city school."

She continued to look over the forms. Frowning, she inquired. "Your home address, Mr. Townsend? Is this a mistake? I believe the address listed is Miss Broadnax's Boarding House."

"Yes, it's temporary, but I'll let you know when we move."

Mrs. Greer didn't appear at all understanding of this particular small fact, but as she considered a response, Ella took the reins.

"We call her *Miss Bee,* and her house feels like home. She's almost the nicest woman I ever met. She checks on us when Pop is gone and gets milk for us every afternoon. Usually cookies, too. She won't like us to leave… ever."

Ella flashed her broad smile at Mrs. Greer before looking at her sister. "Right, Rose?"

Rose hesitated only a moment before nodding and looking up at Mrs. Greer with her own adorable smile.

"Well, then," replied Mrs. Greer, once more agreeable, "everything seems just fine. Ginger Lee will take the girls to their classrooms and introduce them to their teachers. You may go along with them, Mr. Townsend."

Still puzzled, Mrs. Greer observed them as they left her office. *Living in the boarding house—unbelievable. I've never known Irma Rae Broadnax to allow children. Moreover, that's surely the first time I've heard her referred to nicely in twenty years… she's an old sour-puss.*

Less than twenty minutes later, the girls were in their classrooms and Russell was ready to leave.

At the front entrance, Ginger Lee put her hand on his arm. "You need anything, let me know. May I call you Russell? Most of us go by first names."

"Of course. Thank you."

She beamed as he left. *He liked me, his smile was one of interest. And I don't care about the two kids. Good looking... polite... educated. His eyes... I've never seen such dark blue against such beautifully-tanned skin. I'm for sure gonna check him out further.*

Russell contemplated her as well. *First names right away. She said to let her know if I needed anything. And she's attractive. A bit bold, but perhaps she's simply outgoing, trying to make a newcomer feel welcome. But, I don't have room in my life for a woman. She'd never understand. After a while perhaps... but I can't live always looking back. I must look forward... to re-building our lives.*

~~ 5 ~~

Two weeks into the school term, Dare stopped at the school to give Doreen a ride to the mechanic's shop to pick up her car.

Just as Doreen reached her car, she stopped to speak to a student. Keeping the conversation brief, Dare heard the child say, "Thank you, Mrs. Miller."

Dare smiled. "Doreen, you've been married five years and it still sounds strange to hear you called *Mrs. Miller.*"

"I know, it doesn't seem possible I've been a married lady so long... been a *good* five years, though. Hey, thanks for the ride. It's worked out fine for Bobby to drop me off in the mornings and Connie has been sweet about taking me home. I didn't want to ask her to drive all the way across town, though." She laughed, "Much easier to inconvenience my sister."

"You know I don't mind." As Doreen got out of the car, Dare called out, "Hope your car's good as new. See you Thursday night."

Dare always looked forward to time with her older sister. With only a two-year age difference, they enjoyed a close relationship though Doreen was very protective.

At home, she unlocked her door and kicked off her high heels. "Ahhhh." Within a few minutes, she'd removed her stockings and slipped on her favorite house slippers. In the small kitchen, she poured a glass of iced tea to carry to the front porch and the recently purchased outdoor rocker. *One of my favorite times of the day. Between work and the evening routine of supper, phone calls, correspondence, and readying for the next day, it's heavenly to do nothing but stretch out and relax.*

She began to rock comfortably as she looked about the neighborhood. The air remained hot, but she felt a slight breeze, reminding her she'd soon see the first signs of fall. Dare loved this old neighborhood. When she began looking for a house, she'd had three neighborhoods in mind and was determined to wait until an affordable house was available in one of them.

When the real estate sign went up, she'd phoned the same day. Papers were signed by the end of the week and she'd lived here almost a year. *Old, but well-built and brick. Many on the block are two-story houses, lovely, but not what I needed—this is one of the few smaller homes. I knew I'd love it before even walking inside. It's perfect for me and my budget.*

She sighed, realizing an hour had passed. As she rose, she heard children playing in the distance. *Probably the Mason girls—what sweethearts.* Unbidden, the image from the previous week returned... *the father with his daughters, I can clearly picture them. Him... the dark, thick hair, a little unruly, as a young boy. His laugh, robust and genuine... I could hear it through my open car window. What an intriguing man...* with *two lively daughters.*

**

Dare had invited her sister for supper Thursday night, as Doreen's husband, Bobby, was out of town a few days. They had always been close. Though different in appearance as well as personality, they shared almost everything.

Doreen was tall with light brown hair, described by her as *mousy*—Dare saw it as *soft*. Her eyes were a bright blue, and her skin, admittedly, less than perfect. "Good thing I have this drop-dead figure," she'd laughed. "Bobby says he loves me for my sparkling personality and lilting laugh... but my personality wasn't what caught his eye in the first place."

Doreen wasn't exaggerating about her figure and, despite her sister's description of herself, Dare thought her appearance quite regal. Because of her happy personality and love of making people laugh, she inadvertently gave the impression of being a scatterbrain in spite of the fact that she was a school teacher. But she was the most generous, kind-hearted person in the world. She generally saw the best in people, but had an uncanny ability to see past the presented image straight to the person inside—the real personality. And she spoke her mind… always.

The sisters were both outgoing, but Dare saw herself as more cautious, less trusting.

After supper, they settled onto the sofa with bowls of ice cream as Doreen reported the school news. "Nothing very interesting, obviously, when our main topic is the new cafeteria menu. It even tops discussing the new teacher—she'd been substituting a year, so we already knew her. And, she's so *nice*, there was not a single snide remark from any staff member," she laughed. "What about *your* job, anything exciting there?"

Dare worked at the American Tire Corporation, the area's largest employer, known as *ATC* to the locals.

"Well, something I'll share with you, though I'm sure it's been noticed by others. As I've feared, Jenny Lewis is involved with a new supervisor. He's been here six months and is at least ten years older than Jenny. He's never been married and, admittedly good looking, but I think there must be a *reason* for his never marrying."

"People will say that exact thing about *you* in a few years…"

"Never mind your meddling in *my* life… point is we don't know much about this guy. He came from Washington State. I wonder if he may have been married and isn't being honest.

I don't think they do enough background checks. At the same time, I tell myself it's wrong to be so suspicious."

"Jenny is about nineteen, isn't she?"

"Yes, and Mr. Harrell is at least thirty, a little older than *me*. I'm afraid she's making a big mistake. I haven't said anything but wonder if I should. I don't think Jenny has dated much. She has a bit of inferiority complex due to her weight, making her more vulnerable. But she's such a good person, always has been… kind-hearted and giving."

"So… you were never interested in him? He's the right age for *you*."

"When he walked in the first day, I thought *maybe*… tall, charming, sharp dresser. By the end of the week, I changed my mind. Can't say why exactly. Maybe *too* nice a package."

"But, Dare, you do tend to find fault with any new male who shows up. You don't *want* to be interested, honey."

"Possibly… but I'm really worried Jenny is making a big mistake. It feels wrong not to speak up when you think a friend may be walking into a fire."

"People in love rarely listen."

"I guess. I think she may be infatuated and mistaking it for love. And he's leading her on—I know he is. I'll think about it a while but I believe I need to say something to her about it."

As casually as possible, Dare changed the subject. "Speaking of good-looking, *interesting* men, what about the guy with the two girls who just moved into town?"

"Russell Townsend. Nice. Cordial. Attractive, I guess. You know I stopped noticing those things when I got married."

Spoken so seriously, Dare absorbed every word.

Doreen burst into laughter. "Of *course,* I noticed. I'm not shopping, but I can still *admire* the market."

Dare giggled. "Bet you don't confess that to Bobby."

"Well, no, and I tell him not to be looking around at other women, but I'm not crazy and he's not blind, after all. It's just like noticing whether you have long or short hair, or whether you're wearing jeans or your Sunday best... you notice when someone is good looking."

"I get it. But you have a way of going all around something without getting to the point."

"The point? Oh... Mr. Townsend. Good looking in an unusual way and seems pleasant. Everything is about his girls, though. No one who's talked with him has learned much other than he's from the Chicago, Illinois area and is a widower, which, to my knowledge, he hasn't actually discussed. It seems his wife's death was fairly recent. Tell you what I'm thinking—I think her death was connected with the *seiche* in Chicago. It was in June, and they came from that area. *And*, he doesn't seem to want to talk about it—such a horrible event would certainly be unsettling to discuss."

"The *what*? I have no idea what you're talking about."

"Sorry. You know me, always the school teacher. This summer I saw an article in our newspaper about a tragedy in Chicago caused by an unusual storm. It intrigued me enough to look it up in the encyclopedia in the library. One of these days, I'm going to buy a set of encyclopedias to have at *home*—you can find anything, it's fascinating. I want *Britannica*. I'm not exaggerating, you find *every*thing. Mark my word, in twenty years, every home will have a set—you won't be able to get through school without it. *And*, you'd never get rid of them because history doesn't change; you just buy their updates every few years. *World Book* is good, too."

Dare was losing patience. Her sister was wonderful, her favorite person, but she did tend to talk too much and often forgot the point of her own conversation.

"*Teacher*... please. What about this... *thing* you believe caused Mr. Townsend's wife's death?"

"I've done it again, haven't I?"

Dare rolled her eyes.

"Okay. The newspaper reported on a rare storm, *seich,* in Chicago, in June of this year. I looked up *storms* in the encyclopedia. This type is spelled s-e-i-c-h-e, but pronounced, *saysh,* like the bow we tie on the back of a girl's dress. It's a rare storm surge. When the storm front has passed, the water rushes back into place.

"The one in the newspaper in Chicago had a towering wave estimated to be *eight feet high* sweeping up the shoreline! The article described it as similar to an inland tidal wave.

"Anyway, a number of people were killed. Mind you, honey, Mr. Townsend didn't *say* how his wife died. He hasn't given any details. It was just easy to put two and two together. It must have been horrible."

Sad to have his wife die so tragically, and suddenly, leaving him with two little girls. No wonder he wanted to get away from the area and make a fresh start. He must have a deep loneliness, but he hides it well.

~~ 6 ~~

Dare had driven the same rural route to work for eight years. It was generally a twenty-minute drive and had become her best time to think. Driving in Friday morning, she was aware how little had changed—perhaps a house being remodeled or a trailer being moved to or from a lot, but that was all. Today, as she crossed the unused railroad tracks, she noticed a stack of wood beside what appeared to be the remains of a small building foundation.

I wonder what the wood is for?

She drew more than one appreciative look from men in passing cars. Traffic was sparse on this back road, but she drew appreciative looks everywhere. She was an attractive woman, with expressive pale blue eyes, and honey-blond, naturally wavy hair, worn slightly below the shoulder. She had a figure her closest friends envied—the one physical attribute she and her sister had in common. Her mother had described her as a *classic beauty,* which had honestly aggravated her.

Sure, except for the fact that I'm barely five-foot-two. I have trouble finding clothes in styles that aren't childish. Can't reach anything in the grocery store, and have to wear high heels to look professional or dressed up. I just hate being short. Dad and Mom were tall, and Doreen is five-eight, leaving me to feel like the family midget. Mom would say, 'It's who you are, honey. Your sister would give anything for your perfect skin and blonde hair. My goodness, maybe the Lord didn't give you more height to keep you humble,' her mother laughed.

Now, at twenty-six-years-old, I'm a humble, classic beauty. I have a job and a small house, for which I am

thankful, but I seldom go out and go home alone each night.
Not much of a resume, after all.

Dare had no desire to attend college after graduating from high school, though encouraged by Doreen. She'd enjoyed typing and shorthand classes in high school and was hired by ATC soon after graduation. Gradually moving up from file clerk to the clerical pool, she was selected to her current position of division secretary three years prior.

As well as being the largest company in the area, ATC was the best-paying company as well. Friends, acquaintances, even people she barely knew, often phoned her home or stopped her in town to ask assistance in getting a job. "They're not satisfied to just be told where to get an application. Doreen, I promise you, I'm going to start telling everyone that I drive those big ol' trucks to test industrial-size tires."

She'd been almost angry. Doreen, on the other hand, found it comical and began to laugh heartily. "It is *not* funny, Doreen. You're not the one who receives calls practically every night."

"Oh *yes, it is*," her sister choked out between laughter and snorts, "I've got this picture in my mind of you with an *ATC* cap pulled down over your ears while your short little legs try to climb up in that big ol' truck! *That*, little sister, is hilarious!"

Presented with such a vivid picture, Dare began to smile, finally giggling along with her sister. Minutes later, they were doubled over in laughter.

Later Dare declared, "This calls for a double-chocolate sundae, your treat. You owe me one for all the ridicule I endure."

Truth was, Dare was secretary to the director of the personnel division, where all the hiring (*and* firing) was done. Not only did she not readily share specific information, she avoided it at all costs. But it wasn't easy to sidestep when you lived in a town of less than twenty thousand people.

Fridays were always particularly stressful at work and she happily looked forward to the weekend. *Another work week finished. But what am I going to have for supper? It's hard to cook for one.*

She recalled her mother telling her she needed to learn to *wait.* "Good things… *better*, things will come in time."

The nostalgia came over her again. *Mom's been gone almost three years, but I miss her every day—and Daddy, too, though he went long before. They both died too young. Thank God for my sister—we're still a family. Doreen and Bobby are thinking of growing their family—that will change things.*

She turned on the car radio, choosing music with a lively beat.

At home, depositing her keys in the glass dish on the kitchen counter, she glanced around at the sunny yellow walls. "It will help me start my mornings cheerfully," she'd explained to Doreen and her husband, Bobby, when they helped her move.

Bobby grinned. "You get any more cheerful, we're gonna have you examined."

As she tossed a dish towel at him, he laughed and headed out to the truck for another box.

I am *happy. I'm blessed with a good job, my own home, my sweet Doreen and Bobby, good health, and friends. Is it my aspiration to come home to a quiet house and cook for one the rest of my life? Maybe it is. I want a simple life. In my experience, men tend only to complicate life, which I never want again.*

She woke at eight o'clock on Saturday morning.

It's delicious to sleep in after five days of getting up at five-thirty. She stretched lazily and remained in bed a few more minutes before rising to go into the kitchen. She plugged in the percolator, which she'd readied the night before.

Doreen said she was over-organized, which she denied. The phrase came to mind as she picked up her To-Do list, which included the amount of time to accomplish each task. Well... *maybe.*

A trip to Connor's Hardware Store was a treat. She wasn't especially handy with repairs, but she always found interesting items, and Daniel Connor was such a nice guy. He greeted customers as if they were old friends, and many were. Additionally, no other store had free, hot, fresh popcorn at the entrance every day.

"Good morning, Daniel. It's a little early for popcorn. May I get it on my way out?"

"You bet. What are you looking for today? I'm at your service."

"Need a new mailbox. It needed to be replaced when I moved in. Standard size. You still add the house number free?"

"Yep. We have a good stock. There are a few variations. The wall-mounted boxes are on aisle nine. Go on over. I see Mandy signaling me to the phone, so I'll meet you there in a few minutes."

"Sure. No hurry. I enjoy browsing here." Watching Daniel cross the store, she observed him speaking to everyone he passed. *Doubt there are many guys like that big, towering man anymore. His heart is as large as his stature. He's been married to the same woman forty years and speaks of her almost as if they were still on their honeymoon.*

She looked over the mailboxes, more varied than expected. All were black, but there were several differences in what she'd called standard... sizes of mail slots and location for outgoing mail.

She'd almost decided when a pleasant male voice came from behind. "Daniel sent me over. He had a phone call."

She turned to face Mr. Townsend.

"How may I help?"

Taken aback, she replied, "Oh... I think I know... this one looks fine." Dare was suddenly aware of her casual appearance and wished for her slim skirt and high heels.

He smiled... the smile she seemed to have memorized from afar.

He held out his hand. "I'm Russell Townsend, fairly new here."

"Hi. I'm Dare Perry," she replied, holding her hand out to him.

"You do need to consider the back of the mailbox. Some hang differently. Do you know how your current box was put in place?"

It's so unfair that a man in comfortable work clothes can still look good. He has sawdust scattered over his shirt.

She turned the mailbox over. "I haven't taken the old one down, but it is flat against the brick and this size."

"You're probably safe then, and I'm sure you are aware you may bring it back if it's not right. Is there anything else you need?"

"No, thanks. Nice to meet you, Mr. Townsend."

"Call me Russell. Seems everyone here is on a first-name basis."

He has a bit of sawdust in his hair, too... it's so thick and dark... his handshake is strong...

"And call me Dare. I saw you at the school one day. You were picking your daughters up and they were so happy to see you." Realizing she'd been more detailed than necessary, she laughed and explained, "I was waiting in my car for my sister. She teaches there."

Russell liked Beacon's small-town atmosphere but wasn't sure he liked people knowing his every move. "Yes, it was the first time I'd met them after school. If there's nothing else you need, I'll get back to the lumber yard. Nice to meet you, Dare."

And he was gone.

She watched as he departed abruptly. *I must have made a great impression on him. He couldn't get away fast enough. And I think I'd like to get acquainted with him. Maybe I won't be such a blabbermouth if I see him again.*

As she checked out, Daniel came to speak with her again. "Sorry to desert you, but I 'spect Russell took good care of you," he winked. "Widower, you know, his wife was killed in a *seiche* in Chicago. He's a really nice guy and a good worker."

"He introduced himself. Didn't seem especially friendly, though."

"What? Hard to believe. Any guy with eyes in his head would be friendly to *you*. Maybe he was intimidated. I'm not teasing—he could have been. Either that or not as smart as I thought."

"Have a nice *day*, Daniel," she laughed, as she left munching the hot popcorn she would consider lunch. Looking down at her old jeans and worn tennis shoes, and aware she'd taken no time with her hair, she doubted Russell Townsend had been intimidated.

**

Walking back to the boarding house after work, Russell's mind was a flurry. *How long can we live in one room and without a car? I need to make better progress with my work situation... but I'm thankful for a job, and when I work on Saturdays, it's only a half-day, which is good for Rose and Ella.*

Miss Perry... Dare... was attractive. My reaction to her telling me about seeing me with the girls at the school was perhaps unreasonable. It was the thought of someone secretly observing us that was upsetting—but it wasn't that way, and I was rude. She's beautiful... petite... I almost thought she was a child when I turned down the aisle. Stunning, even in jeans... perfect skin and a smile so open when she introduced herself, accepting of a newcomer. Until I turned on the ice and abruptly walked away. Perhaps I'll get another chance.

~~ 7 ~~

Rose and Ella discovered the game of Jacks the first day of school. Hearing about the game they enjoyed so much, Russell made a stop at Woolworth's Dime Store. He was surprised to see how small the entire package was... a miniature ball and ten small metal game pieces. It was an inexpensive, quiet game they could play in their room. He could enjoy it with them as well, though it proved to be more difficult than he'd expected—bouncing the ball and quickly picking up the tiny Jacks. Perhaps his larger hands were a handicap.

They were playing when he returned from work.

"Hi, Pop," they greeted.

Rose bragged, "I'm getting better at Jacks. Some of the girls play at recess. Sometimes Teacher won't let us, though. She thinks we need to be running or skipping rope."

"Her name is Mrs. Jennings," Russell reminded.

"It's hard to remember so many new names. I knew everybody at my old school. It's not fun being new." Rose's mood had changed quickly, not unusual for her, but Russell couldn't let the mood linger.

"So many new friends, though. They seem to like you."

She brightened. "I'm the prettiest girl in my grade. That's why the boys like me."

Ella was dismayed. "You're not 'sposed to call yours*elf* pretty. Your friends will think you're stuck up."

"Don't *you* think I'm prettiest?" Rose asked her sister.

"Of course. You are the prettiest girl in all the world."

"Okay, girls, whose turn is it to go first?" Russell asked. "We have about an hour before dinner."

"Rose can go first," Ella declared. "And it's *supper* here."

Ella had smoothed things over with Rose and corrected him in one fell swoop. Rose's mood had passed again. She eagerly shook the Jacks in her tiny fist before letting them fall to the floor. "*Ones*," she laughed.

"Ones are easy. I don't like when I get to the fives," Ella commented.

Russell had been pleased to get home early today, though *home* wasn't the word he should have used for their current residence. A *room*. In a boarding house where the other tenants were working men. But they had become comfortable.

The day he'd first visited to inquire about a room had been interesting. Miss Broadnax answered the door. Before he said a word, she'd given him a thorough inspection, clearly taking in the whole picture... to include two small children. Entering the wide front door, he'd immediately felt it a good place. The aroma of fresh bread baking reminded him of his early childhood. Mixed into the aroma was a whiff of furniture wax—the house was spotless.

Miss Broadnax was relatively tall. He would describe her as *sturdy*, not overweight, but muscular. Her attire could best be described as practical. She wore no makeup or jewelry and her hair was pulled back tightly in a bun. He'd guess her to be in her sixties.

"I don't rent to folks with children."

This was not to be a simple task. It had taken some fast talking to convince her to let him have a room. "I just need this temporarily, ma'am. A safe place for them while I work. Until school begins, of course, and an hour or two in the afternoons after the school term begins. They're very well behaved. I hope, of course, to be able to get an apartment or house before long. Miss Broadnax, I understand you generally rent to working men. But you run a reputable, clean place, for a reasonable price, which is exactly what I desperately need."

"Folks 'round here will tell you I generally mean what I say."

He suspected the reason she finally gave in wasn't due to his pleading, but Ella's.

Miss Broadnax's gaze went downward. *Well, I'll be... that'n is sidling up to me just like she knew me.*

Ella held her small hand out for her to take as she looked her straight in the eye from her lower vantage point.

"Me and Rose are scared in the motel. Your house is nice." She did not waiver as she held Miss Broadnax's gaze. "Please?"

"Humph. I tolerate no noise interfering with anyone's sleep, day or night. Some of my boarders work the night shift, you know."

"Yes, ma'am. We promise," the girls nodded energetically.

"What about their mother—where's she?"

Russell cast his eyes downward. "No longer on this earth, ma'am. We prefer not to talk about it."

She was flustered but satisfied. She wouldn't mention the mother again in front of the girls. No reason to unduly upset them. They seemed well-mannered and close to their father. The poor man had his hands full. He could use a break, for sure.

"Alright. We'll give it a try. There's a clock radio in each room. They can have it on durin' the day if they keep it low."

"Do we have a television?" asked Rose.

"Onliest one is in the front room. Doubt they'll stay in style long anyways, just a waste of time." She turned her attention to Russell. "Don't wanna see them watching it without you, though—all men here and it wouldn't be proper."

Russell nodded. "Thank you, Miss Broadnax, you are very kind."

A large burly man walked by. Overhearing the statement, he jerked his head toward them. *I'd beg to differ,* he thought, *but none of my business. He'll find out soon enough. She ain't got a kind bone in her body. Shame, too, she's a right handsome figure of a woman under all her bluster.*

Russell was barely aware of the low grunt coming from Frank Weathers. Frank worked for a builder who would possibly be in town for a year. He'd learned to remove his work boots and shake the dirt from his clothing before entering the house. He even removed his shirt if it might have collected any debris. *Worth it for a clean room and the hearty meals she sets on her table. Abide by the woman's rules, pay on time, and it's a right fine place to stay. Can't believe she's takin' in kids, though... first time they bother me, I'm telling her that kids were not part of the deal.* He gave them a quick once-over before walking to his corner room on the main floor.

Miss Broadnax saw his scowl and determined to keep an eye on him. He was a big one and as unpleasant as they came with his straggly, greasy hair, and smells she could not describe. Muscular, though, right nice build—she'd noticed when he removed his shirt one day after work. *And those dark, brooding eyes—read the description in a book once and think it fits him. He can turn on a bit of charm when he wants an extra serving, too. Never mind, I'll not put up with any trouble. But I can't afford to lose Frank—I upped the price when I picked up on his employer's name—he could afford more than most. And he pays on time... in cash.*

After Russell agreed to her rules and paid the deposit, Ella hugged her. "Thank you, Miss Broadnax." The stern businesswoman blushed. "You can call me Miz Bee."

Rose and Ella were thrilled. Though not large, the upstairs room was pleasant. There were two beds, and they liked sleeping together. Two comfortable chairs had been placed in front of the floor-to-ceiling window, which was covered with light curtains. There were also window shades that could be pulled down in cold weather. The floral wallpaper was noticeably faded, but not a speck of dust to be seen. They had a good view of the tree-lined street. The large bathroom at the end of the hall would be shared, but most boarders left for work very early. The few remaining were sleeping.

"You won't have to keep the curtains pulled, girls, though the rules about the door are the same. The exception will be for lunch. School will begin soon, but in the meantime, you may go downstairs for lunch at noon, locking the door and taking the key with you. Miss Bee will keep an eye out until you return upstairs."

Comprehending what she had agreed to, Irma Rae Broadnax shook her head. She thought Mr. Townsend a nice man, though, and a dedicated father. Obviously, the girls were devoted to him. *Handsome guy, slender and in shape, not especially tall... mighty neat looking under the circumstances. Too bad about his wife. His daughters must look like her.*

Russell was relieved to be here after a week in Beacon's First-Stop Motel. Remembering the hot August night when he drove into town, he'd been impressed by the brightly-lit, freshly-painted sign beside a miniature lighthouse.

Welcome to Beacon, Alabama
Come to Visit - Stay for Life
Population: 19,592
(Give or Take a Birth, Death or Two)

It had been just over a week since they'd left Illinois. He'd driven rather aimlessly, stopping randomly for a night or two, before stopping three nights in a small Kentucky town after seeing a sign advertising Mammoth Cave National Park. The girls had never been to a cave and were excited about going to the longest cave in the world. Though a tiring tour for little legs, they begged to return the next day, which he indulged, taking a different tour.

"That's the most fun place in the whole world," they declared.

"I knew you would enjoy the wonderful formations and colors."

Ella answered, "We did—they were so many colors! But we liked when the guide talked about the *spee-cees* animals."

"*What* animals?"

Excited, Rose explained with authority, "The man said there were lots we couldn't see, but we saw bats, I think they were the *Indian* ones. He said they were all kinds of shrimp... we saw some in the water... and fish, too. You can't see some of the *spee-cees any*where else."

Contemplating, Russell realized his visit to Mammoth Cave had been unique seeing it through the eyes of children. "You two are absolutely right, and I'm glad you listened so well—I might have forgotten some things the guide explained. The word is *species*; they're not animals—it means a special kind of living things. I remember the bats; they were *Indiana* bats. It is a wonderful place indeed. I'm glad you liked it so much and I'm especially glad *I* got to see it with *you*."

"I didn't like when they turned off the lanterns, but I wasn't scared 'cause you were holding my hand tight," added Ella.

Rose declared, "I wasn't scared, but I was glad when he turned the flashlight back on."

They spent the next night in Cullman, Alabama, a lovely small town that was home to Ave Maria Grotto, or Little Jerusalem. They toured the outdoor scenes the morning they left the area. There were more than a hundred famous religious structures in miniature, built largely from rock, by hand, by a monk. It was one of the most beautiful, inspiring places Russell had ever seen. The girls enjoyed it immensely but didn't fully appreciate it. They referred to the miniature masterpieces as 'great dollhouses' as they skipped along the well-planned pathways.

**

When Russell first drove into Beacon, Alabama, he was weary of living on the road and stopped at the old motel. He liked the overall look of Beacon, located in central Alabama surrounded by beautiful mountains. The town was more than a wide spot along the highway, but not too large. The impressive architecture and well-kept old buildings and homes had taken his eye as well.

The girls had been amazing, taking everything in stride and lifting his spirits at every turn. While at the motel, he'd had to leave them most of the day while he looked for work. He'd rented the room for a week. "If I find a job, we may stay here a while, not in this motel, but in the town." Returning to the motel, he would use his key to open the door as far as the chain allowed. "It's okay, girls. You may remove the door chain."

A motel such as this would have humiliated him even to visit in years past, not especially clean, and the noise of traffic barely twenty feet from the door, but the price was low. He instructed the girls not to open the door for anyone, to keep the door chain on, curtains drawn, and the television on—he was thankful they *had* a television, but when they checked in, the proprietor had proudly informed, *With the weekly rate, ya'll get a room with a telly.*

"Other than the television noise, you are to be quiet."

It wasn't a good situation, but he had to work. His money was almost gone—he hadn't planned well enough. *I was in a bit of a hurry.*

They hugged him tightly upon his return each day, chattering about the television cartoons and games they'd played during his absence.

After turning in the rental car, they had to walk most everywhere or call a taxi, another reason to like the area as everything was close.

The third day he'd applied at Conner's Hardware. "Been short-handed for months, Mr. Townsend," Daniel Conner explained. "If you want the job, you can start tomorrow. And if you need to change the hours you work because of the children, I'm flexible most days." He would work in the lumber yard, taking orders and helping with loading trucks. The pay was fair and the owner, who had asked to be called Daniel, appeared to be a nice guy. With a place of employment, he could find a better place to live.

While at the motel, each evening followed the same routine. "Okay, girls, time to escape. I know you're tired of staying inside. Put your shoes on and grab your caps. We'll pick up burgers or sandwiches and go to the park to eat. Afterward, you may run or swing till your heart's content, or at least until dark."

Because he didn't want to draw attention, Rose and Ella's daily attire was jeans, tee shirts, and baseball caps. Watching them in the park, he thought how important they were to him.

Rose was a beauty. She had gorgeous blond hair, long and wavy... that is, until he cut it the second day on the road. She cried, which broke his heart, but he had to do it. "Honey, I'm sorry, but it will be easier to take care of for now. I'm not as good at washing it as your mother. It will grow again before long." He didn't explain not wanting to draw attention to them.

Long or short, Rose's blond hair was a perfect frame for her equally-perfect face, creamy skin, and sparkling blue eyes. At seven, she was quiet, appearing to think things through before speaking; and giving the impression that she was confident and poised beyond her years. *That's what the rest of the world sees... confidence and poise. But she's insecure somehow, moody, and unpredictable. Brenda's death impacted her most of all.*

Ella was a year younger, six years old, and equally attractive to him. But she did not have the beauty of her sister. She was livelier, a bit on the pudgy side, and her hair, though blonde, was unremarkable. *But she's got the cutest little pug nose I've ever seen—not the nose of a typical beauty, but the nose of her mother. And she's grounded, even at six. She takes care of her older sister like a little mama. Both delight me, but it's Ella's personality which is capable of winning over the most difficult disposition.*

Russell watched as they climbed the monkey bars, laughing and calling to him every time they made a new move. So precious.

They ran back to him.

"Pop?"

"Yes, Rose?"

"When will we go home? I'm having fun with you... but, I wish we could be in our house."

"Rose," interrupted Ella, "Pop explained, and you have to act big."

"I promised to take care of you. And I will. It's okay to ask, just not around others. I know you don't understand. But, for now, back home isn't the best place for us. I need you *here,* with me."

Proves my point. Ella is the one to make things right. They don't understand, of course—they can't. I needed a fresh start. We needed to get as far away as possible. Everywhere I turned was bad news. Losing my job, then worse heartbreak, and the weather fluke, the seiche, on everyone's mind and lips continually. At home, others telling me what to do, not giving me any part in decisions. I felt inadequate, others judging. There was no comfort—I had to leave and bring them with me.

He was thankful the First Stop Motel was history and they were at Miss Bee's, which was only a few blocks from the hardware store. Perhaps not much progress, but he was working, getting acquainted, the girls liked school, and they were comfortable—all were steps toward rebuilding their lives. It had been a while since he'd felt hope.

I might get in touch with Ginger Lee, see if she'd be interested in doing something casual to include the girls.

~~ 8 ~~

Returning home just after noon, Dare put the groceries away and poured a glass of tea before pulling off her tennis shoes. *The blessing of Saturdays and bare feet.*

She picked up the new mailbox and headed to the front porch. As she opened the screen door, the mailman walked up her sidewalk. Billy Carl Hicks had delivered her mail as long as she could remember. Her mother had known his family all her life. He could have retired years ago but enjoyed his job.

"Good afternoon, Billy Carl, you'll be happy to see I was just about to replace the ratty old mailbox. Got time for a glass of tea?"

"Yes, ma'am. I'm hearing on the news it's looking like snow up north, but it's still sweltering in Alabama."

"Remember that when you only need a jacket in January and they're shoveling snow—count your blessings. Have a seat, and I'll be right back."

"Hand me the mailbox. I'll swap 'em out for you."

"Thanks."

As she returned with another glass of tea, Billy Carl was adjusting the new mailbox.

"You got a new one just in time. Old one is almost rusted out on the back. New'un fit perfectly. Got it at Connor's, I guess."

"Yes. Except for groceries, I get most everything at Connor's or Woolworth's. If I don't find it there, I figure I don't need it," she laughed. "Sit down in my new rocker. I'll sit in the other. I'm sure you could use a break."

"Yep. I'm glad to have these old neighborhoods on my route, though. Sidewalks are shaded in the summers, and plenty of nice offers of hot chocolate or coffee in cold weather." He laughed. "Truth is, once I was near freezin' and hadn't seen anybody home, so I rang Esther Benson's doorbell and told her I was in pure *need* of a cup of coffee. She had a nice fire going and let me warm up inside, even served up warm cinnamon bread to go with the coffee. She teasingly mentioned that if Miz Scott saw me come inside, she'd deny it and call her senile."

"Quite the scandal, alright, you with a wife of nearly fifty years and great-grandchildren."

"Not to mention Esther Benson being a nun."

Dare broke down in laughter.

"I've known Esther since grammar school, so I forget to call her *Sister*. Regulation sez you cain't even sit a spell… like this… much less go inside a customer's house. But, those of us in Beacon figure folks who wrote the regulations just didn't know our ways. We *know* our customers. Speaking of customers… not that he's gotten any mail, but have you met Mr. Townsend, the guy with two little girls working at Connor's?"

"I did, just this morning."

"He seems a right nice young man. I talked with him a good little while when I took the mail in the other day. He was on a break and having a cup of coffee out front. I sez, *kinda hot for coffee, you oughta be having iced tea.* He sez he's used to drinking coffee all day no matter what time of the year it is. I sat with him a few minutes and asked about his little girls. He's kinda quiet, but a family man if I ever saw one. Sad about his wife getting killed in the *sike*, though."

She realized Daniel Connor had mentioned the same fact when she was in the hardware store… now Billy Carl. She asked, "You mean, the *seiche*, the storm in Chicago? How did you hear about it?"

"Don't recall exactly. A customer on my route told me, guess he told somebody at the school. Anyway, sad. Such a nice man and those girls are as cute as I ever saw. They spoke to me one day when I delivered mail to Irma Rae's. She came to the door and they were right there with their cookies."

"Who's Irma Rae?"

"Oh, you probably know her as the *boarding house lady*, but I knew Irma Rae Broadnax's whole family before she was born. She was the youngest of six. Seems to have soured as she grew up, but those little girls sure seemed happy with her.

"Well, I've stayed too long, Miss Dare. Glad you got us a new mailbox. Guess I'll see you at church Sunday."

"I plan to be there. Have a good afternoon." She watched as he walked away. She hadn't noticed how much he'd slowed down over the past years. It appeared each step was an effort.

Sweet old guy. Wonder how much longer he can keep his route. I'm worn out trying to keep up with his whole conversation, though... he rambles worse than Doreen. But two people in a short period of time have informed me Russell Townsend is a nice guy. He had me with those eyes. Well, until he seemed to turn to stone and left abruptly. What did I say wrong? I guess Doreen was right about how his wife died—seems common knowledge.

She reluctantly rose and walked back into the house, wishing she had more time to sit in the porch rocker.

I need to get ready for my date with Thomas. Should be an interesting evening—we've been speaking for two years at work yet know so little about each other.

She smiled wryly at the thought. *Working in Personnel has its advantages. I know Thomas Gray's age, address, income, marital status (never married), education background, where he's lived, as well as his height and weight as of January this year.*

Wish I could have discovered his thoughts on religion, politics, and whether he has a real sense of humor. Why do I let Doreen talk me into these things? Trying one more time, she says.

~~ 9 ~~

Rose and Ella were comfortable walking from school in the afternoon, and Miss Bee had volunteered to keep an eye out for them and let him know if they did not return on time. She had been unexpectedly helpful.

There were nine rental rooms in the old home, partitions having been added in the basement years earlier, creating three additional bedrooms. Rent for the smaller basement rooms was less.

Miss Bee's large bedroom and private sitting area was on the main floor, along with the kitchen, formal sitting room (containing the lone television), large dining room, and two single bedrooms. On the top floor were four bedrooms, each containing two beds, for which she charged more if rented to a single occupant.

"I run a clean place, meaning floors *and* reputation," she'd explained. "No pets, overnight guests or loud noises. Beds are changed once a week—I take care of the beds and clean towels in the bathrooms. Personal laundry is all yours. I know several women who take in laundry and will pick it up here and deliver back to you, or there's a laundry on Main Street. Breakfast and supper are included in your rent. If ya'll need lunch, you can have a sandwich and a glass of tea, no extra."

She seldom smiled when doing business. She wanted boarders, almost entirely working men, to know she would not hesitate to lock them out of their rooms if need be.

Russell learned from others that once Miss Bee became acquainted with her boarders, she was cordial, even joked at times, but none had called her friendly. The boarders, however, observed a marked difference soon after the Townsend family arrived.

"Nary a smile most of the time, but the moment those girls and their daddy appear in the dining room, Miss Bee starts chattering all over the place. You'd think royalty had arrived," Dennis Sims remarked to another on their way downstairs one night.

"Yep, kinda nice, in a way. Didja hear about the crazy storm called *seiche* his wife died in?"

Boarders came in and out of the dining room according to their work schedule. Breakfast was served from five until seven every morning, with cold leftovers left on the sideboard until eight. Most boarders left for work before dawn.

Supper, never called dinner, was from five-thirty until seven every evening, no exceptions. Large bowls or platters of food were set on the huge table, which was covered in a brightly-patterned oilcloth, and served family style. There was much conversation as they passed the dishes and a definite lull as they began *diggin' in.*

An enormous bowl of dry beans could be expected every night, varying only between butter beans and pinto beans. One could also count on cornbread, cornbread muffins, or cornbread sticks, sweet tea, sweet milk, and buttermilk. Meats were fried chicken (often), pot roast, corned beef with cabbage, pork chops, or chicken and dumplings. Soup could be counted on once a week, and it was different every time, depending on the leftovers. Toward the end of the month, if there was a larger array of vegetables and no meat in the soup, one best make no mention of it. Dessert might be chocolate or caramel layer-cake, vanilla pudding, cookies, apple or buttermilk pie. Only one dessert was available each night, but each was delectable—baking definitely her specialty.

Russell was surprised at how quickly Rose and Ella adapted to dining with a group of strangers, as well as the differences in foods. Though worlds apart from the manner of food preparation to which Russell himself was accustomed, he also adapted and learned to enjoy most dishes Miss Bee served, especially fried chicken and gravy. An exception was known as Thursday bread, which the other boarders nearly fought over. Their first Thursday night, Mr. Sims... he'd asked to be called Dennis... told him to expect it. "The boarders called it Thursday bread way before I got here, but we can usually expect it then. You hadn't heard about it? Just wait. No need to describe it. One taste will tell the tale. It's delicious."

When the mystery bread was passed, he realized it was cornbread and was unsure why they thought it different. He liked cornbread, especially hot, with dripping butter, so he took a large piece and buttered it generously before biting in.

Crunnnch—he'd bitten down on something in the bread. Holding it out to look closer, he saw pieces of... *something* throughout the bread. Whatever it was, the others considered it a treat, so he resumed chewing... and chewing, finally swallowing quickly just to get rid of the disgusting taste.

"What'd we tell you?" asked Dennis, grinning. "Good thing you got a big piece first go-round, 'cause it's not likely to come back to you."

Pleased that his disdain for Thursday bread hadn't been obvious, he nodded before asking, "What exactly *is* this?"

"It's cornbread with cracklings... crackling bread."

"What are cracklings?"

"Cracklings are made from the skin of a hog, with a goodly layer of fat and salt—wish she'd make it more often."

Upon hearing the description, Russell was sure he would lose his entire meal, but drank more tea and managed to make it through. Glancing at Rose and Ella, they apparently had no problem.

While adjusting to their new life, Russell also realized others were adjusting *for* them. Their first evenings at supper, a boarder would begin a conversation, others joining in, and one would stop mid-stream, seeming to swallow a word or change direction.

These hard-working, tough men were cleaning up their language and conversation out of respect for the children. The girls soon became *Little Misses*.

We are among good people. A diverse group, decidedly different from my family and neighborhood, and they probably work harder and have less financially. But they care enough about us to change their conversations.

Weekends were different at the boarding house as many boarders went home for two days. Breakfast was coffee, juice, biscuits and an array of homemade jams. Saturday's supper consisted of fewer dishes and any leftovers from the week. A large lunch was served on Sunday from one until two-thirty. "After two thirty on Sundays, my kitchen is closed," she stated. "The Lord's Word tells us to rest one day a week… and heaven knows, I need more rest than just an evening off, but I know I deserve that much."

After the girls left for school one morning, Russell went down for another cup of coffee. Even when the kitchen was *closed*, a fresh pot of coffee was always available on the dining room sideboard. Miss Bee was tidying up. Her long apron reminded him of his mother—how he wished she were here now.

"Russell, you're a good father. You tell them girls something an' they take it to be law. It's good training, and the reason they will always be good girls."

After a moment's hesitation, he replied, "Thank you. I appreciate your keeping an eye on them. I wish you would allow me to pay you."

"It's a *favor*. I told you, folks don't pay for favors."

"Thank you."

She watched as he left the dining room. *So polite. Formal-like, though, and not fully trusting, I think—wonder if that's his Chicago ways. Hated to hear how his wife died in a terrible storm. A violent death is hardest on the family.*

At work, Russell thought about the town of Beacon, a decent size with a small-town feel. The residents were friendly and took pride in their history, including taking care of the old city buildings. Perhaps the beautiful old architecture had drawn him to the town when he stopped the first night. Architecture was in his blood.

The schools are good. I might not mind settling here... if I can ever come to grip with things.

"Why are so many people at school called by two names?" Ella asked one evening. "Me and Rose just got one name, and Mama did, and you."

"I think it's a Southern custom. You'll find different names in different parts of the world, even different spellings—only what people are accustomed to."

"I heard my teacher call one of the other teachers Dixie Gail. That's too long for a name," added Rose.

"Rose, you have another name, you are just not called by both. Your full name is Brenda Rose Townsend. Ella's is Ella Susanne Townsend. It just isn't a custom where we come from to use both names."

Rose brightened. "I was named for Mama. From now on, I want to be called Brenda Rose."

Ella looked downtrodden, out of character for her. "Well... if you want to. But it's a big name and I don't know if I can get used to it. Besides, Mama was Brenda... and she's not here anymore. I don't want to call you Brenda."

This line of conversation was heading for trouble. "Your mama called you by only one name because it's what she preferred. Two names are fine for some, but I think we should stay with what your mama called you. What do you think?"

Ella looked at Rose, acquiescing to her sister, as usual.

"Oh... okay... I guess. It wouldn't sound right to think of Mama calling me two names when she didn't."

Relieved, Ella asked. "Know the funniest one I've heard?"

"What?"

"Ima Belle."

Rose giggled. "You're making it up."

"No, it's a girl in third grade. No one else acts like it's funny, though."

"Well, then, let's not make fun of the names of others. They might think *our* names are funny or the different ways we pronounce words, and we wouldn't like it if they laughed at us. It's almost time for lights out. I'll read you one story before bed."

Lying in bed, the moon gave enough light to see most of the room. Russell's eyes took in the sweet scene of two small sleeping angels. T*hey're okay. And things will get better in time. They liked my surprising them at school the other afternoon—might do that again soon. And I might get a chance to get better acquainted with Miss Ginger Lee.*

**

Russell finally bought a car, a black 1950 Ford, custom V-8, four-door sedan. The dealer had steered him to a station wagon, but he balked. *Way too old family-man style. What I really like is the convertible, but it's not practical.*

Returning to the boarding house, he walked in with car keys in hand as Miss Bee walked from the kitchen. "Wondered how long you'd make it without a car," she commented. "Glad to see you drive up this afternoon. How in the world did you get all the way from Chicago without a car, anyway? I know the bus comes right through here... you just don't look like the bus type... 'course, there's trains, and friends, all kinds of ways of traveling these days... just thought you looked the type to have your own car... none of my business, 'course, just wondered."

He smiled and gave her a playful hug. "Thank you for your concern, Miss Bee. I'll probably continue to walk much of the time, but the car will allow us to branch out."

She watched him walk up the stairs. *Well, I shouldn't have pried... serves me right. If'n I don't watch out, I'll become the old sour biddy-body everybody already thinks I am. He's as nice a gentleman as I've ever met. A catch for any girl, even with two young'uns, and handsome as a movie star... kinda makes me wish I was ten years younger.*

Irma Rae Broadnax smiled at her own thoughts, commencing to hum as she returned to her kitchen.

～ **10** ～

*R*innnnng, rinnnnng, rinnnnng.

"Hello. Hi, Doreen, is everything okay? You don't usually call at night. What? You are in *charge* of the baby shower; there's nothing you didn't plan. Why are you really calling?"

"Aw, Dare, you know me too well," her sister snickered. "I just feel possessive sometimes, like a mama. I was hoping you'd tell me more about Thomas. I know you've been seeing him regularly. Is it serious?"

"*Good grief*, two dates do not constitute seeing someone regularly, or time to get serious, nosy sister."

"You know it's just 'cause I care. I'm sorry."

Dare felt bad. She'd hurt her sister's feelings. Of course, she knew she'd only asked because she cared... she *was* a bit nosy, but she loved her.

"Oh, it's alright. I'm sorry, too, but you do jump to conclusions. I have been out to dinner and a movie with Thomas, and to a going-away party for a guy at work—that's it. I like him—well, he's okay, and we'll probably go out again. But I'm not ready for him to think he's the *one* in my life. I told him I was really busy."

"Is it because you do like him a lot and are getting cold feet?"

There she goes again. "Doreen..."

"Sorry. Well, he seems nice, and oh my goodness, he's good-looking, and those muscles—must be something for him to... well maybe after two dates, you'd kiss him goodnight."

"Enough. He has not kissed me good night, and I will not tell you if he does... or when and if I allow it."

"Well, that tells me you've already decided just how many dates before you'll allow a kiss. I don't mind telling you I made Bobby wait… okay, the third date, but you know we already liked each other before we had a real date."

"*Quite* enough." But Dare was laughing. Her sister was one of a kind, and yes, she thought her sister and brother-in-law were probably already in love before he had enough nerve to ask her out.

Unlike Doreen, her brother-in-law, Bobby Miller, was the shy type, but Doreen had a jewel. Bobby was a good-looking guy, slightly over six feet tall, with blond hair and a sprinkling of freckles, giving him a boyish look, and he had a robust laugh. More importantly, he was a godly man, kind-hearted, sweet, honest, a hard worker, and humble. But, if need be, he could stand his ground with Doreen or anyone else.

**

Dare and Thomas were to attend Beacon's Fall Festival together. It was a family event and everyone she knew would be there. When Thomas had asked her out and she suggested the festival, he'd hesitated. "What do you do? I thought those were for children. I'm way past Halloween costumes."

"The festival is for the whole family, the last Friday in September every year, so it's not Halloween. Dress is casual. There will be hot dogs and corn dogs, apple cider, caramel apples, all kinds of goodies, and a cake walk. There will be a variety of booths set up, and fun things for every age."

He hadn't been enthusiastic with her plan but balked completely when she suggested they double-date with Doreen and Bobby. She had delivered a file to his division at work and stopped to make the suggestion. "It'll be fun, Thomas."

He'd glanced around before placing his hand on her shoulder, moving it in a caressing manner and lowering his voice. "I'd prefer just the two of us. I'd thought we might drive to Birmingham… a romantic drive and dinner for two. Tempting?"

Dare was suddenly uncomfortable. He hadn't exactly been inappropriate. Perhaps it was his tone, but she wasn't ready for this. As casually as possible, she removed his hand from her shoulder, saying pleasantly, "Maybe another time, Thomas. But it's important that you get acquainted with my sister and her husband. This will be the perfect time."

He beamed. "Oh, get to know your family? Good idea."

Shoot-fire, now I've done it. He thinks I'm working him into my family. Well, I'll just deal with one thing at a time.

Thomas picked her up at five o'clock, wearing a suit and tie.

"I mentioned this was a casual event, didn't I?"

"Yes. That's why I didn't wear my pin-striped suit."

Does the man not notice I'm dressed in blue jeans? He does look good, though.

They drove to Doreen and Bobby's to pick them up and arrived at the Beacon Activities Center at five-thirty. The festival was in full swing, noise level high with music from a local teenage band combining with children's laughter, and adults calling out from their respective booths. The smell of hot dogs and roasted peanuts wafted through the air.

"This makes fall official. I love it," laughed Dare. Glancing at Thomas, she was certain he didn't share her sentiments. She squeezed his arm. "It gets better, honestly. Let's go get a hot dog basket and find a place to sit."

Bobby replied, "Doreen and I like the corn-dog basket—comes with two dogs. We'll want cake later, 'specially if we win one in the cake walk. Let's get going."

"I'm not walking in circles for a cake," Thomas grumbled.

"I doubted you would. Don't worry. There are plenty of other choices."

A few minutes later, laden with food and drinks, the foursome scanned the area for a table.

"Table to your right, make a run for it," shouted Doreen.

Just as they arrived, so did Russell Townsend, with Rose, Ella, and Ginger Lee. Dare stood with Thomas as Doreen and Bobby claimed two of the chairs, leaving four.

Thomas glared at Russell. "We were here first, fella." He sat and motioned Dare to the chair beside him.

This was awkward. Thomas had a point, though Doreen was the one who reached the table first, and he sounded like a bickering child.

"Quite right. We'll find another spot," answered Russell politely.

Dare replied, "There are still two extra chairs here, and there's plenty of room. Let the girls have a seat while you and Ginger Lee score two more chairs."

He appeared doubtful.

"Russell… I'm not sure you remember me. We met at the hardware store recently, and Ginger Lee and I know each other from school."

Assured the girls were in safe hands, he agreed. Within minutes they returned with two chairs.

Thomas grumbled, "It'll be too crowded."

Dare answered, "This is not fine dining, Thomas. Everyone can scooch up and we'll be fine."

In unison, Russell and Thomas echoed, "*Scooch?*"

The women laughed. "Oh, for goodness sakes, just move the extra chairs in and scoot them closer together," Dare explained.

Doreen looked toward Rose and Ella. "Girls, I'm happy for a chance to get acquainted. I've seen you at school, but I teach third grade."

Rose smiled as Ella answered, "Yes, ma'am, I've seen you in the hall. I'm Ella. I'm six. Rose is seven."

Proper introductions were made, and they settled into eating and exchanging conversation about the weather and the festival itself.

"I like this," Russell commented. "I've heard of school festivals, but not for the entire community."

"Yeah," grumbled Thomas. "At least it will be a year before another."

Russell studied him. Was he so unhappy with his surroundings... and his date? At the very least, he was rude.

They had been here less than an hour but Dare already regretted suggesting it to Thomas.

Full of giggles, Ginger Lee turned her full attention to Thomas. "Mr. Gray, I know you've lived here a few years, but where are you from? I do hope you've found Beacon a good place to live."

"Ah, *Miss* Cotton... please call me Thomas. I was reared in Virginia and moved to New York City after college. I loved the city. I heard about a position being open at ATC, which is what brought me to your small town."

Bobby took offense. "Beacon isn't exactly small potatoes, Thomas. Last count, our population was near twenty thousand."

"The city welcome sign... oh yes. Nevertheless, it doesn't compare with New York City. You have no theaters, upscale clothing stores, or even grocers with ethnic foods or specialty items."

Russell joined the conversation. "I've lived in a large city, and I find Beacon refreshing. It's a beautiful town. The citizens know each other and care about what's going on in their town."

"Thank you, Russell," Dare answered.

Ginger Lee focused on Thomas. "Oh, Thomas... I guess you know everything about the New York theater."

Dare raised her eyebrows as she glared at Ginger Lee. *Gag... she's drooling over him, same as she was over Russell a few minutes ago.*

Leaning closer, Ginger Lee cooed, "Thomas, I can surely understand missing the theater. I heard it's wonderful. And I'm always saying we don't have up-to-date styles available here. I myself often drive to Birmingham to shop."

Dare glanced at Doreen, surprised she had not joined in. *Why, I believe my big sister has been rendered speechless.*

Bobby stood. "You finished eating, Doreen? Let's go check out the booths. Not needin' the kissing booth anymore, but some of the other booths look interesting."

"Okay with you, Dare? Are you and Thomas coming with us, or do you just want to meet up later?"

Thomas answered. "We'll meet you at the front door in an hour. Quite enough time, I'd say."

At seven-thirty, Doreen and Bobby were rushing toward the front door. "We didn't have time to talk to anybody," Doreen complained.

"No more double-dating with Thomas. I'm firm on that," replied Bobby.

As they rushed up, they spotted Thomas and Ginger Lee sitting to one side of the entrance, laughing and appearing quite relaxed as Ginger Lee rested her hand on Thomas's knee. He had an arm draped over the back of her chair.

Dare appeared with Russell and the girls, walking quickly from the direction of the *Go Fish* booth. Dare was laughing, holding cotton candy and an oversized teddy bear. Doreen was again speechless. She looked from one side to another, eyebrows raised.

"Hi, everybody," Dare greeted. "We've had a great time. Rose and Ella have a sack full of candy and prizes, and

Russell and I are stuffed with candied apples. Oh, and the teddy bear belongs to the girls, too."

Doreen stared. *I haven't seen her in a mood this happy since before Mama died.*

"Goodnight, girls… and Russell. Thanks for letting me tag along with you tonight. I had a wonderful time." Turning to Thomas, she asked, "Ready to go, Thomas? Doreen… Bobby?"

Thomas and Ginger Lee stood. Russell touched Dare's arm. "Good night, Dare. I enjoyed being with you this evening."

Doreen was practically leaning to be sure she missed nothing.

Dare answered, "Good night, Russell. Thank you."

Ginger Lee moved closer to Russell, taking his arm possessively.

They said their goodbyes before going in separate directions.

Driving to Ginger Lee's home, Russell thought, Now *she wants to be with me, not any other time since meeting Thomas. She is a knock-out. When I picked her up tonight, I thought how radiant she was in the gold dress and commented on it. The matching high heels showed off her legs… couldn't help noticing as I helped her into the car. She was over-dressed for the occasion, but I was delighted to have her on my arm… at least when the evening began.*

Rose and Ella were almost asleep in the back seat when he reached Ginger Lee's. He walked her to the door.

"Thank you for going with me, Ginger Lee."

She reached to put her arms around his neck, holding her face up to him, clearly waiting for a good night kiss.

He put his hands around her waist and leaned in to give her a quick kiss.

Her eyes widened. "Honey, we can do better than that."
She lifted her chin and pulled him closer.

"Ummm, better. The girls aren't watching—they're asleep. I had a great time tonight. Call me soon."

"Goodnight, Ginger Lee."

Leaving a gorgeous woman at the door who is obviously making herself available, why am I thinking of the woman who was only being friendly, and wore jeans and a sweater?

That woman made me laugh.

~ 11 ~

"**W**hat, in the name of Santa Claus, *happened* tonight, Dare?"

After the festival, Thomas had driven Bobby and Doreen home, then drove Dare to her house.

Dare had been inside no more than fifteen minutes when her phone rang. She knew it would be Doreen.

"Why, sister, what *do* ya'll mean?" Dare answered in her slowest, most dramatic Southern drawl.

"Don't *make* me come over there. You know exactly what I mean."

Dare answered, seriously. "I honestly don't know, Doreen. Really. After you and Bobby left the table tonight, Ginger Lee continued to flirt shamelessly with Thomas and he clearly enjoyed it. After a while, I asked him to walk with me around the festival to see the booths. His response? *I'd really prefer to sit and relax.* I might mention he was looking at Ginger Lee as he answered and she was nodding agreement. Russell stood and asked, *Would you join the three of us, Dare? We're anxious to see what else is here. That* is what happened. And I had a fabulous evening, up until the ride home."

"Yeah, and we stayed out so *late*, too," Doreen answered sarcastically. "Even old married couples expect to stay out later than eight o'clock, but…"

"Let me finish filling you in, Doreen. I had a delightful time with Russell and those darling girls. They are the sweetest things I've ever seen, polite, funny, and very well behaved. And watching Russell with them is total pleasure— it's as if he's fully in love and enthralled with them. But not obsessed. I mean, he talked with me, too, and I enjoyed getting better acquainted.

"Since the four of us rode home together, you know there was almost no conversation. There was none on the drive to my house, either. Thomas got out, opened my car door and walked me to my door without either of us saying a word. *Then*, if you can believe it, he put his arms around me and leaned in for a kiss."

"After his behavior?"

"Yes. I pulled back and he looked at me with the goofiest expression I've ever seen. I think you'd call it moony, love-sick, or attempting the *look*, anyway. He said, *Dare, darling, tonight didn't go at all as I'd hoped. Ginger Lee made a play for me and I'll admit I let it go on too long. But I hope you know how I feel about you. I want to take our relationship further... beginning tonight...*

"He leaned in again, holding me more forcefully. I jerked away, saying, t*here will be no going further, Thomas. Your behavior tonight was atrocious. The only effort you made was to enjoy Ginger Lee's drooling over you. You can have her.* You won't believe his answer."

"What?"

"He responded, *Oh, baby, she's more loser-Russell's type, just a receptionist—great build, but way too obvious. I'm much more interested in a more gorgeous, petite little package.* He paused to tilt his head, evidently thinking this move made him irresistible, and added, *I foresee you becoming a supervisor at the company someday. We'll make a great team.*

"Then... then...!" Dare was getting angrier by the moment." I won't repeat the rest of what he said... and did."

"Dare, are you okay?" Doreen held the phone away from her mouth, and yelled, "Bobby, get in here, we're goin' to Dare's... now!"

Dare interrupted, "Doreen, no—I'm fine, other than being so mad I could spit. I slapped the jerk's face…" She finally began to cry. "I went in and slammed the door in his face."

"Honey…"

"No, it's okay, I'm just mad. I've never slapped anyone before or felt so stupid—not seeing what kind of person he was. His personnel file didn't give me the information I needed, after all. I'll be fine, and I'm begging you not to show up at my door. I'm going to get some hot chocolate and go to bed. But I'll see you at church Sunday. I love you."

"If you're sure." To one side, "No, Bobby, we don't have to go. I'll explain later."

To Dare, she said kindly, "Sleep well, honey. Call if you need me."

Dare's family had always attended Beacon's First Church, as well as many of their friends. It comforted her to look across the aisles to see old friends like Billy Carl Hicks and his wife, Daniel and Mabel Conner, Jenny Lewis, whom she'd known since Jenny was born, Doreen and Bobby, Miss Broadnax, who she'd just learned was Irma Rae, Joe, who taught her Bible class, and his beautiful wife, friends from work, and so many others.

After church Sunday morning, Dare went for lunch at Doreen and Bobby's.

As they began to eat, Bobby commented, "I saw Russell with his daughters at church today. He was on the opposite side from us. Has he been before?"

Dare answered, "I think I've seen them a few Sundays."

"Seems like a nice guy."

"Yes," answered Doreen, "I think he is. I did see him with the girls at church last week, not sure about before." She turned to direct her conversation to Dare. "Honey… I don't know what's going on in your mind, but I just want to say something. I was so glad when you told me about the date with Thomas. We know now he is a huge jerk, but I was glad for you to be going out again. It's been way too long... since..."

"Doreen..." Bobby began.

"Ya'll know I'm going to finish what I have to say. Dare, I'm angrier than you about Thomas. But if you're interested in Russell Townsend, I'm sorry to say, but Thomas made the right call. I don't mean I see him as a *loser*, but he seems to be carrying quite a load, even though I think he's a nice guy and, granted, *very* good looking. But all we know about him is he came from somewhere near Chicago, his wife died in a weather tragedy, he has two small children and a low-paying job with no future. God knows *how* he arrived here in the first place. He didn't even own a car. Dare? You agree, don't you?"

"Yes... it was nothing more than a fun hour at the festival. Quit worrying." She knew Doreen was right. She was a good judge of character.

Returning home, Dare admitted privately she was becoming depressed.

Why do I always do the wrong thing with men... or choose the wrong ones? I thought I had come to grips with what happened... so far back. I don't think I can do it again.

Rinnng, rinnng, rinnng.

"Hello... hi, Jenny. No, I've been to church and lunch— just relaxing at the moment." *I'm not relaxed—I am depressed and wanting to scream...* "What, honey? You sound troubled, are you okay?" *What am I doing asking if she is okay? I'm in no condition to help anyone.*

"Dare, did you know I've been... seeing Mr. Harrell?"

"I knew you appeared interested in one another."

"Larry, I mean Mr. Harrell, is really nice. We've only been out twice, but he's been to my apartment several times. I love cooking for him. He especially likes my Italian dishes. Anyway, he has to be careful not to cause any talk at work, and being older than me, he knows people would get the wrong idea. He is a perfect gentleman."

Who's she trying to convince, me, or herself? "Jenny, I'm not sure why you called. Did you just want to tell me about him?"

"No, not exactly."

She's been crying.

"Dare... I got a phone call last night. From a woman, but she wouldn't say who she was. I don't believe it was anyone I know, but she was trying to change her voice... holding something over the receiver, maybe."

Jenny's voice broke and she began sobbing. "The woman... told me she'd seen me with Larry and I didn't know who he really was. Said I wasn't his only one, just the youngest and latest. She was *so* mean and ugly." Sniffling, she continued, "She told me to drop him before I got in deeper than was good for me. No one has ever talked to me that way."

"Honey, could you come over, or do you want me to come to your place?"

"No... I just don't know what to do. Should I call Larry, uh, Mr. Harrell?"

"*No.* Look, how about we go out for lunch tomorrow? We'll just pick something up and have it in the car so we can talk privately. Okay?"

"Alright... thank you. I'll see you tomorrow. Good night."

Dare's problems seemed insignificant now. She was more concerned about this young, innocent girl than before. She should have spoken to her when she saw her heading for trouble.

**

Sitting in the car with their lunch, Jenny was quiet.

"Dare, I'm sorry I called you. I believe whoever phoned me was just jealous. Larry came in to see me at break this morning. He was *so* sweet. He wants to come over Thursday night—he has something important to discuss." She was giddy, breathless as she spoke. "I think he might *propose*. Oh, Dare, I love him, and he makes me feel wonderful. I know you don't understand... you... oh, I'm sorry, that was a terrible thing to say, I didn't mean it."

"Jenny, it's okay. But I've been worried about you... with Mr. Harrell. I've been wrong not to talk with you before you called. Honey, I believe he has different ideas for you than marriage. I don't know what the woman meant, but I think there's a lot about his past we don't know."

Stricken, Jenny became angry. "I'm sorry I talked with you. Take me back to work."

"Jenny, I've known you all your life. I attended your parent's funeral after their wreck. They were strong Christians, and I know you have high moral standards as well."

"Don't talk about my parents."

"Just think about it. When you're with Mr. Harrell... Larry, think about whether you would be proud to tell your parents about your relationship with him."

"Take me back to *work*. You *don't* understand. Maybe *you're* jealous."

Startled, Dare drew a deep breath. Jenny was being defensive.

"Okay." Backing out of the parking space, she stopped for a moment and turned to Jenny. "I love and care about you. I'm sorry I haven't been of help. I know you're mad with me now, but you can still count on me if you need something later. I hope you'll remember that."

There was no further conversation.

Dare's depression returned. She hadn't been a good friend. She'd failed Jenny. Perhaps if she'd talked with her when first aware of the situation, things wouldn't have gone so far. Now, she was honestly afraid for her friend.

A friend loves at all times... she thought...*but love* acts.

Is this my life? I've failed at so many important things... and people... beginning in high school.

~~ 12 ~~

Having an early afternoon off from work. Russell decided to forgo his other project and meet the girls after school on this clear, warm day.

Before the final buzzer, Ginger Lee exited the school, waving happily. There was no one in sight other than the line of parked cars and school buses. He glanced toward them in hopes she was waving at one of them—no, she was looking directly at him. He should have realized he might see her. By the time he returned the wave, she was standing in front of him. She wore high heels and a slim, close-fitting green skirt with an off-white high-necked blouse, very appealing.

"Hi there, saw you from the window. I've been expecting you to phone. Are you bashful or just waiting so as not to appear anxious? You don't have to play games with me."

He had no idea how to deal with such a forward woman. He'd dealt with others, but she was in a special category.

"Well, I'm very busy, not much time left after work and children." He hoped mentioning the children would give her second thoughts. She'd obviously not enjoyed them on their first date.

"I *love* children. I work in a grammar school, after all."

She flipped her hair back. Looking around, she placed her hand on his arm, giving it a quick squeeze. "This will give everyone something to talk about. *Do* call soon. You could do a lot worse than this Southern girl. I go to church, too… Beacon Memorial."

Buzzzzzzzzz, buzzzzzzzzzz, buzzzzzz…

"There's the last buzzer. People will be lining up in my office. Bye for now." She turned to run back inside.

His eyes were drawn to her movements as she disappeared into the school building. *I'm only human, after all… she's got quite a figure. What was the remark about going to church? Maybe only that she knew I was going elsewhere. I believe I know enough about Ginger Lee.*

Dare was completing her nightly routine before getting into bed.

Rinnng, rinnnng, rinnng.

It's late for anyone to phone.

"Hello."

"Dare? This is Russell Townsend. Do you remember me?"

An uncomfortable lump came in Dare's throat. She felt weak. "Yes. I had a lovely time with your girls at the festival… *and* you. How is Ginger Lee?"

Not expecting that particular subject or question, he paused. "Ginger Lee is fine. I spoke with her today while waiting for the girls after school."

He decided to use a bit of directness himself. "Honestly, seeing Ginger Lee is what brought *you* to mind… not for the first time, but *again*. I remembered how much we enjoyed the festival. The girls have talked about you—wanted to know when they could see you again. I wondered if you might go out for a picnic lunch with us after church on Sunday—I've seen you there."

No, I don't want to like you, I'm enough of a mess all by myself.

"I understand if it isn't a good time."

"Yes.... it is. I'd love to see Rose and Ella again. Shall I make sandwiches?"

"No, thanks. We're still at the boarding house. I asked Miss Bee if she would prepare a lunch—she's been wonderful to us, a very special lady."

Dare remained doubtful. *Why did I agree? This can go nowhere and will only make those little girls believe I'll be around more. I'll just enjoy the afternoon, then tell them I'm very busy. I'll make it clear I won't be seeing them again.*

"Shall we meet you in front of the church after the service?"

"Yes, fine."

"Wanted to ask about Sunday school. We've only been attending worship, but I want to get the girls back into classes. Can you tell me where theirs are located?"

"Sure. Just go in the side entrance closest to the front. There's a map showing each class location. Someone will more than likely grab you when you come into the door and point you in the right direction."

"Thanks. Which class do you attend?"

"There are two adult classes. One is in the main auditorium. The one I attend is in the hallway off the auditorium. It's a beige door with a poster of Noah—it's a younger group. You're welcome to join us... studying the Gospels at present. Joe, our teacher, generally puts a practical spin on it."

"Good. And thank you. I'll probably see you in class."

What have I done? I'd already agreed to a picnic, after all, and couldn't exactly avoid answering questions about Bible classes. Well, it's a big class.

To avoid raised eyebrows and questions Sunday morning, she told Doreen about the picnic ahead of time.

"No more questions, Sis, it's only a picnic *with* his children. I wish I hadn't agreed, but I won't let myself get roped into anything else. End of discussion."

After worship, Dare got into Russell's car, the girls happily piling into the back. She'd worn a blue sundress with a hint of a sleeve, dangling beaded earrings, and flat shoes.

"You look lovely," he commented.

"Thank you. I wanted to be comfortable for the afternoon."

Blue is her color. It brings out the color in her eyes. But she was as lovely in jeans. The clothing doesn't matter—in this case, it's the woman who makes the clothes look good.

"Miss Bee told me about a place on the edge of town, up the mountain slightly, called, Beacon's Far-Away, but I haven't checked it out. Sound okay?"

"It's great—the best park in town—and I haven't been there in a long time."

A different variety of trees began to appear as they drove up the mountain. They had begun to turn glorious shades of yellow, orange, and red, fluttering slightly in the light breeze. The day was crisp and sunny. Russell didn't think he'd ever experienced such a clean, fresh smell. They passed families flying kites, children on bicycles, and gatherings in front yards as younger groups played ball nearby.

I don't miss the city. Beacon is peaceful. People speak, wave from cars, socialize, laugh. I think I'd forgotten laughter.

About halfway up the mountain, he saw the sign— Beacon's Far-Away—A Place to Get Away Without Leaving Home. Beside it was a beautifully-crafted miniature lighthouse, exactly like the one at the city welcome sign. He parked in the spacious graveled lot and got out of the car. Beyond the sign was a thickly wooded area and a wide path of small pebbles. After removing his jacket and tie and rolling up his sleeves, he unloaded the car, handing the girls blankets after Dare picked up the small cooler.

They walked less than a quarter of a mile on the pathway when they came to a large clearing. The picnic areas were separated by at least sixty feet, each somewhat secluded by a small grove of trees or large shrubs.

Dare put her hands on her hips. "You need to look at each area before you decide where we will picnic. Each is different."

They strolled to each section. The first, *Serene*, featured a man-made waterfall with goldfish swimming below and a long picnic table beside a wildflower garden. *Paris* featured a miniature replica of the Eiffel Tower, with small individual tables giving it the feel of a sidewalk café in France. *Safari* was a larger area toward the rear of the park resembling a wild animal safari, with life-size animal statues, a small pond with a stone hippo, and a replica of a safari vehicle, sturdily built for children to climb in and upon.

There were several other areas, *Circus*, *Farm*, and *Christmas*.

The girls ran from one area to the next, trying to decide where to picnic. They had the choice of any section except *Paris*, where a couple sat holding hands.

Russell marveled, "Lovely... so peaceful and quiet today. I've never seen anything comparable. I wish I'd thought of it... a great addition to most any development."

"What?" Dare asked.

"Oh, nothing. Daydreaming, I guess."

The girls chose the *Safari* area. "We're going to eat our lunch in the safari jeep and pretend the animals are waiting for our leftovers."

Dare appeared concerned. "Russell, didn't you bring play clothes for them to change into? They'll ruin their good dresses."

"No... they'll be okay."

"Hey, Pop, I brought play clothes in the car. Can me and Rose go back to change?" Ella called out.

Embarrassed, he answered, "Yes, go ahead. I forgot to lock the car." Looking sheepishly at Dare, he admitted, "Sometimes Ella is the better parent."

Dare answered sympathetically, "It's generally the woman who thinks of these things. Don't worry about it."

Russell and Dare had the table to themselves, talking comfortably, laughing at the girls' antics, and discussing likes and dislikes they had in common.

"Roller coasters?" asked Russell.

"Definitely no. Also, no Ferris wheels, but I'd love an actual wild animal safari," she laughed.

A few hours later, Russell dropped Dare at the church to pick up her car. He came around to open her door, telling the girls to stay put.

"I've had a wonderful afternoon, Russell."

"As have I. Dare…"

"Yes?"

"The girls like you—you're great with them."

"They're pretty special. You seem to have coped well since your wife died." She was immediately aware of the cloud coming across his face. "I'm sorry to have brought up sadness. It's been a lovely afternoon."

"Yes. I haven't relaxed like this in a long time."

Trying to change the mood and get herself out of this, Dare continued. "You need to get out more. What *about* Ginger Lee? I know Thomas wasn't serious about her, though they had a silly flirtation. She's a nice person." *I didn't phrase it exactly right. I meant to steer him in another direction, let him know I didn't want a relationship… but it sounded as if I were checking out the competition. Good grief, now I'm blushing.*

Completely captivated with this lovely woman, Russell heard little other than the name of Ginger Lee. *Why is she talking about Ginger Lee? I've thought little of her since the festival. Even when I took her home, I was thinking of Dare.*

"No. I mean *no* Ginger Lee… Dare, will you go out with me again? Without Rose and Ella? Do you have plans this weekend? If I can get a babysitter, I'd like to take you out… to dinner, or a movie… whatever you enjoy." *I'm talking too much.* "Sorry, I just… May I phone you?"

She'd rehearsed her answer. *No, I'm sorry—I'm very busy these next months.*

But she heard herself clearly replying, "Yes, I'd love to go out with you."

∿ 13 ∿

Russell was aware he might not be doing the wise thing. But Dare was one of a kind. *I made the decision to move forward. Things are going well. My immediate problem is to find a reliable babysitter.*

He recalled his last attempt at getting a babysitter. It had not worked out well…

He'd just returned from work. "Hello, sweethearts. You must have had a wonderful day at school."

Rose's little arms were tight around his neck, making first claim on his attention. "Mrs. Jennings said my picture of the farm was one of the best, 'cause I did more animals than anybody and mine were really farm animals, not zoo. Bobby Jenkins had an elephant on his, isn't that funny? You can see it on the bulletin board on family night."

Ella, growing impatient, planted a kiss on his cheek. "I got all my letters *and* numbers right."

"You are both doing great. But I'm pretty hungry and we better get downstairs before Miss Bee starts clearing the table."

Rose agreed. "Okay. Hey, did you know Miss Broadnax is Miss Bee 'cause Broadnax starts with a *B*?"

"He knew *that*, Rose."

Smiling at the rare moment of competitiveness, Russell held out a hand out to each to walk downstairs for supper.

Later that evening while Ella was in the bathroom, he'd told Rose his plan for a babysitter for the next day, which was Saturday.

"I have to work a few hours tomorrow, though not late. I've asked Mrs. Johnson to take you to the park."

"*No*, don't leave us with her, Pop!" cried Rose. She began the loudest, most frantic crying he'd ever heard. He attempted to calm her, but she would not quieten.

Returning to the bedroom, Ella looked alarmed.

"Ella, I told Rose Mrs. Johnson was going to keep you in the morning and take you to the park for a while, and she became upset."

"We never want to stay with *her*, Pop."

Ella's tears began to flow, though she wasn't screaming. Russell was at a loss to understand.

"Mary Nan Johnson, Miss Bee's friend… you know her, don't you?"

Their cries become louder.

Holding them close, trying to soothe, he murmured, "Okay, okay, I will not leave you with Mrs. Johnson."

They generally like everybody. And they've seemed to enjoy Mrs. Johnson when she's visited Miss Bee. But I trust their instincts—if they're afraid of her, there must be a reason.

After a few minutes, they had calmed somewhat.

"Since Mrs. Johnson is Miss Bee's friend, a nice neighbor *and* I thought you liked her, I was sure she would be the perfect babysitter. Has she done something I don't know about?"

"*Pop…*" Ella answered calmly, with an expression which caused *him* to feel like the child who needed an explanation. "I guess you don't know about her. She *is* nice and we like her."

"Well?"

"You know she comes to visit Miss Bee a lot and we hear them talking. One day she said she'd lost her father. She was crying and real sad."

"That *is* sad; you should feel bad for her."

"We do."

Rose interrupted, "Yesterday Miss Bee was on the phone and told somebody Mrs. Johnson had lost her *best friend* now and was a lonely woman. She said, 'She lost her husband first. Now the poor woman has lost almost everybody she's ever cared about.'"

He contemplated all he'd heard, remaining puzzled.

"Shouldn't you want to be her friend and stay with her to cheer her up?"

They began to cry again.

"Girls!"

"Pop," sobbed Ella, "We do want to be her friend and cheer her up, but *please* don't leave us with her. Me and Rose don't want to be lost, too—you *need* us!"

Russell's eyes widened. He finally understood.

"You believed Mrs. Johnson had actually *lost...* completely *misplaced*, her family and friends, never to be found again?" After he stifled his amusement, he pulled them closer. "I love you so much. You make my life."

They were clearly delighted, grinning and happy once more. He gave them another squeeze before explaining some people used the word *lost* to mean the person had died.

Still puzzled, Ella asked, "Why don't grown-ups say what they mean? Mommy always said *die*, not lost."

Rose agreed. "Die means you go to heaven. Lost means your family doesn't know where you are and you might be with a mean person or in a bad place."

"You're right. It's just a term, though, and now you will know what they mean. You must be sad for Mrs. Johnson if so many people she loved have died lately. But I'll just work until noon. I'll let Miss Bee know you'll be here and I'll take you to the park myself in the afternoon."

"Okay. We'll play paper dolls while you're working."

All the upset of a few minutes before was forgotten.

He'd had to phone Mary Nan Johnson and cancel, knowing he was defeated. Maybe someone younger would be better, anyway.

After supper, the girls headed upstairs. Russell held back to speak with Miss Bee.

"Do you know any babysitters, Miss Bee, possibly a teenager who could play with the girls? Someone you wouldn't mind being here to keep them, perhaps for an evening?"

"Sure. Your boss, Daniel, has a granddaughter who babysits. I don't know her, but if she's a Connor, she's okay."

"Thanks, Miss Bee, you've saved me again."

"Going out, are you? With Dare Perry?"

He didn't know what to say. Did people here know *every*thing? He collected his thoughts and smiled. "Just going out."

She grinned.

Maybe this isn't a good idea for many reasons. But I like Dare. She makes me feel alive. She's unpretentious… genuine.

He spoke with Dare about Friday night and made arrangements for Holly Jo Connor to stay with the girls. He promised she would play Jacks *and* paper dolls and would take them downstairs to watch the new television program, *Lassie,* a popular new program about a collie dog. They were excited about the prospect of a new friend. Russell was confident Holly Jo would be pleased to have the television to keep the girls quiet for a period of time.

As for him, he had not been as excited about an evening in years. *I've been to theater openings, corporate galas, and the most exclusive restaurants and clubs in Chicago over the years. I was nervous about a few of those nights, but not as excited. It's the person who will be with me that makes the difference.* He needed to calm himself and not expect too much. However, he could not keep this petite, vibrant woman out of his mind. *She looks so delicate—the lovely porcelain skin, lively, sparkling eyes, and golden hair. She has three tiny freckles on her nose... a delightful touch.*

He'd first noticed her across the church sanctuary. At the festival, he saw her beauty come to life in such a charming, sometimes amusing manner. She was as comfortable with the children, and *him*, a relative stranger, as with the townspeople. She seemed to know everyone—which came from living in the same small town all your life. He reminded himself Beacon wasn't considered small by its residents, but it was certainly small compared to Chicago.

∼∼ **14** ∼∼

When Russell phoned Dare to confirm their date, she suggested they go to the local museum before going out to eat. "You could pick me up at six if the time works for you. The museum is open later on weekends during October, hoping for part of the Halloween business, but it closes at eight. Wouldn't an earlier evening be better for you? I know you had to make arrangements for Rose and Ella."

With everything else, she's also considerate.

"I appreciate your thinking of them."

He rang her doorbell at exactly six o'clock, surprised to find her ready and waiting. *In my experience, unusual for a woman.*

She wore a long beige skirt with a soft brown blouse, and the turquoise earrings he'd noticed before, the combination lovely.

As she directed him to the museum, she gave an overview of the *Fall Museum Experience,* as titled by eminent city leaders. "The first good thing is the prices are cut. Secondly, they've decorated many of the displays for the season. Some are funnier than scary, but it's become a tradition.

"Seriously, though, you'll most likely be surprised at the quality of our museum. The collection of World War Two artifacts is quite large. They were brought back by a member of one of Beacon's founding families. Some items have caused a lot of speculation as to how he obtained them," she laughed. "Nonetheless, it contributes a great deal to our museum."

Russell was intrigued… by the museum… more so by his companion. "You have certainly elevated my curiosity."

"And," she continued, "the initial reason I thought you might enjoy it, is the overview of our town's history. I believe it's good to know about the place you live... especially if you're considering making it your home for a while."

She's blushing. Even in the darkness of the car, I can feel her unease at perhaps presuming too much. She's wondered whether I plan to remain in Beacon.

"Turn right, just at the end of this block. Park wherever you can."

"I've not adjusted to there being no parking meters," he mentioned.

"There are a few in town, but it was fought vigorously," she laughed.

As he reached the passenger-side door, her hand was on the inside handle. "A gentleman always opens a ladies' door, madam."

She held her hand out to him.

"Prepare to be amazed," she laughed. "Maybe even frightened. If so, I'm warning you, points will be lost with me."

"Oh? I'd be interested in knowing how my points are adding up so far."

Embarrassed again, she replied, "Not at all what I meant."

"I presume *you* do not frighten easily."

"Never. My sister's friends tried to scare me every Halloween, and it always bombed or backfired."

"On my guard, then. I can be somewhat of a coward in a haunted house, but I'll try not to be obvious."

As they exited the museum later, Russell commented, "I enjoyed that very much. The history of Beacon was interesting—I'd wondered how the town got its name since it isn't near any large body of water."

"Yes, we're rather proud of the fact that our founding fathers wanted it to be a place of hope, which is one meaning of the word, beacon."

Nodding, Russell continued, "And you were right about the World War Two artifacts. Larger cities would be envious. I enjoyed all of it, though, including the Halloween touches and, thankfully, it was mild enough not to bring on fear I couldn't subdue."

She hit his shoulder playfully. "I'm happy on all counts. They did a better job this year with the decorations. I'm starving now, though. I know the timing was my idea, but it's pretty late for supper."

In the city, parties and dinners are just beginning.

"Too late for barbeque?"

"You must have been asking around. Barbeque is my favorite."

"Well," Russell admitted, "I did ask Daniel what he would suggest."

She laughed heartily. "Have you had barbeque since you've been in Alabama?"

"No."

"Then you're in for another treat. The South *knows* barbeque."

Driving her home, Russell hated for the evening to end. It was only nine, but they'd agreed on an early evening.

As he parked in front of her house, she turned to him. "It was a fun evening, Russell."

"Thank you for coming up with a perfect plan. I enjoyed it all." He hesitated a moment. "I enjoyed being with you, Dare. I suspect it wouldn't have mattered where we went or what we did."

She lowered her eyes. "Well, we did agree on an early evening… you need to check on your girls."

He'd said too much... sounded too serious. He knew even as the words rolled out of his mouth. He answered cheerfully, "Yes, time to see you safely in."

She had gathered her purse and sweater when he opened her door. *She's suddenly in a rush.*

On the porch, she unlocked the door. "Again, Russell, thank you. Good night."

"May I call you next week, perhaps go to a movie?"

"Russell... I'm really very busy... with work, family... you know... probably can't do anything anytime soon."

He didn't respond, trying to think of how to repair what he'd obviously done wrong.

She had opened her door and stood inside her house. "I know you're busy with your daughters when you're not working, too. Had a nice time, though. Good night, Russell."

"Good night, thank you for a lovely evening."

As she closed the door, he turned to walk to his car. *She doesn't want to see me again—it seemed to be going so well. I rushed her, that was it... but, if I liked her yesterday, I can't think of a word to describe how I feel now. She's comfortable to be with, has a great sense of humor, and her laugh... a big laugh coming from such a small woman. She is all woman. Come on. It's not as if I'm in love. She's just the first woman I've enjoyed being with since...*

But she is special— I won't give up.

~ 15 ~~

While Fridays were always harried, Monday was the busiest work day for Dare. Messages from late Friday had to be handled, as well as the backlog of weekend mail. Additionally, Mr. Matthews was generally in a less congenial mood. He was a good supervisor, all business, and Dare respected him, but she suspected he was a weekend drinker. She'd learned to be quieter and not allow anyone to rock his world on Mondays. Today, she didn't feel her best either. She hadn't slept well.

She wanted to check on Jenny. She had only seen her in passing the first of last week and hadn't seen her at all on Friday, nor at church on Sunday. *She was probably avoiding me, still angry, but I want to see for myself. Best wait until lunch.*

"Jenny isn't here and hasn't called in—unusual for her, isn't it?" she asked June, the secretary for Jenny's section.

"Yes, she was out Friday, too, but she phoned late morning. I talked with her myself." Lowering her voice, she added, "She sounded bad, not sick, though. I'm not saying she wasn't, but she sounded more down-and-out, you know? She said she had a stomach virus. I asked if she wanted to speak with Mr. Harrell, and she became even more distraught. So, I told her I hoped she would feel better by Saturday."

"Thank you, June. Have you phoned her today?"

"Yes. Mr. Harrell asked me to, but she didn't answer. Perhaps she'd gone to the doctor."

Back at her desk, Dare looked at the clock. It was one o'clock. Jenny not contacting work was totally out of character. She dialed Jenny's home number. She let it ring over fifteen times before hanging up. Looking up, she was startled to see Larry Harrell.

"Oh, Mr. Harrell. Good afternoon. Do you need to see Mr. Matthews?"

"No. Yes. Well, not now, my business can wait." He appeared uncomfortable. *Had Jenny told him she'd talked with her?*

"Miss Perry..."

"Yes, sir?"

"I know Miss Lewis—Jenny—is a friend of yours. Have you spoken with her over the weekend?"

"No, I haven't heard from her. Have you?" *Shoot, I didn't mean to ask that. He'll think I'm being a smart-mouth.*

"Of course not. But I'm concerned she hasn't phoned."

Boy, this guy is cool. He didn't miss a beat.

He continued, "You know, though... she hasn't been as efficient lately. She may have found another job... not even having the decency to give notice... just like these young people." Dismissing the entire subject, he turned to leave. "Have a good afternoon, Miss Perry."

Decency? Young people! You leech. Dare was steaming. But her desk phone demanded attention.

She steamed as she worked. At two-thirty, she had another thought.

It isn't like Jenny not to contact someone. She was upset a week ago... but expecting to see Mr. Harrell on Thursday night... hoping for a proposal. Perhaps the evening didn't go well. What might her state of mind be? She pulled Jenny's personnel file to verify her address.

"Mr. Matthews. I have somewhat of an emergency. Not me, I'm fine, it's a friend of mine. Could I take the remainder of the afternoon off?"

Asking for time off on a Monday. I'm out of my mind, too.

Though he appeared surprised, he answered considerately, "Of course. You wouldn't ask if it were not important. I'll handle things."

"Thank you, sir.

Thank God for a decent supervisor.

Driving faster than usual, Dare was knocking on Jenny's front door within thirty minutes. No answer. No movement inside. Yet, she sensed she was home.

"Jenny, it's Dare. I'm worried about you. Please come to the door."

No sound.

"Jenny. If you don't come to the door, I will phone the police. Seriously. I'll wait only another minute."

Still no sound, no movement. Dare was genuinely alarmed. Jenny's apartment was an older home turned into duplex apartments. If someone was home next door, she was sure they would have already heard her. She would stop there first... hope they would let her make an emergency phone call. As she stepped off the small porch to walk to the other, she heard the door open.

Jenny looked a wreck. She must have been crying for days. Her hair was a tangled mess, her makeup obviously days old and smeared. She was dressed, but from the rumpled look, she appeared to have been in the same clothes for a while.

"Oh, honey. Let's go inside."

As Dare entered the house, her concern grew. The house was dark, closed curtains and no lights. Everywhere she looked were broken items amid strewn magazines, pillows, and overturned kitchen chairs. An array of pill bottles sat on the kitchen counter, others scattered about on the floor.

"Jenny, honey... talk to me."

Jenny glared. "Talk? You haven't talked to me since I poured my heart out to you. You didn't phone or come to see me at work—you don't care. I have no one left who cares!"

Dare stood, unmoving. *I thought she needed space. I was excusing myself... not wanting to get deeper into her problems. No wonder she won't talk to me now, I haven't shown myself to be a friend... when she desperately needed one.*

"You're right. I made the wrong call. I assumed you wouldn't want to talk with me. Then I became worried when I went to your office today and found you hadn't called in."

Jenny wouldn't look at her.

"Then... when Mr. Harrell talked to me about you, I got so angry I..."

"Larry? You talked to him about me?" Jenny was incredulous.

"*No.* He stopped at my desk to ask if I'd heard from you. I replied no, and he became so rude, I knew something was really wrong between you two. Honey... he is not a decent person. He's not worth your time."

"I know... now. I wanted to be the woman he could settle down with. He made me feel important. For a while. No one ever made me feel like a woman before... *desirable*, you know?"

"I do." Dare sat on the sofa as she looked at Jenny. "Could we sit together for a minute... to talk about this?"

Jenny hesitated but seemed to give up a measure of her anger before sitting on the opposite end of the sofa."

"Jenny, did something happen?"

"He came here Thursday night. I thought he was going to propose. Honestly. I was so excited, actually planning a wedding in my mind. I lit candles, had on a soft pink lounging outfit... romantic music... but he didn't propose.

When he realized what I'd expected, he made it plain he'd *never* had it in mind." She took a deep breath before continuing. "So... I asked *him*... I asked him to marry me."

"You are not the first woman ever to propose to a man."

"No? Do most men *laugh* at the woman?"

Dare was speechless. How could he be so cruel?

"Yes. He laughed. Then he tried to console me, caressing me gently, and I went into his arms and cried. After a few minutes, he wanted to be romantic again... he said we could still *enjoy each other*. I clung to him and told him I loved him and begged him to say he loved me—he'd made me think he did, but he wouldn't say it. He only said he could still *show me a good time*, kissed me and..."

"What *happened*, Jenny?" Dare asked, not sure she wanted to hear the answer.

"It was ugly. When he wouldn't say he loved me, I began to pull away. He laughed again and called me a child. He told me he was *fond* of me, that my naiveté was charming. I finally realized I didn't really matter at all. I was just entertainment. He tried to kiss me again... but I finally made him leave."

Dare was relieved, able to breathe again. "So..."

"I am so stupid. And no one cares. I don't have a single real friend."

"Jenny, I'm sorry. I *haven't* been a good friend. Please forgive me. And... forgive yourself. Cruel men have been doing this for centuries. He took advantage of your sweet, good heart. He called you naïve because you didn't know people like him existed in your world. You expect good from people."

Jenny's response nearly broke her heart.

"I believed he loved me," she whispered weakly. "I almost... I was going to let him... I wanted to... you know..."

"But you didn't." Dare looked at this pitiful... *child*, so hurt and disillusioned. She moved closer and took her hands in hers.

"Jenny... why are the pill bottles scattered about?"

"You *know* why." She appeared to be calming. "I thought of taking them. I don't have anything of worth in my life. And no one would miss me."

Before Dare could respond, she confessed, "I'd already changed my mind... *God* gave me life. I believe it's His decision when mine is over. I may have forgotten for a minute, but I wouldn't have done it."

Dare's tears began to spill over. This sweet, innocent girl had nearly been crushed.

Jenny continued. "I also realized I would not give the rat the satisfaction of thinking someone would be willing to *die* because of him." Her hand suddenly went to her mouth. "Oh, no—I'm awful! I meant besides Jesus. Jesus died for everyone. Dare, I *am* awful. I think I'm going crazy."

Surprisingly, she began to giggle. "Larry Harrell really is an old *poot*, isn't he? And he didn't get what he wanted. I'm *glad* he laughed—it was probably what saved me from being completely over-the-edge foolish."

Dare hugged her. "I'll be a real friend, I promise. I could use one, too, after all. How about you go take a shower, and I'll straighten up a few things. Then we can go out to eat, or just pick something up if you want."

As she picked up clutter around Jenny's apartment, her anger grew. Jenny considered taking her *life* because of this guy!

Another one, Thomas, had me thinking I might try again at caring for a man... which ended with my slamming the door in his face. I've said it before—I'm done. I have a good life and it's enough.

Russell, though... he's a gentleman... no, I've given him the brush-off. I made the right decision. Besides, he has a past... and two children.

~~ **16** ~~

Jenny returned to work the next day. Considering her recent experience, she was doing well. She and Dare agreed Larry Harrell would be as anxious to avoid her as she would be to stay out of his way. In the meantime, Dare began working on her transfer to another department.

Please, no more drama for a while. A quiet evening with canned soup for supper, a hot bath, and climbing into bed with a good novel and a chocolate bar.

She and Jenny had made plans for a movie within the week, with Jenny assuring her, "I want a friend, but I don't want you to feel responsible for me. I *do* have other friends. I cut them off. I've realized it was my fault—I think I'm growing up," she laughed.

**

Craaacck…

As Dare crossed her porch, she heard a faint sound. She turned to walk back to the steps. A spot in the porch felt weak—she was sure she'd felt it give a bit.

After work the next day, she stopped at the hardware store and asked for Daniel.

"What's up?"

"I heard a faint cracking sound in the middle of my porch yesterday. When I walked back across, it seemed to give a little. Not an emergency, but I hoped you might recommend someone to look at it and possibly repair."

Daniel raised his hand into the air. "Russell," he called, "Come over here for a minute."

"Oh, no, Daniel, I don't want to bother him. Couldn't you recommend someone else?"

"Russell seems to have expertise in this area, and yours is a small job. I've had several folks this week refuse to buy wood until they could talk with him. He's been giving good advice, even figuring how much wood they should buy—not everyone can handle figuring, you know. I've just given him a raise, hoping to keep him a while."

"Is Daniel singing my praises? Hope so." Russell looked directly at Dare. She couldn't read his expression… hope, or disdain?

Daniel walked away as Dare explained, "I only have a weak spot in my porch, too small for you to be bothered."

"Look, Dare, it's business. I'll stop by when I leave here this afternoon and look at it. If wood needs replacing, I'll measure and take care of it for you. No problem at all."

She was uncomfortable.

He asked, "Is it a problem for *you*?"

She looked up, finally meeting his direct gaze. She attempted to appear calm and business-like. "No. I'd appreciate it. So… I'll see you later."

She walked away, leaving Russell questioning whether he should have handed this off to someone else after all. But he wanted another chance. He had a feeling she was worth the effort.

Lord, am I going in the right direction? I'm not doing a good job straightening out my life on my own. Trying to do it alone may have been the problem for a number of years.

As Russell walked up the sidewalk, Dare opened her front door.

Not a good sign, no chit-chat.

"Just walk slowly toward the door. See if you feel a slight give."

He walked back and forth several times before leaning down to press the wood at the center of the porch. "I think you're right, but it's slight. I brought a flashlight to look at the underside."

She sat in the rocker as he walked down the steps to the opening at one end of the porch, bending to look before crawling underneath. Appearing again in only minutes, he came back to measure a spot. He hadn't uttered a word. He measured and wrote on a small pad, tore off the page and stepped over to hand it to her.

"I can do it if you want. My estimate is close to what it will cost. I wouldn't charge you because it won't take long. But you can keep the figures and call whoever you like. Just let me know." He turned to leave.

"Russell?"

He stood on the top step. "It's okay." Heart pounding out of his shirt, he so *badly* wanted her to see him as someone who could at least be a friend. Whatever he'd done wrong, he'd weigh every single word if she gave him another chance. "As I said, just let me know what you decide." He walked toward his car as she rose to follow him.

"Russell."

She'd stopped at the first step. He was almost to the street as he turned around.

"Russell, please sit with me for a few minutes... to discuss the repairs." Trembling, unsure, she questioned herself. She'd gotten what she asked—he'd walked away and made it clear he wouldn't bother her. She returned to the rocker and he pulled up the other chair. Neither spoke for a minute.

He smiled weakly. "Do you want me to do the repairs?"

She hoped he couldn't see the quivering she felt coursing through her body. "Um... yes... I'd want to pay you for your time. I'm sorry for being so abrupt the other night. I *am* busy, though, and didn't want you to get the wrong idea. Could we leave it there, and be friends?"

His heart was doing flips. She'd offered kindness and friendship, a step in the right direction. He grinned. "I can be a great friend."

"Good."

"About the pay… I have a solution."

"Oh?" More relaxed, she smiled.

"If you don't want to do it, no bad feelings." He laughed, attempting to keep the mood light. "I get what you'd call *home cooking* every day—Miss Bee's version. I don't want anything fancy, but a meal not cooked for a crowd would be nice for a change. One without dry beans, perhaps—would you pay me with a meal cooked for four… me and the girls, with you?"

To his relief, she laughed. "You've obviously not heard much about my cooking, but I think I can come up with one meal. It's a bargain."

They shook hands to seal the deal. Not the touch he desired, but he would wait. If right, it would work out.

Russell prayed. *Lord, I'm listening. I'm trying to learn to wait. Direct me—show me the way to go. I've made a mess of my life. I don't know whether it can be made right, but only You can help—I know that now. I'm falling in love with this woman… but I don't want to hurt her… or anyone. If I'm going in the wrong direction, please let me see.*

He was thankful for the progress made with Dare and he would weigh his words with the hope of building a relationship. He knew she was fond of Rose and Ella, and they adored her—a good foundation on which to build.

He phoned her the next evening. "Would it be convenient if I do the work tomorrow afternoon? The girls have a birthday party to attend after school. Their friends' mother will bring them home about six-thirty. I can probably finish by then, but if I'm somewhat later, it will not be a problem."

"Yes, fine with me."

"You don't have to be home. I just wanted to check with you. I'll have everything I need. And… let me know about the other whenever you want."

Teasing, she asked, "You mean when I'll *pay up*?"

"I was trying to be subtle."

"*If* I'm satisfied with the work," she laughed, "I think I can have a satisfactory meal for four on Thursday night. Would that work for you?"

"Absolutely. Thanks. Have a good evening."

"Thank you, Russell…"

Replacing the receiver, he smiled. *She's relaxed again. It almost seemed she wanted to talk more. But I'll wait.*

He was growing more content at Connor's. Though not the work for which he'd been educated, it did involve building. Daniel was relying on him more often and had given him a raise, which in no way compared to his salary a few months ago, but on the plus side, he didn't have nearly as many expenses. Additionally, he had no work worries to carry home. He liked and admired Daniel Connor. He was a good man. On numerous occasions, he'd observed him giving away materials or information to save money for his customers… even when a sale was lost.

"Hey, Russell, how about sitting down with me for a lunch break? My wife sent an extra pimiento cheese sandwich, and she makes the *best*."

"Sounds good."

The other employees had already taken their break. They had the small room to themselves.

"Russell, I'm curious about your background. You're more knowledgeable about building than anyone I've ever had working here. You know more about the details than I do."

"Well... I..."

"Look, son, I'm not asking for information you don't want to share. I know you're a widower and about your wife dying in an unusual storm. But I have a feeling there's more to your story... more that made you want a fresh start. I'm only trying to say I like you and hope you'll stick around. I doubt you'd be sticking here at my little store because you're qualified for more. It's obvious you're educated. I only wanted you to know I'd noticed. So, if you ever want to talk about anything, just know I'll listen."

Russell had never known a man like Daniel. He clearly knew there was more to Russell's past, yet made it easier.

"Thank you, Daniel. I appreciate it more than you know. You're right, I do have extensive experience in building. And... I experienced more than a few dark days before landing in Beacon. I'm trying to work through them."

"Alright. 'Nuff said. Now, enjoy your sandwich so I can tell Mabel."

"Daniel, have you always lived in Beacon, born and reared?"
"No."

As Daniel mentioned his home community, Russell's eyebrows shot up, completely unnoticed by Daniel as he continued to explain. "We had a church, general store and grammar school. That was about it.

"I met Mabel at a church revival, the first night I went. You know, one of those traveling tent meetin's. Didn't especially take to the preacher. He was too loud and a bit *un-holy*, in my opinion. 'Course, I was judging, which is wrong, but he just wasn't someone I'd want to sit down with if I wanted to discuss God's love. Anyways, I hadn't thought of lookin' for a woman just yet, planned to build up a nest egg before I settled down.

"You never know when your plans will change, though. Life is just a plan, similar to first-draft blueprints. We think we got 'em just right, then someone or something comes along and alters them. Sometimes we agree, sometimes we don't, but it doesn't matter. We have to deal with the changes anyways."

Russell was momentarily uneasy. *Life is like a blueprint? Is that insight... or suspicion?*

With a belly laugh, Daniel continued. "Anyways, I went to revival every night... to get to know Mabel. I thought she was a follower of this preacher, which I was just willing to overlook. Found out later she lived in Munford and came with a group the first night. She didn't like the fella either but came back because she liked me. Now, how do you like *that*? I was just as charming way back then as now."

Russell was enjoying this. Daniel was not only a great guy but a good storyteller.

"How long before you asked her to marry you?"

"Funny you should ask. We married the next month. Mind, we were both twenty-one. Anyhow, Mabel liked small towns. Her family was originally from a small town in Tennessee called Mt. Seasons, where Mabel was born, but they moved away when she was in grammar school. Her mother was a Marshall and she still has cousins she visits now and then—one of them married a Russian named Nordin... but that's another story for another time.

"Mabel liked Munford, but it was *too* small. She wasn't kidding—though it had my stompin' grounds beat by a stop sign—the only thing she asked was that we settle in Beacon."

"But you said you were not from Beacon."

"No."

Russell could see Daniel was having a great time with this story. "Where are you *really* from?"

"Thought I said."

"Daniel, I knew you were kidding… it caught me by surprise, but just because I'm not Southern…"

"True, not many people have heard of it but I wasn't kidding about where I grew up…"

"I find it hard to believe you would even *say* the name… the word. How would a place ever get such an ugly name?"

"What in the world are you talking about, son?"

As Russell repeated the name of the town Daniel had mentioned, Daniel began slapping his leg and laughing so hard, Russell actually thought he might fall out of his chair. Quickly the laughter grew out of control as he doubled over. His laughter was so contagious, Russell began laughing with him.

It *was* a comical name, but still…

Russell looked up to see two employees at the open door, curious as to what was going on.

Gaining a measure of control, Daniel explained, "I just told him where I was from." He lost control again, tears rolling down his face.

The guys looked puzzled.

Still laughing, Daniel explained. "He thought… when I told him where I was from… he thought I said…ya'll will never believe this… he thought I was from a place called *Shit*-bone!"

Now three guys were howling with laughter, and Russell decided he had simply missed something.

They finally explained. The name of the community was *Shin*bone… for real, but not what he believed he heard.

As they settled down and the others returned to work, Daniel and Russell began clearing the table. "Sorry I laughed so hard, Russell, it just got away with me," Daniel grinned.

"I get it… *now*," Russell laughed, "but I knew that word was out of character."

Daniel nodded.

"Changing the subject, Daniel, may I ask a serious question?"

"Sure."

"You've known Dare Perry a long time, and me for only a short time. *And*, there are blanks about me you'd like filled in…"

"What's the question, son?"

"Do you think I'd have any chance with her? We've only had one actual date and we're at a rather fragile friendship level just now. But, I'm very fond of her. She's special. Do I stand a chance?"

"Russell, I'll be honest. She's carrying a burden in her heart which seems to trouble her relationships with men. I agree with you—she is a very special woman, a *good* woman, and it's no myth they are hard to find. But, your chances? Possible, but I wouldn't bet on it. I'm sorry."

"Has she been married?"

"No."

"Then, what…?"

"No, I'll not be telling you about her burden. It's hers to share or not. I'd advise you not to ask her—you would assure the *end*, son."

What burden could Dare have? She appears so carefree, has many friends, a good job… home… family… faith… never married… How would she react to my background and past? Not good. I must get things resolved. I'm only coasting… I have no more of an answer now than when I left the other life behind.

I'm thankful to have Daniel as a friend. He's a wise man who seems to see through to the core of people. I'd do well to heed his advice.

~~ 17 ~~

Russell delayed telling the girls about plans for supper with Dare. He returned from work shortly after they came in from school, finding them dutifully doing homework.

"We're almost through, Pop. Can we watch television after supper?" asked Rose.

"I'm glad you've almost finished because I have a surprise."

He had their attention. "After you clean up, you may wear your favorite dresses." He paused, teasing them.

"Why? Where're we going?" they shouted.

"Do you think you might enjoy going over to Miss Dare's for supper tonight?"

As predicted, they could not get ready quick enough, talking constantly, asking question after question.

"What're you wearing, Pop?"

"Me? What do you think I should wear?"

Rose considered the question seriously. "I guess it doesn't matter what boys wear, does it?"

He chuckled. "Not like girls, for sure. I guess I'll just get a shower and change from my work clothes, maybe not smell like sawdust. Okay?"

"Use your perfume. It smells good." Ella suggested.

"Guys don't wear perfume, honey. We wear after-shave lotion."

"Oh. Well, it smells good. Hurry up—we can't wait." They were no more thrilled than he.

Arriving at six o'clock, Dare welcomed them inside.

As Russell walked in, his arm brushed hers. She was more than aware of the feelings coursing through her, at the same time appreciating the light aroma of his after-shave. *He wore dark blue dress pants... most men would have been more casual... and even I can appreciate the fine quality... and a casual white shirt... against his dark skin....* He looks as comfortable in dress pants and shirt as in work clothes.

She wasn't sure she recognized the feelings she was experiencing, but she was suddenly nervous in his presence,

Russell observed Dare approvingly, as well. She was lovely in casual soft brown slacks and a white ruffled blouse with plain low-heel shoes. Once again, her earrings and necklace were turquoise, but a differently-designed set. She generally wore little makeup, perhaps less tonight for a casual evening, but she'd added a flattering touch of coral to her lips.

Putting aside her momentary anxiety, Dare said happily, "I'm glad to see you girls again. I hope I've cooked things you like. I'm not worried about the dessert, but that will be a surprise."

"Look, Pop, she's got a television," Ella exclaimed. "Can we watch it tonight?"

Dare answered, "If it's okay with Russell... *after* supper, we'll have dessert and watch one of my favorite programs."

"*What*? Timmy's dog, *Lassie*, is our favorite, but it's not on tonight."

"You'll see. Miss Broadnax has televisions at the boarding house, doesn't she?"

Russell answered. "She has only the one in the front room, well, *sitting* room. She thinks it's a fad."

Dare laughed. "Almost everyone has one now. There are quite a few good programs, movies, and the latest news. Occasionally, on nights when I'm not sleeping well, I wish it were on after midnight."

"Doubt Miss Bee knows much about the programming. I've never seen her watch it. We're just hoping she will have inside bathrooms installed before long," Russell answered.

"How horrible!" Dare gasped.

Rose interrupted, "We've *got* bathrooms, Pop."

Russell grinned.

"Russell Townsend, you're teasing me. I *believed* you!" Dare laughed. "Okay, I've been warned—you are not always honest."

She continued to delight him. He grinned as their eyes met. Seriously lost in thought and the moment, he finally replied earnestly, "You have a hearty laugh."

Flustered, she turned toward the kitchen. "It's ready. Everyone, have a seat."

She had prepared the table and place settings for a true dinner party, complete with a fresh floral centerpiece. Russell seated the girls before coming around to pull a chair out for Dare, who was clearly surprised.

"You've prepared a fine meal and set a beautiful table for us. May I seat the hostess?"

"Why, yes," she acquiesced.

As he sat, she looked from Rose and Ella to Russell. "I enjoy setting a pretty table now and then. Russell, would you ask the blessing?"

He hesitated for an instant. "Yes. And thank you. We have a lot to thank God for tonight, and I've been remiss since we began traveling."

Rose had already bowed her head. "Mama didn't let us skip prayers," Ella commented.

Russell mentally reprimanded himself. "And we won't skip them anymore."

Dare had prepared a roast with potatoes, carrots and onions, a leafy green salad, a fresh fruit mix, and hot rolls. As they began to eat, Rose commented, "Mama cooked roast like this on Sundays. I like it."

Fork in air, Russell stopped to look at Rose. For months, she had rarely spoken voluntarily outside family. She'd suddenly begun to open up.

Dare answered, "It's a good Sunday meal because you can leave it to cook while at church."

"That's what Mama said."

Dare glanced at Russell. It was obvious to her that he was surprised by the conversation. "I'm glad you like it, honey," she replied.

Rose continued, "Did you know I was named for Mama? My whole name is Brenda Rose Townsend, but she just called me Rose… 'cause she was Brenda. Where we lived, people don't use two names."

Ella added, "My name is Ella Susanne."

"Your names are beautiful," Dare answered, "like both of you."

"Thank you," the girls answered together.

After a minute, Russell resumed enjoying the meal, and conversation turned to other things.

"The meal was delicious, Dare, the fresh salad a treat in itself. Miss Bee's green offerings are green beans, cooked to death, or turnip greens, which I do like, but she is overly generous with grease."

Realizing four small ears heard every word and the girls might repeat them at the most inopportune time, he added, "But we like her cooking, don't we, girls? And she truly bakes the best cakes anywhere."

Ella added, "We liked your roast, Miss Dare, and everything, 'specially rolls—Miss Bee makes good cornbread and biscuits, but she doesn't have rolls."

"I'm glad you enjoyed it. I thought we might enjoy sitting in the back yard for a while before dessert. It's nice out this time of the year. I think it's too late in the fall to catch lightning bugs, but I enjoy listening to the crickets after dark and hearing the old owl in the tree next door."

"Lightning bugs?" echoed the girls.

"Girls," answered Russell, "we have them in Illinois. You probably know them as fireflies; I believe they're the same, aren't they, Dare?"

"Yes, I'd forgotten they were known by another name."

"We didn't have any in Evanston," Rose insisted.

Russell smiled, shaking his head. "Shameful… maybe there were too many lights and you didn't see them."

Dare carried light blankets as they walked outside. "If it's cool, we'll put these around us."

Russell put a blanket around the girls as they huddled together. Returning to sit beside Dare, he picked up another, placing one end around her shoulders and one around his, careful not to sit too close. He enjoyed sitting peacefully without conversation. The stars sparkled and shone above, thousands visible, appearing as tiny flickering lights in the night sky. A light cloud cover had partially hidden the moon, making the night darker and seemingly all their own. The absence of street lights was a blessing.

How I wish I could take her hand, look into her eyes and tell her how special she's become.

Instead, he sat quietly, enjoying her nearness.

Rose and Ella adored sitting in the dark listening to sounds of the night, whispering about what they heard.

After a while, Dare whispered, "They're amazingly quiet. I hate to interrupt such peace."

"Let's enjoy it a little longer. I'm as content as they are."

She pulled at the blanket and seemed to inch closer—maybe he imagined it, but he knew they were sharing the serenity of the moment.

"You look lovely tonight… as always."

"Thank you."

Her light hair shone in the moonlight. He sensed a faint aroma of orange blossoms. Even in the darkness, she seemed to glow with an inner beauty.

Dare felt his warmth as they sat comfortably close, breathing the night air. She felt his eyes on her and realized she didn't mind. She had known few responsible, solid men. Responsible in careers... but in personal lives, it wasn't often true. This man was raising two children on his own. She'd never heard a complaint, not even a comment about any difficulties. They were a part of him and he obviously loved it. And he'd maintained a sense of gratitude and humor. Rare.

She looked at her watch. "Sorry to break up the fun, but it's almost eight. Let's go inside. You can turn on the television while I get dessert ready."

The peace and quiet of the evening gone, the girls shouted gleefully as they ran inside.

Russell and Dare folded the blankets. He took them as they began to walk inside.

"Dare, this has been as nice an evening as any I've ever experienced."

She stopped to look up at him. "For me, too."

"The television is on the right channel. Turn it on and get comfortable. I'll bring the dessert in to you in just a minute."

"We *never* ate in the living room before," Rose informed.

Russell looked around the kitchen while she busied herself with dessert. "You have a lovely home... and solid-built."

"Thank you. I've been here a year and really love it. I like all the older houses in this neighborhood. This is one of the few smaller ones."

"I noticed most are older two-story homes. The architecture in the area is beautiful."

"One of my favorites, a couple of blocks down, has been vacant quite a while. I know I'm silly, but it looks sad without a family. There are not many in the Pennington family left, and none of them want it. More than likely the inside is in bad shape by now." She turned from the counter. "There's talk of the cost for repairs being too much—it may be torn down."

Russell was visibly dismayed. "I noticed it... because of the remarkable trim and details in the roof line."

"Most people pay no attention," she said, appreciatively.

"I like history and old buildings. They have character." He winked, continuing, "And I agree with you—the old place needs a family."

"Dessert is ready. Let's join the girls."

As she walked into the living room with desserts on a tray, she announced, "Thankfully, I didn't bake a cake—doubt I could compete with Miss Bee, but I think this is a treat... ice cream with hot fudge sauce. With big napkins on your lap, you can eat it while we watch *Father Knows Best*, my favorite program."

"We never *heard* of that one," the girls commented as they settled down on the floor.

"Well, I'm sure you'll like it. She looked at Russell. "Can't mess up ice cream and heating fudge sauce out of a jar."

"All perfect," he answered.

It *was* perfect... until a small crack appeared... a crack less perceptible than the one in the porch, but there, nonetheless.

"We liked *Father Knows Best*, Miss Dare." Ella proclaimed. "We wanna watch it every week."

"We'll try to do that," agreed Russell. "I enjoyed it, too. But it's time to get going. You do have school in the morning, and you're going to be late getting to bed. Thank Miss Dare and get into your jackets."

At the door, he wished he could prolong the evening. "Thank you, Dare. The evening has been a treat for all of us." She looked so soft and happy. His hopes were building, but he would say no more tonight.

Before the girls ran down the sidewalk, Ella, "Goodnight, Miss Dare. Me and Rose liked the dark night and ice cream, and *Father Knows Best*... the daddy was nice, and he was funny with his children, like our daddy was."

Russell's heart seemed to thud and stop.

The girls were halfway to the car. He paused briefly on the porch steps and half-turned to catch a glimpse of Dare's face. She'd heard. Maybe she wouldn't read anything into it. After all, who can understand children?

"G'night, Dare," he called out cheerfully. "See you soon." *A perfect evening. Almost. Children say the strangest things... I won't focus on possibilities. I'll focus on the future and resolving the past. I can see a future here in Beacon. I'd like to think of Dare as part of it.*

Dare stood at the door until she could no longer see his car. Closing the door slowly, she thought, *A lovely, almost magical night. Sitting outdoors in the crisp fall air, sharing the blanket...there's no question about it... I've grown attached to Rose and Ella. I adore them. And their relationship with Russell is beautiful; the love they have for each other is almost tangible. He's so good and caring with them. And the same with me—it's who he is. I could almost...*

When I think I've conquered my past, something happens inside. This time, though, maybe it wasn't just me... Ella said, the way our daddy was. Daddy. *They always call him* Pop. *She said* was... *not, the way Daddy* is. *A casual remark from a six-year-old. Maybe it meant nothing, just repeating what most children call their father.*

Then, why can't I calm my inner being? I want this feeling of foreboding to go away... because I'm falling in love with him.

∼∼ **18** ∼∼

Going down for supper later than usual, they filled the last three chairs at the long table. Russell was surprised to see Miss Bee seated at one end. She'd never dined with the boarders before. As he surveyed the group, he realized her friend, Mary Nan Johnson, was seated to her right. *Mrs. Johnson... Mary Nan, the neighbor who had 'lost' everyone she cared about. Miss Bee is a good friend, trying to help.*

Frank Weathers sat on the left side of Miss Bee. At least he *thought* it was Frank. This man's hair was combed and *clean*. He had on a plaid shirt, unlike any work clothes observed prior. The biggest change, though, was his smile. *Perhaps Miss Bee has seen more in Frank than we have. She's trying to get him together with Mary Nan. They're all talking... even laughing... rare for Miss Bee, but mind-boggling to hear from Frank Weathers.*

"Mr. Weathers, didja get a haircut? You sure look different tonight," Ella observed brightly.

Lord... even Ella noticed. Please control her words.

"You look nice."

Poor Frank appeared mortified. He coughed and sputtered, before stammering, "Thank you, Little Miss Ella." Miss Bee's expression hinted at being amused, though a bit embarrassed as well.

Russell tried to hurry the girls through the meal before either could make further observations. He should warn them about saying such things, but what could he say? He decided to let it go.

Roughly hewn Frank Weathers and very-proper Mary Nan? I guess anything truly is possible, for which I should thank God.

The thought reminded him how much he wanted to phone Dare... hoping she might go out with him again. But he wasn't sure. He reminded himself he'd vowed to take it slow if given another chance. *A door has been opened. She was happy being with us the other night. The three of us, though, not a date with me. I have to wait. Do I have* time *to wait?*

**

Dare looked forward to lunch with Jenny. They'd decided to take an extra hour to allow time to talk.

Jenny wore a new peach-colored dress, the style and color flattering, and shoes with three-inch heels. In addition, she had a new haircut.

"Jenny, you look great."

"Thanks. I'm feeling better about myself and everything in general. I'm trying to lose a few pounds but, you know, I've decided not to lose any sleep over it. All the females in my family are big. What's new with you, though? I have a feeling something *is* new. Am I right?"

Dare didn't usually talk about private feelings with friends. Even Doreen had to pull it out of her. But she felt a need.

"Yes, in a way. I'm interested in someone. Or think I am. My brain and heart seem mixed up. I'm sure you know what I mean."

"You always seem to make good decisions, Dare. This man must be a good person if you like him. What's the problem?"

"There are things about his past I don't know, and I have no idea whether they're important. One moment I'm questioning, the next moment I see him smiling and helping someone, and my questions disappear.

"There's something else...about *me* that few people know. I need to sort it out and I'm not doing that at all well. You know my sister, Doreen… she's tried. I'll think I'm past it, then it rears up again… usually when I'm beginning to be interested in someone."

"Dare, you can trust me if you want to talk."

Dare poured her heart out and Jenny listened patiently. Afterward, they cried together.

"Dare, you're a good person. I hope you can put this behind you. The guy you have feelings for sounds great—he'd have to be for you to be giving him any thought at all."

"Thank you for listening. I believe I needed to relive my guilt and cry again. I still don't know what to do. Somehow, though, I feel stronger."

Walking back into the office building, Dare stopped suddenly. "Oh, Jenny, I haven't given you a chance to talk at all. I've been concerned about you and have prayed for your recovery from what Larry put you through."

"I'm honestly all right, thanks in a big part to you. You helped rescue me from myself," Jenny laughed. Today was *your* turn."

"Thank you, Jenny. I thank God for you."

Jenny vowed to herself never to reveal any part of what Dare confided.

**

Dare remembered something barely catching her eye last month as she drove to work. A glimpse from her rear-view mirror. A man was carrying a few old planks of wood, placing them carefully on top of a small stack, several hundred yards from the railroad tracks she'd just crossed. Perhaps he was a hobo, she couldn't tell much with the cap pulled low over his face. It wasn't quite time to collect wood for a winter fire. Maybe he was planning ahead.

There appeared to be an old foundation at the site, a slab of concrete no larger than fifteen feet square, as if there had been a building there of some sort. Good place for a fire when the weather took a turn. Yes, it must be a hobo.

Driving past the property again today, she glanced at the pile of wood. It had grown. In one stack were boards from old buildings, different lengths, some with noticeable peeling paint. The smaller stack appeared to be new wood. There was something else—on the existing slab, a small building was being framed in. Though the wood was mismatched, the builder seemed to know what he was about.

She could see nothing desirable about the area. There were a few houses, trailers, and other nondescript buildings, most in poor condition but cared for. She had observed women hanging wash on clotheslines, men working on old vehicles, and children playing happily. *Well, I haven't seen any appliances on front porches yet.* She reprimanded herself—they were doing the best they could.

Before she reached home, she thought again of Russell. She'd seen him at church Sunday, but he sat across the auditorium, as he had when she'd first observed him there. He looked in her direction, smiled and nodded, and she did the same. *Perhaps he'll come over to speak after the service.*

She spoke to those around her before looking across to Russell's empty seat. He'd left without coming over. *It's what you indicated you wanted... space, friendship but nothing more.* She felt warmed to know worship was important to him. She couldn't have a relationship with anyone who didn't believe.

Relationship? It came to mind so easily. Maybe I do want more from Russell Townsend. Oh, God, let me see clearly. What's in his past I should know?

**

Rinnng, rinnnng, rinnng.

Dare had just walked in from work.

"Hello."

"Hi. It's Russell. I didn't know what time you got home. Do you have time to talk?"

"Yes. I just walked inside." She laughed nervously. "I'm removing my shoes this minute." She tugged at her hose and garter belt, as well... *information for which he has no need.*

"I wanted to walk over to speak to you after church yesterday but wasn't sure I should intrude. I did want to thank you again for the meal and such a nice evening."

"I thought you would come over to say hello."

"I enjoy being with you, Dare, but I don't want to be pushy. Everything we've done together... the museum, the evening at your house..." He felt foolish, like an insecure teenager.

"How about taking me to a movie?" she interrupted, surprising herself.

He had to catch his breath. "I'd love to. Tonight?"

"Russell, it's five o'clock."

"Then, when?"

"Can you get a babysitter for tomorrow night?"

"Yes."

She giggled. "You can't *know*. How about calling me at work tomorrow? The number is ADams-4565."

"I have it written down. Six o'clock, okay?

She suggested getting a babysitter, which means she does want to be with me, *not just the girls.*

Dare replaced the phone receiver. *I want to be with him. Lord, I am alright with the world. I really think I am going to be okay. Thank you.*

~~ 19 ~~

*R*ear *Window*, starring Grace Kelly and James Stewart, was a perfect date movie with its tension-building story and touch of romance. Dare leaned forward in a tense scene and grabbed Russell's hand. She gripped it for several minutes. When she relaxed to lean back, she didn't let go.

Driving home, she chatted about the movie. "One of the best I've ever seen."

"I agree, couldn't predict the next move. Of course, at one point the pain in my hand was so intense, I lost concentration," he grinned.

"I did *not* squeeze hard." She looked at him and laughed. "Besides… I think you liked it."

More seriously, he answered, "I hated for the movie to end."

At her door, Russell determined to keep things light and do nothing to make her uncomfortable.

After she'd unlocked the door, he put a hand lightly on her shoulder. "I enjoyed tonight. I hope we can do something again soon."

Happy and relaxed, she looked up at him as their eyes met. He leaned in and gave her a quick kiss on the cheek. "Good night. Thank you."

He took a step backward as she reached for his hand.

"I won't squeeze this time. It was a lovely evening, Russell." Seeming to ponder, she asked slowly, "Could we meet over the weekend, just the two of us? Later I'd like to include Rose and Ella, just not this time."

"Later? You're thinking ahead?"

"Is it possible?"

"I hope so. Oh, God, I hope so—I've prayed not to do the wrong thing again."

"I *meant*, is it possible for us to meet over the weekend to talk. I don't think *you* were the problem. I like you. There are things we need to talk about, though, things I need to tell you. For now... could you kiss me goodnight?"

He was afraid to speak. He leaned in to put his arms around her, resisting the temptation to hold her tightly. As he came close and his lips covered hers, she responded, her arms going around his waist. His arms tightened around her as she moved her hands up to the middle of his back.

Breathless, he relaxed his arms and moved back.

"Russell," she whispered.

"Dare... I've never felt what I feel for you. I was almost engaged once and never felt this."

Softly, she asked, "What do you mean?"

He wasn't thinking clearly. Continuing to talk almost in whispers, he answered, "There's no one like you, not for me. I'm trying not to rush, but I care for you so much, so deeply."

"What about Brenda?"

"Brenda was different."

"We've known each other only two months," she said tenderly.

"A lifetime."

The desire was strong to take her in his arms again. But, he knew he should leave. He touched her lips. "Goodnight... thinking of you will keep me warm all night."

She sighed. "This weekend?"

"Yes, I'll call you."

She stood watching as he walked to his car and drove away. She wanted to hold on to this feeling. But they had to talk before anything more. There were things he needed to know about her, the things she'd shared with Jenny.

**

The girls were going home with a friend after church on Sunday. Russell would pick them up at five o'clock. The timing was perfect.

"I'll make sandwiches and we can drive to the park," Dare suggested.

"Let me take you out to eat first. It may be too chilly to sit out at a table," he commented.

"There's nothing open on Sunday, remember?"

"Oh. I knew alcohol couldn't be served but thought a few places were open."

"No. I'll bring the sandwiches. If it's too cool to eat outside, we'll just talk in the car. It's a pretty area."

Russell commented, "Beacon's city planners apparently saw the value of parks. There seems to be one in every area of town, all well-kept."

His first, positive, impression of the town had only grown in the short time since he first spotted the welcoming sign. But he was apprehensive about the discussion to come. He and Dare had been so close a few nights ago. Happy. He'd felt renewed hope. Now he worried about her questions and prayed not to lose her. She made it clear she had things to tell him about her*self*. But other times she had hinted at questions she had about him—could he answer? He'd have to wait for her to take the lead. There was that word again, *wait*—it seemed to come to his mind involuntarily… over and over.

The heavy jackets felt good as they ate at a picnic table. Though the sun shone brightly through the bare trees, the air was cold and crisp.

Russell hadn't thought of the city in weeks, but its image came to mind—windy, much colder, people rushing through the crowded streets in their heavy coats and boots, anticipating the ice and snow to come. Those people could pass by him by the hundreds and none would speak—he wouldn't speak either because he knew none of them... by choice, he realized. He would be intent on getting to his job, or a business before it closed, or to a restaurant to meet acquaintances with whom he had little in common. He didn't miss city life.

Did the city fail him? No, the failing was within. He'd been ambitious, climbing the corporate ladder, meeting and greeting, but never *seeing* people.

There were exceptions... Katherine... he'd *thought* he was seeing her, knowing her. For more than a *year*, for Pete's sake. He was upset when she left him. At first. But he soon realized he didn't miss her. He was upset because he was accustomed to their routine dinner dates, more often relying on her as a date to business occasions disguised as formal dinners. She'd been more of an accessory he took for granted.

Brenda. She was the one he saw and truly knew. More importantly, she knew him, *everything* about him, and loved him anyway. She'd always been there for him. *Until she was gone.*

"Russell? Did you hear me?"

He'd been staring in the direction of the pond and a family of ducks, though seeing none of it. "What? I must have been daydreaming. I'm sorry."

"You certainly were. I'm freezing. Let's get back in the car and run the heater a few minutes. And talk."

"I'm sorry I let you get cold." He gathered the trash to place into the nearby can and hurried to unlock the car.

It didn't take long to warm up and remove their jackets. Dare turned toward him and leaned back against the passenger door to stretch her legs as much as possible. He turned the heater low and turned to face her.

"Dare, you wanted to talk?"

"Yes. I'm not sure I made it clear the other day… about not wanting Rose and Ella around. I *love* and enjoy them. But I needed to talk with you seriously about things you need to know about me."

"They're fond of *you*… and *comfortable*. I'd been meaning to tell you that when Rose told you about Brenda cooking roast on Sundays and that she was named for her… it was the first time I'd known her to initiate a conversation with anyone in a long time. It was a breakthrough for her, and a touching moment for me. Thank you for being so good to them."

"They're easy to love."

He took her hands in his as she looked into his eyes. They sat quietly for a moment before she let go of his hands and leaned back. "Russell, you need to listen for a while."

"Nothing can make a difference in what I feel for you."

"Maybe not. I don't think it will. But it might explain a few things about me. I need you to understand what burdens me. It rears up when I least expect it and changes my moods, my way of seeing things, being able to love… my view of life."

"I'm listening."

"Okay. I had the same boyfriend all the way through high school. His name was Edward Champion, an all-around good guy. We were in the same grade, attended the same church, shared the same group of friends. He played football, made good grades… the complete, wonderful package.

"Other guys flirted and I was interested in a few. But Edward was my constant. I was comfortable with him, could be myself—*fixed up*, you know, hair done, makeup… or *no* make-up, old jeans, he didn't care. I knew other girls were interested in him, too, but I don't think he ever noticed or cared. I'm not being conceited. I was the one for him, period."

"Dare..."

"I'm explaining. I want you to understand. He was a *wonderful* person, a great young man, a strong Christian. And *handsome* on top of everything else."

Tears had filled her eyes, spilling down her cheeks.

He reached to gently wipe away her tears. She took his hand and held it.

"After graduating from high school, Edward began talking about our future, his attending college and what we'd do after we married... he hadn't proposed really, but that wasn't the problem... I realized his dream wasn't mine. I wasn't in love with him. He was my best friend, a wonderful, loyal friend. Sure, we'd kissed and what you might call *making out*... in our circle, it meant hugging close in the movie or in the car before saying goodnight." With a weak smile, she admitted, "And, yes, a number of long kisses. But I became physically sick realizing he had plans of which I didn't want to be a part. I wanted to remain his *friend* and go out with some of the other guys who'd flirted.

"So, I avoided seeing or talking with him for an entire week. Then he phoned and Mother called me to the phone. She told me to talk to him... to do the right thing. I broke up with him... over the phone..."

Her voice was barely above a whisper. "He came to the house and Mother insisted I see him. I walked out to the porch to talk with him. I told him I liked him as a *friend* but I wanted to date other guys. He couldn't believe it. He begged me to think it over. I repeated, no, and added I'd wanted to do it the year before but had been confused. I said, *I am not confused now. I am not in love with you, Edward.* I told him I was *sure*—to please accept it and go on with his college plans without me."

Her voice was so low, he strained to hear.

"I walked into the house, closing the door behind me."

"Dare, honey, you broke his heart. But you weren't in love, you were only honest."

"I haven't finished. Wonderful, decent Edward... the Edward I used as a best friend for three years, but didn't love... *that* Edward... drove away, hurt and angry.

"Mrs. Champion, his mother, phoned late that night, about eleven. He'd wrecked his truck fifty miles away. She didn't understand why he'd driven so far, she said. Edward was... *dead*. He was dead... because of me."

She was sobbing, shaking, as he held her. He had no words. His mind searched for words, but there were none. *She's heard all the words over the years. But she's still weighed down with guilt.*

After a while, the sobbing quieted. He continued to hold her, softly rocking as he'd done with Rose and Ella.

Finally, she looked up. Questioning. Waiting for a response.

"Dare, I know better people than *I* have expressed this—you are not to blame for Edward's death."

He waited.

"But your pain remains. You have to *forgive yourself*... for any part you feel you played in the boy's death. I have no doubt that you know God has forgiven and forgotten... for the part you *feel* you played."

She nodded.

"I want to say the right thing, but I don't know what it is. You wanted me to know this, to understand more about you. You were not in love and he was, always a bad situation. You can't choose those things. You had to do what you did.

"You are a wonderful, caring, loving person. *I*... am in love with you, Dare, deeply and completely. Wait... I had to say it, to tell you, though I know it's not the right time. But, I *won't* say it again unless you want to hear it because I'd be adding another burden to you. We haven't known each other long enough, and there's more you need to know about me, too. This, too, could be another case of one loving, the other not, but it's a part of life—an honest, often painful part.

"I had to tell you how I felt... but now is about *you*. I'll begin praying for you to be able to forgive yourself and put it in the past."

She looked into his eyes, then scanned his face, almost as if she were studying him.

He gently kissed her forehead. He could feel her breath, her sweetness. They were growing closer, and every step with her made him love her more. She'd shared such intimate feelings. He needed to be honest with her, too.

"Dare, I haven't been in the right place with God for quite a while, but I'm finding my faith again... slowly, since I've been in Beacon."

He saw a hint of a smile. "What is it?" he asked.

She leaned closer. "Russell, I haven't dated much since high school, but *never*, then or since, has a boy... or man... suggested he would pray for me. It means everything to me."

He kissed her tenderly, then pulled away. She appeared calm and relaxed, a big change from only minutes before.

"It's time to take you home. It's been quite an afternoon."

She moved close as he started the car. Laying her head on his shoulder, she answered, "Yes, it's been good. You know, I recently told someone they needed to forgive themselves. Thank you for the reminder that it applies to me as well."

Hours later as Russell's eyes closed for a night's sleep, he thought of Dare, the extraordinary woman he loved. And she cared about him.

He hoped it would grow into love, but he would not rush her. He thanked God and slept more peacefully than in months.

~~ 20 ~~

Dare drove in to work earlier than usual. She had final preparations to complete for a noon meeting. She looked toward the mysterious pile of lumber and the small building in progress. One of the men she'd seen previously was there. This one didn't have the look of a hobo. His cap was again pulled low and jacket collar turned up against the morning's cold. She could see a red plaid shirt collar, probably flannel, perfect for the windy October morning. *I'm curious to see what is to come.*

The meeting went well. Mr. Matthews actually praised her in the presence of his associates. "I must thank Miss Perry for the excellent organization. I assigned her a daunting task, usually handed over to the graphics department. Dare, you may have prepared too well—I'll be assigning these projects to you more often." Everyone laughed appreciatively.

"Thank you, Mr. Matthews." She sat back to take notes for the remainder of the meeting, a bit surprised to have been given credit. *If supervisors only knew how much a compliment means.*

Driving home, she remembered she needed batteries. She could get them at Woolworth's, but Connor's was convenient and she always found what she needed. *Maybe I'll see Russell.* As she looked through the batteries, she saw him at the far end of the store talking with a customer. She felt the warmth coming from seeing a friend. She was becoming more confident about her feelings. He turned as the customer left. Their eyes met. He smiled and she waved him over to her.

As he walked over, she observed something else. Her smile faded, questions returning. The warmth she'd felt earlier turned to a knot in her stomach.

"Hi. Good to see you this afternoon. Need some help?"

She'd frozen, unable to speak. *This is crazy, the men around the stacked wood are hobos. The shirt is a coincidence and means nothing.*

"Dare?"

His eyes melt me... "Russell?"

She had motioned him over, but she sounded uncomfortable, leaving him confused.

"You're wearing a red plaid flannel shirt."

"Yes, it's warm for these cool days—bought it *here*," he grinned. "Daniel knows what to sell his customers *and* employees."

"Were you by the railroad tracks this morning... working on a building of some kind?"

His smiled faded. "Yes... I sometimes go before work."

"Why?"

"It's hard to explain. I'm helping out... it's hard to explain," he repeated, "but I'd like to try. Could I see you tomorrow... lunch... whenever you say?"

"I went in earlier today so it will be no problem to take off earlier tomorrow. I'll be home before three. Could you come by then?"

It's a small thing, but another that I don't understand.

"I'll ask Daniel if I may leave early."

**

The next afternoon, she opened the door as soon as he knocked. They walked into the living room. She sat on the edge of an armchair. He sat on the end of the sofa nearest her.

"Dare, you are so special..."

128

"Russell, for once I want to understand you. I poured my heart out to you to explain *my* behavior but every time I've had questions about *you,* well, you do something that causes me to put them aside. I'm tired of being confused. I want to know about your work with hobos by the railroad tracks, apparently building a... I don't *know* what... and I want to know why Ella said her daddy *was* nice—I want to know who you were before you came to Beacon." She fought back tears, determined to stand her ground.

"Dare... okay, I'll make an attempt to put things in order. My life has become so tangled, I'm not sure I can *ever* get it right. Most of it was not my fault, honestly, but I've made mistakes, bad ones."

"Russell?"

"Okay. The first thing you should know is... I am an architect."

She slid down into the chair.

"I'll try to shorten my story. It's a lot to absorb but a vital part of my life and who I am. I wanted to be an architect before going into junior high school. After graduating high school, I went on to study architecture, worked my way through, and did well. As a result, I was hired immediately by a large, prestigious firm in Chicago. All my dreams were beginning to take shape.

"The founder of the company was my immediate supervisor. He promised if I worked hard, followed instructions and didn't get impatient, I'd most likely get ahead in the firm, which meant becoming a partner. Work went smoothly the first years. I worked as many as sixteen hours most days, loving every minute."

He observed the woman he loved, whose love he desperately wanted. Her expression told him nothing.

"After a while, I was assigned to a team to oversee a unique office building expected to be the talk of Chicago.

The company who contracted it asked for a brand-new look. They wanted to be the talk of, not only Chicago, but of the entire country. When it began to take shape, literally seeing the unusual outline, my adrenaline was as high as the building. It was very exciting."

He paused, hoping for a comment, but she continued to look at him as if he were a stranger.

"I'll try to summarize what happened afterward—how my life began to fall apart."

Her voice low, she spoke. "I'm still confused."

"I know. My explanation may not make sense even when I finish. I can only explain what's inside my muddled mind."

"All right."

"Blueprints are the most valuable thing in any building project. They include every detail for the building, from the foundation to the last light bulb. Blueprints for the McGuire building were in my keeping even before I was assigned to the building team. While in the process of studying, making notes, and lining up material, I made the mistake of a lifetime. Someone came to my office with a bogus story, which I barely questioned and never actually suspected to be sabotage. I handed over the original prints... just handed them over.

"They were returned to me the same evening and I carefully locked them away before I left for the evening. Never gave it another thought. Months after, when we were at the point of the new building taking shape, I was summoned to a meeting with the board of directors. *All* the partners had gathered to confront me. They had photographs of an almost-completed building in another city. It was an exact replica of the supposedly unique building we were building. It was obvious to all, including me, the blueprints had been stolen and the other group got an earlier start.

"Upon questioning, I remembered the young courier coming to me to get the blueprints, supposedly for the originator of the blueprints, to make a file copy. I told them about it, the young man's name and everything I remembered. Thing is, no such employee or courier existed, and the originator of the blueprints vowed he'd never sent for them. I had no viable evidence. I was fired on the spot, allowed a few things from my office and escorted out of the building. They promised I'd never work as an architect again. I knew they could make good on that promise."

His voice cracking, he continued, "Dare, I am a planner and builder who isn't allowed to do it any longer. It's a stretch to say the hardware store is in my line of work, but at least I deal with people who *are* planning and building."

"Russell, this breaks my heart. I know you would never have done anything dishonest. And I'm glad to know more *about* you... but I still don't understand why you're building a *shanty* with hobos."

"I know it doesn't make sense. I saw the foundation where a small building had been and thought it could be put to use. You mentioned seeing others there?"

"Yes, at first. The reason I especially noticed you was because the other guy, maybe *two* others, had a different look and never wore a hat."

"Those two *are* hobos. I made a small delivery in the area for Daniel one day. You know how generous he is. The order wasn't big enough for a truck delivery, but the folks had no way of getting the supplies home. Well, I noticed those guys that day—they were building a small fire on the square of cement. I felt bad for them and got the idea. I contacted the owner of the house a couple of acres away, He owned the property and gave me permission for a small one-room building. These men live under bridges, boxes, or whatever they can find. They aren't like you and me, I'll agree, not much on-the-ball, most would say, one probably physically disabled. But I think they are decent guys, certainly mean no one any harm, and they deserve four walls and a roof without leaks. Doubt it could be more, but it could mean a great deal to them.

"So, I promised to make it happen. It doesn't take an architect to do what I'm doing, four simple walls and a roof. But, somehow, it's helping *me*. They've collected scrap wood, I've found some, and have been given new wood from the hardware store left from an order—you know about Daniel's generosity. Those two homeless guys stay there after dark every night, *to protect their property,* but disappear most other times."

She moved to the edge of the chair and leaned toward him. "That's the kindest thing I ever heard."

Tears in his eyes, he answered, "Don't credit me. Six months ago, I wouldn't have even *talked* to someone wanting a dollar to *help* with something like this. I've learned a lot since I lost my job."

"And you lost more than a job…"

"Yes. I left what I called home. Truth is, I *ran away*. And when I stopped, I was in Beacon, Alabama."

She stood to move to the sofa, sitting close. "In Beacon, Alabama, with Rose and Ella. Thank you for telling me."

He watched her. She appeared about to say more but stopped to consider her words.

She attempted to absorb all he'd told her, which had been a great deal. "I'm glad you stopped in Beacon."

He had not answered all her questions but had shared *so* many details. He'd shown her another layer of himself, a humiliating, painful part of his former life. He was a good man.

"I know this is only *part* of your story, Russell, but it explains a lot. When the time is right, I hope you'll share the rest."

He nodded, sensing her hope that he would continue unveiling his past. He wasn't ready.

She lifted her face to him, whispering, "You become dearer every time I discover another side of you." She raised her hand to his face, touching him gently, then moving her hand slowly to the back of his neck. "Russ..."

Her touch was everything. She still cared. His arms encircled her as their lips met, each feeling the warmth of love unspoken. He stroked her hair and neck, breathing in her sweetness, their kisses becoming more urgent. Her hands moved to his back, caressing, and pressing in to bring him closer as the outside world faded away.

"Oh, Russ..."

"Dare," he said hoarsely, "my sweet..."

Bong... bong... bong... bong.

As the clock struck four, Dare's hands fell to her side as she pulled her head back slightly. He opened his eyes, reading hers, as they slowly straightened, sitting close on the sofa. She put her hand to his cheek again, not wanting the warmth of his touch to end.

"You have to go."

He nodded, understanding, but not wanting to move.

She stood. "Call me tomorrow."

He stood to kiss her lightly before leaving for *home,* the boarding house and his little angels. *She said she would wait for the complete story, knowing there's more. How will I explain? But she called me Russ.*

Dare closed the door and leaned back against it, holding the feeling of his nearness and knowing she hadn't wanted him to leave. He'd allowed her to see more of who he was. She dismissed the other questions. He was a good man—that was enough for her to know. He would tell the rest when the time was right. And she would wait.

She would sleep well tonight, dreaming of Russ and his arms holding her.

~~ **21** ~~

The girls were asleep and the house quiet. Needing water for the bedside table, Russell quietly closed their door and walked downstairs. Though only ten o'clock, this house was silent and almost completely dark. Most boarders began their work days before daybreak.

Might as well grab a late-night snack while I'm here. Miss Bee always left a few things on the dining room sideboard, covered with a napkin. He lifted the napkin, delighted to find several pieces of pound cake.

Returning to the stairway, he heard low voices coming from the front room. Looking intently from the bottom stair, he realized there was a bit of light. *A break-in? Anyone in the area would know this place was shut tight and asleep by ten.* If he attempted to use the phone, he would be heard. He was in no mood to be a hero. He remembered reading the best thing is to let intruders know you are home—hoping they would make a quick getaway.

He asked loudly, "Who's here?" He waited a minute before stepping into the living room to turn on the bright overhead light. The scene before him was the last he would have imagined. Miss Bee sat in the corner of the sofa with a blanket over her lap and a tiny night-light glowing from the corner. Standing over him was a very angry Frank Weathers. Russell looked from one to another. What was going on?

"Something you want, Mr. Townsend?"

Though obviously attempting to keep his voice down, Frank's question seemed to boom and bounce through the room, his eyes angry, cutting him down to size. Russell looked at Miss Bee, confused.

She's blushing. The TV is dark. She and Frank were cuddling in the dimly-lit room! Stammering in an attempt to remove himself from an embarrassing situation, he finally answered, "Mr. Weathers, I apologize. Miss Bee, I'd come down to get water, trying not to disturb. I didn't realize you were watching television while trying to keep the house quiet." He backed out of the room as he spoke. "Good night. Sorry I disturbed you."

Back upstairs, Russell thought he would lose control but he'd managed to stifle his amusement. It was not the *neighbor* for whom Frank Weathers had cleaned himself up, it was for *Miss Bee*. The night at the supper table when he assumed Miss Bee had invited Mary Nan over for Frank, he was completely wrong. She'd invited her as a buffer for *herself*, a chaperone of sorts. This was the most humorous development he'd ever witnessed. *Good for her.*

**

As they went into the dining room for breakfast the following morning, Russell wondered whether Miss Bee would acknowledge the incident.

"Good morning, Miss Bee. I trust you had a good evening."

"Good morning, Mr. Townsend... Rose... Ella. Yes, I slept right good."

Uh, oh. I've been Russell to her since the beginning. She's more upset than I thought.

"Mr. Townsend, I'm happy I had bits of pound cake left for you last night when you came downstairs. Mr. Weathers and I found the best television show and couldn't turn it off without seeing it to the end. It ended as you came in."

He answered seriously, "Yes, ma'am. Everyone is discussing the variety of shows available now."

She appeared satisfied. But he couldn't help himself—still holding her attention, he grinned and winked before turning to take a seat with the girls.

**

Arriving to work early, Russell spoke to Daniel at the coffee counter.

"Morning, Russell. Day startin' off good?"

"Absolutely. I've wanted a chance to ask you about Miss Broadnax, though. You know how good she's been to us. You said you'd known her a long time and I've been wondering about her. Was she ever married when she was younger?"

"No, Irma Rae never married. I tell you something, though, she took care of her parents and everybody in her family before most died. Then she made her family home, the one she was born in, into a boarding house. She's gotten the reputation for being a sour old woman. Maybe she is, but she's a good woman, Russell, and not as old as you probably think."

"How old *is* she?"

"Hmmm, forties I reckon, mid to late."

Daniel saw Russell's expression of surprise. "Yeah, she's had a hard life. Worked every day since age ten, I 'spect. She had a good, loving family, but dirt poor. They worked hard, but never seemed to get ahead. Two older brothers died while she was in grammar school—one drowned, one run over by a tractor. Tough. But she was the youngest and everything just seemed to fall to her early on."

"Is there no family left?"

"There may be a brother but he moved away long ago. I don't think she hears from him, not since she bought out his part in the old home."

"She *has* had a hard life. She deserves some happiness."

"Yeah, but she's probably doing what she wants, and makes a good living. Most don't ask much more."

But she might just want someone special to love, like most.

Going in for supper, Russell noticed Frank sitting at the far end of the dining table away from the kitchen. He'd remained consistent with his new look which, in a nutshell, was *clean*. His hair was trimmed, though longer than most, and it appeared he shaved every day *and* changed clothes. Actually, not a bad-looking guy. Since the night Mary Nan Johnson had visited, Miss Bee had continued to sit with the group of boarders who ate later, which included Frank. She couldn't be called jovial but had begun conversing rather pleasantly. Frank generally managed to sit to one side of her or close by. It was to him she'd directed most comments.

Tonight, however, Miss Bee was not seated. As she came in and out of the kitchen refilling bowls and removing empty dishes, her conduct was all business, little to no conversation and a dry expression. Frank's eyes remained down, and she never looked in his direction. What had happened? He hated seeing things going backward for these two. He'd enjoyed envisioning Miss Bee smiling with someone who might share life with her. Perhaps a stretch of the imagination, but there had been a spark between them, he was sure of it.

He'd enjoyed the new atmosphere and realized he'd truly enjoyed getting acquainted with the other boarders, each with his own unique story and talent.

Tucking the girls into bed, Rose commented, "Why didn't Mr. Weathers talk tonight, Pop? He looked sad. Ella told me not to ask."

"I don't know, honey. Maybe he worked harder today and was more tired. But now it's time for prayers and sweet dreams."

Russell nuzzled Rose's neck as she giggled and pulled the cover over her head, their nightly ritual. He then went to Ella's side of the bed to lean in to kiss her neck. She reached up to put her arms around his neck, pulling him down. He whispered, "Do you know how much I love you, Ella-Pella?"

"Nooooo, don't call me Ella Pella," she giggled. She kissed his cheek, loudly smacking, before answering, "You love me a million-billion and more."

"Right."

"Me and Rose love you bushels and bushels of kisses."

With a muffled giggle coming from under the blanket, Rose agreed, "And hugs."

"G'night Ella-Pella and Rosey-Posey."

They giggled for about five minutes before falling asleep.

Russell woke earlier the next morning. He had something on his mind. He dressed quickly and walked downstairs in sock feet, hoping to find Miss Bee alone in the kitchen. She was humming while turning the sizzling bacon in a massive iron skillet, the smell of buttermilk biscuits wafting through the room. He noticed an enormous bowl of beaten eggs on a work table, and pitchers filled with freshly-squeezed orange juice.

He didn't want to startle her. Standing several feet away, he coughed. She turned immediately, appearing surprised. There it was again—she was embarrassed. Now he knew for certain. She had been humiliated at his discovery of Frank alone with her that night.

"Miss Bee, I came down early to talk privately."

"As you can see, I'm mighty busy this time-a-day. You need me to keep an eye on the girls, just spit it out. No problem."

"No. I wanted to say I'm sorry I interrupted you and Frank the other night."

"You did no such…"

He raised his voice slightly, though the last thing needed was to be overheard. "Miss Bee, I know Mr. Weathers appears rough, but I think he's shy. *You* are careful with your reputation, as you must be. But you two have become friends and you believe I have the wrong thoughts about it. I don't."

She raised her eyebrows.

He stepped closer, placing his hand lightly on her shoulder. "Everyone needs friendship, *even* Frank Weathers. And you might be just the person who can make a friend out of him. It's a good thing, my dear, and I assure you I have told no one or made any remarks. Please don't change anything you… had in mind about building a relationship… on my account." He grinned and leaned in to kiss her cheek before turning quickly to leave the kitchen and scurry up the stairs.

Irma Rae Broadnax was flabbergasted. *The nerve of young Russell Townsend!*

Nevertheless, a smile slowly crept across her face. She resumed humming as she finished breakfast.

Just so happens, he's the second *man to kiss me this week.*

Before going downstairs that evening, Russell cautioned both girls about asking questions. "I know you were concerned about Mr. Weathers appearing sad last night. Maybe you can be sure to speak to him, though. I know he likes you."

Pleased to see Miss Bee at the table again, he took his place, determined not to look at her. As he moved his tea glass, he ventured a glance. He was taken aback when he realized she was looking straight at him. She grinned, winked, and turned her head to speak to Frank.

Touché, Miss Bee.

Returning upstairs, Rose remarked, "Mr. Weathers was happy tonight. I guess he didn't hafta work hard today. I didn't ask him anything, though. I like it when Miss Bee eats with us, don't you, Pop?"

"Yes, honey, I do."

-~~ 22 ~~

"**I**'m glad you called, Russell. I'm so excited—Doreen and Bobby are going to have a baby! She just saw the doctor today. You know, you can't go until you've missed two..." Mortified that she'd almost mentioned something so personal with women, she stammered, "Um... you can't see the doctor for two months even if you're *sure* you're expecting. The due date is the first of March; she was further along than she thought. She's hoping for a girl since she had so much fun taking care of me when I was a baby, and she loves Rose and Ella. We haven't been around baby boys much..."

Laughing at her enthusiasm, Russell asked, "So, you're a *little* excited?"

"I know. I get carried away at times. But they've been married five years and have been anxious about this. A baby—what *could* be more exciting? I'm sure you remember when you heard Rose was on the way."

"Yes, but Dare, I'm on my break at work. I called to see whether you'd go with us to the parade tomorrow afternoon."

"Parade?"

"Where have you been? President Eisenhower is visiting the Anniston Ordnance Depot and will make a stop in several nearby towns. Beacon is one of them, and they're having a parade in his honor. Daniel said they didn't have much notice."

"I'd forgotten, but I'd love to go. This will be different, perhaps similar to a Veteran's Day parade. Most parades I've been to have been at Christmas. What about the girls?"

"Just Christmas parades. I'll pick you up at two. We can park behind Connor's, but they will begin to block the street soon after. Daniel's closing the store for a few hours. It will be exciting to see a president in person."

As Dare hung up the phone, she smiled contentedly.

My life has become more interesting. I feel good about my relationship with Russell—we're growing closer each day. Difficult to realize it's been less than two months since the day I saw him at the school. And Doreen and Bobby's baby on the way—I'll be an aunt.

So many good things...a baby in the family, a chance to see a president in person, and... Russell. I am so happy with my life right now.

"Yay! Mrs. Crown talked about president *I-sin-how-er* yesterday and we were excited school would be out right after lunch," babbled Ella. "I didn't think we'd get to go, though."

Rose added, knowingly, "It's *Eisenhower*, Ella. It starts with an *E*, even though it sounds like an *I*. In second grade, you learn to write it out, even though it *is* hard," she admitted.

Ever supportive, Ella replied sincerely, "Rose, you are so smart. Isn't she, Pop?"

"How did you two both get to be so smart and cute?" Russell laughed, grabbing them into his arms. "I might not be home from work when you get here after lunch tomorrow, but I'll be here soon after. If you haven't gotten too dirty, you might not have to change clothes for the parade and we'll take your hats in case it gets cooler. We'll go by Dare's house first, then straight to the hardware store to park. We'll have to wait for the parade to begin, but we can have popcorn as we wait."

Dare was ready when they pulled up in front of her house.

"Rose and Ella were as excited about your going with us as they were to see the president."

Looking toward the back seat, she answered, "I am excited to see *you*, girls."

The parade began on schedule and the weather was nice enough for President Eisenhower to ride in the convertible with the top down.

"I *like* him," Dare commented. "I believe he enjoys seeing us sometimes. You know, *regular* people, even though I'm sure it's tiring."

"I heard that our First Lady, Mamie, made this trip with him, but had a cold and had to stay in," Russell answered.

Rose and Ella waved at everyone, excited about the day. Ella shouted over the crowd noise, "I *like* parades! We've never been before... can we go to every parade from now on, Pop?"

"You bet. And you'll always remember seeing the *President* of the United States in person."

Dare asked, "Haven't you been to Christmas parades?"

"No," Ella answered. "It was always too cold."

Dare looked at Russell, but he turned his head. *How could he not know they'd never been to a parade? But he did say he worked long hours—I guess he thought his wife took them.*

Returning through the hardware store to the car, Daniel spoke to Dare and the girls before addressing Russell. "No need to return to work. I'll probably close up before you have time to get back."

"Thanks."

To Rose, Ella, and Dare, Russell said, "I think we just might all go out for hamburgers."

Thrilled, Rose and Ella grabbed Dare's hands. "This time *we* get to go on your date with Pop."

Giggling with them, she swung their arms into the air, answering, "Hamburgers, here we come—the four of us on the best date ever. *I love this… Rose and Ella… parades… my hand in Russell's, popcorn, hamburgers… sharing.*

**

Changes were taking place at the boarding house. Miss Bee made it clear she would be sitting to eat with the second group of boarders most nights, at the head of the table. Frank sat to her left each evening.

As they came in tonight, Miss Bee was already seated. Mr. Stanley, a new boarder, preceded Frank into the dining room and pulled out the vacant chair next to Miss Bee. Russell watched, amused. Frank touched Mr. Stanley's shoulder as he began to sit. Mr. Stanley turned to find the burly Frank towering over him and looking none too happy.

"*My* seat."

Poor Mr. Stanley. He obviously considered protesting. He glanced around the room, then back at Frank. "Sorry," he muttered, quickly scrambling out of the way, "just as soon sit further down." Miss Bee smiled sweetly. "Think nothing of it, Mr. Stanley. Like most places, we have our little traditions."

"Yes, ma'am, of course."

Frank, now seated, briefly touched Miss Bee's hand before looking up. "Yeah, tradition." The dining room was silent. The men had ceased to eat, staring at the unlikely pair at the end of the table, finally realizing what had taken place. Each man appeared more surprised than the next. Miss Bee and *Frank?* Questions raced through their minds, none vocalized. After a minute or two, Frank spoke, "Irma Rae, would you pass the cornbread… please?"

Even Russell almost choked on his tea. Calling Miss Bee by her given name in *public?* He'd kept his word about not telling anyone of his discovery of them together in the front room, but *this…* he could not wait to tell Dare.

At eight-thirty, Russell walked downstairs to the kitchen to return several glasses. The television was on and men's voices could be heard.

Stepping into the room to ask about the programming, he was further surprised by the vision of Frank and Irma Rae sitting side-by-side on the sofa holding hands… with several other boarders present.

"Just wondering what you all had found to watch tonight," he commented, "but I'll say good night."

One of the other men, whose name Russell couldn't recall, stood. "Think it's time for me to turn in as well. G'night guys, g'night Irma Rae."

This woman they thought they knew was beginning to surprise them all. She straightened her back and replied politely, "I remain *Miss Bee* to you and everyone else here. You just as well tell the rest. Good night, Mr. Denny."

"Yes, ma'am. Good night."

Feeling like cowering himself, Russell turned to walk up the stairs. As he reached his door, he paused to smile in the dimness of the hallway. *Funny situation. All the men here, and most of the town insist on first names. Miss Bee refers to us… usually… in the same manner. But I guess she's decided to maintain a space, a professionalism, perhaps… to remind them she is still the landlady and calls the shots.*

But I'm witnessing a bit of happiness landing right here in an old boarding house in Beacon, Alabama, on two unlikely people who were not expecting it. Thank you, Lord.

~~ 23 ~~

Bobby was out of town for a few days, which meant Dare and Doreen would spend an evening together. Dare drove to Doreen's from work, anticipating laugh-filled hours with her sister and best friend. She wondered about baby names, colors for the nursery... she'd made endless lists and suggestions... and also wondered what Doreen would cook for supper. Opening the front door with her key, Dare shouted, "It's me. I'm loving the smell of your corned beef hash."

Doreen came from the kitchen. Giving her a hug, she laughed, "It's the only time I can enjoy Mom's hash recipe. I don't understand Bobby's disdain of it. I have our baby's fourth birthday meal planned, though. By the age of four, he or she will have learned to appreciate it, and I will not let Bobby say a single negative thing."

"Sis, you never fail to make me laugh."

"I'm one-hundred percent serious. Supper's almost ready. Afterward, you can help me plan the nursery."

By nine o'clock, the nursery had been planned right down to the size of the throw rug on the floor, and the sisters were enjoying a chunk of chocolate cake.

"Dare, what about Russell? Are you getting serious about him?"

Quiet for a moment, Dare answered honestly, "Yes... I think so. Oh, Doreen, I love every minute we're together. He's kind-hearted, honest, patient, and enjoys the simple things of life that I do. He is a great father and I adore Rose and Ella. I'll admit it crosses my mind I might be more to them someday—and I'm saying way, *way* out there, and... maybe."

"Honey, with all your praises of him, I still sense a measure of doubt. I like him… really, but are there problems?"

"No. He's wonderful. I even told him about *Edward*. He said he would pray for me to find peace."

Doreen remained uncharacteristically quiet. She knew her sister had more to say.

"There *are* things, but then I remember what I usually do when I begin to like a man. You mentioned it recently and it's true—I find something to use as an excuse to back away."

For the next hour, they discussed things the girls had said to bring questions to her mind, as well as Russell's random comments. Dare kept little from her sister. "All so insignificant, though." She explained them all away, asserting how much she cared for him, the girls, and their time together.

"Dare, I have a question. He seems to be settling in—you know, working, his girls in school, a car, a routine..."

"Yes?"

"Hon, do you think it's normal for a man to remain in a *boarding house* with two children? And something I noticed early on was that the suits he wore to church were finer than any *ever* seen around here, though it appeared money was a problem, at the beginning anyway. You said you didn't think money *was* a problem for him anymore. Isn't that unusual? And you didn't share the particulars, but you've mentioned he has a higher education, qualified for much more than working as a salesman at Connor's. I see no evidence he's trying to find anything more."

"He's still recovering from his wife's death and moving so far away."

"Honey—something simply does not add up."

As Dare drove home, she was ill at ease with everything. She'd almost become angry with her sister about her questions regarding Russell. *Almost.* In her heart, she agreed. Something did not add up.

But I love him. I realized it fully as Doreen questioned me. I defended the very things I'd questioned. I'm trying to ignore things because I don't want roadblocks.

She gave a great deal of thought to the discussion. But, after all, there was no rush. If her relationship with Russell continued to develop, as she hoped, anything important would clear itself up.

Russell phoned the next night.

"Hey, good news."

"And, how are *you*?" she laughed.

"I'm sorry, I'm not normal when I find I have legitimate time off from being Pop. The girls have a school festival right after school tomorrow and I won't pick them up until seven-thirty. Family isn't invited. Not a great deal of time, but could I take you out to eat after work?"

"Yes. I'll leave a little early, but I won't be home before five. Lou's is a good café if you have nothing special in mind—good basic food and good service. It's right downtown."

"Sounds fine."

She wore a black skirt with a soft gray sweater set, and the turquoise earrings and pendant, obviously her favorite. The earrings brought out tiny specks of turquoise in her blue eyes.

As they waited for their orders, he reached for her hand. "Exactly what I ordered, ma'am. And, how *are* you?"

"As a matter of fact, I'm perfect, thank you. Not me specifically. I have a few things that could be improved upon, but my evening and company is perfect."

At the moment, she saw nothing but him—handsome, smiling, kind, perfect-for-her, *Russ*.

He was lost in her smile, a beautiful, petite package found unexpectedly amid the muddle he'd made of his life.

"You *are* perfect. I know you weren't fishing for compliments, but I find no flaws. I love that you have to reach to hug me, I love the freckles on your nose, three, to be exact, I love that you love Rose and Ella and don't mind their being included. You have a good heart… and I even like your little snort when you're laughing hard."

"Excuse me..."

They looked up at the waitress, who stood balancing plates of food as they held hands across the table. Embarrassed, they released hands. Dare looked down, giggling under her breath.

"Sorry," Russell mumbled to the waitress, making a mental note to increase her tip.

"Perfectly alright… Sir."

After she walked away, Dare giggled again. "The waitress is besotted with you."

"*Besotted*?"

"Smitten, love-struck… come on, you never heard the word *besotted*?"

"Sounds like something from Shakespeare. Also, she is no such thing. She's too old for me."

"Russell Townsend, the girl is beautiful and no more than twenty."

"Well, I didn't notice because I'm besotted by *you*."

"Yeah? I'd throw a plate at you if I weren't so hungry."

After supper, they drove to the nearest park. The darkness closed in earlier this time of year and the night was cold and clear. A few leaves remained on the trees, letting go slowly, singly, to flutter by the window in the whisper of a breeze. In the darkness, they had little need to talk. They sat close, warm and content. Russell's arm was around her possessively, yet tenderly. He could see her in the light of the moon. Leaning in to kiss and hold her, she responded to his every touch, moving closer, but they didn't linger in the moments.

"Dare, honey, will you let me know when you're… *ready*?"

"What?"

"I promised not to rush you. I don't want to—it's just difficult not to tell you how I feel about you."

"Oh."

Relieved, she exhaled slowly. He'd promised he wouldn't tell her of his love again unless she was *ready*… to hear it again.

"When I want to hear the words…?"

"Yes. *If…*"

Her heart pounded. A declaration of love was a promise, a serious commitment. She *did* love him! She felt complete, loved, and safe with him. She hadn't wanted him to leave her house the other night. She *ached* to tell him of her love, to look into his eyes as she confessed it, and to hear him declare his love for her again. She was happy when they were together.

Then, why not? Something held her back… the internal struggle she thought had been resolved. She didn't understand, but something would not allow her to release the words.

She kissed him again. "Soon, I think. Thank you for being patient."

He nodded, stroking her hair. He would wait a lifetime, hoping she might someday want… *crave*… to hear his declaration of love.

Driving from the park, she exclaimed, "I almost forgot. You mentioned the upcoming Saturday being your day off. I have an idea."

"Yes?"

"Let's take the girls to Birmingham. It's less than an hour from here and there's a museum they would enjoy—there's a large section especially for children. We could make a day of it. I'll even buy my own lunch."

"Great idea. But no woman out with me buys her own lunch... even when she asks *me* out."

"Good. Could you pick me up by nine? We'll have all day and can get home before dark. The late-evening traffic is heavy."

~~ 24 ~~

The girls were elated to be going to a city museum with Miss Dare. They were almost ready to leave when Rose abruptly went into one of her moods, which hadn't happened in a while. She stood by the window crying.

"What's wrong, darling?"

"I want Mommy—*she* used to take us to museums."

Russell sat in the chair and pulled her onto his lap. Her crying became harder, sobbing as she pressed her little face into his shoulder. Ella came to stand beside the chair, behaving like a little mother. She began rubbing and patting Rose's arms, trying to soothe. *I'm helpless. I am holding a small child whose heart is broken, with a smaller child attempting to help as her own tears fall as well.*

He motioned for Ella to climb into the chair with them. He began a slow rocking motion, saying nothing as tears flowed from the three of them. After Rose quietened, he leaned further back, causing her to raise her head slightly. Ella raised her head, too, though her arm remained around Rose.

"You know Mommy went to heaven. She cannot return but I believe she watches over us. She still loves you and knows you love and miss her. But she wants you to be happy. You can miss her and still have a good time. I miss her too, very much."

Ella nodded. *Where did this mite of a human being gain such wisdom?*

"Rose, Dare will be wondering where we are. She planned the day for the four of us—she wanted to spend it with you."

"Pop?" Ella ventured.

"Yes, honey?"

"Won't Miss Dare be sad if we don't go with her today?"

"Yes."

Rose wiped her face with her hand. She looked at Ella before speaking, her voice low.

"What, honey? I'm sorry, I couldn't hear you."

"I said, I don't want Miss Dare to be sad like me… can I tell her I miss Mommy?"

"Of course."

They climbed from his lap to finish their hair before slipping into their jackets. Going out their door to the stairway, Rose bounded down the stairs ahead of them. He leaned down to whisper to Ella. "Thank you, honey. You really helped Rose."

"I know." After a hesitation, she asked, "Pop?"

"Yes?"

"I miss Mommy… a lot. I just keep it for nighttime."

Russell's heart was breaking again. "Honey, do you cry at night?" He hadn't heard anything.

"No. I just think of her and say part of my prayer to her. She knows I'm helping you take care of Rose."

He hugged her tightly, marveling once more at her wisdom. Would he ever make their lives good and whole again? Was he enough?

The day was gray and cloudy, but the rain held off until late night.

It began uneasily. As Dare got into the car and turned to speak to the girls, Rose perked up, "Pop said I could tell you I missed Mommy this morning."

"I'm sure you all miss her very much. I'm grown, but I still miss *my* mother. I'm sure your mother was wonderful— she had to be to have two such perfect little girls."

"She was the best mommy in the world. But we're ready for a fun day with *you* in Birmingham," Ella commented.

Russell sighed with relief. Timidly, he reached to place his hand on Dare's. She moved closer and patted his hand to let him know all was well. The drive was beautiful. He loved the majesty of the mountains and the glorious fall colors. Farms were tucked here and there, some small, and some impressive with large homes, classic red barns, and endless acres. Driving into Birmingham, however, he felt tense. He'd been away from city life for months and the feel of it seemed to smother him. He wanted to turn around, return to the safety of Beacon.

"Look at the big buildings. It looks like Chicago," Rose exclaimed, again happy, *as a child should be.*

Dare was delighted with their excitement. "In a few minutes, you'll see a large statue, high on a mountain. It's called Vulcan.*"*

Driving a few miles further, the statue came into sight. "There, look on top of the mountain."

"Wow, it's tall."

Russell, too, was impressed. Fortunately, he'd stopped for a red light and had a good view.

"Vulcan is made of cast iron because Birmingham has been known for its iron and steel industry. It's fifty-six feet high, taller than many city buildings."

Thrilled, Ella commented, "He looks like he's guarding the city."

"Yes, he does. He was made for the World's Fair in nineteen hundred and four, but he's been on *Red Mountain* for a very long time."

"It's nineteen *fifty*-four, now… does that mean he is fifty years old?" asked Rose.

"Why, yes, it does, Rose. That's *very* good arithmetic." She glanced at Russell with raised eyebrows.

"Can we go closer?"

"Not today. Maybe on a sunnier day," Dare replied. "Oh, Russell, turn right up here. We'll be going 'round to the other side of the city for the museum. Just after the turn, look for a food cart. It's usually there, and we can get boiled peanuts to eat until we reach the museum."

Russell turned his head slightly, intent on watching the traffic. "Kidding, right?"

"About what?"

"*Boiled* peanuts?"

"Oh," she answered seriously. "I'd thought you might not have boiled peanuts in the North, but they're wonderful when they're hot—very salty and juicy. I like them cold, but they're best hot. My daddy used to do them at home… maybe the reason I'm so fond of them… it's a sweet memory." To the girls, she added, "You can see Vulcan from lots of places as we drive, though. Just keep watching."

"Pop!" they cried out in unison. "We see Vulcan's bottom!"

Horrified, Ella exclaimed, "He doesn't have any pants and his bottom is showing."

Dare laughed hysterically. Russell no longer had a view of Vulcan from his side and was mystified. "What are they talking about?"

"They're right, his bottom does show," she laughed. "Sorry. I should have explained or told you beforehand. I really don't know why he doesn't have pants. He has the apron in the front… but he's a statue so he isn't cold, and I don't think statues can be embarrassed. I agree, it's not really nice."

Dare tried to stifle her amusement as she glanced at Russell. He grinned and whispered, "*He's mooning the entire city.*"

She popped his arm before saying, "The food cart should be in the next block. Begin looking for a place to pull over."

Rose and Ella loved the boiled peanuts and could not get enough of the museum. They did bring up the subject of Vulcan's bare bottom several times, though. Russell thought it as perfect as a day could be, though not enthusiastic about the boiled peanuts. Leaving the museum, they walked two blocks to a park, where the girls had spotted swings. They played while Russell and Dare strolled the walkways holding hands. By the time they walked back to the car, the girls collapsed in the back seat, almost asleep on the ride home.

They returned to Dare's just before dark. Revived, Rose and Ella wanted to go in for hot chocolate. As she handed each of them a cup, her phone rang.

"Hello. Oh, hi Doreen. Yes, we just returned from a trip to Birmingham." Quiet for several minutes, she listened. Hanging up, she turned to Russell.

"It was about Miss Broadnax."

"What?"

"She fell from a ladder this morning. They've admitted her to the hospital."

"Oh, no!" Visibly upset, his eyes filled with tears.

She realized how much the "boarding-house lady" had come to mean to him. "Would you like to go to the hospital? I don't know whether you can see her, but it might be possible. I can see you're worried."

"I would like to know how badly she's hurt."

"The girls will be fine here." She turned to them, but they were grinning and nodding.

Russell raised his eyebrows in question.

"Russell, go."

As Russell drove to the hospital, he smiled, thinking of the sweet family scene he'd left... his girls sipping hot chocolate, happy and safe with Dare, the woman he loved.

Two hours later he phoned to apologize for being so long. "It took a while to find a parking place and I had to wait to see her. She's badly bruised, but they say she'll be okay. She's expected to be in the hospital only overnight."

"Good."

"Frank was with her. He asked me to stay while he went back to pick up things she wanted from home. I'm in her room but she's asleep. I'll come for the girls as soon as Frank returns."

"It's fine, Russell. Why don't you just let them stay the night? It's Saturday so they don't have school, and they can sleep in my tee-shirts. You can get them in the morning, whenever you want."

As he hesitated, he heard the girls squealing with delight. "All right. I can hear their dismay at staying with you."

"We'll miss you," Dare replied. "Sweet dreams, Russ."

Smiling as he returned the telephone receiver to the base, Russell had no idea what a mistake he'd just made.

~~ **25** ~~

The Time Has Come

Sunday morning, Russell phoned Dare from the boarding house before picking the girls up at eight.

"I'll get them home to change and see you at church. Thank you." He kissed her cheek before waving goodbye. They crawled into the car and began talking about their night. They'd obviously had a wonderful time.

Dare seemed quiet. She didn't say much after asking about Miss Bee. Maybe taking care of two little girls overnight was more than she expected.

"Girls, were you good—did you mind Miss Dare?"

"Yes," they answered in unison.

I guess she was tired.

They weren't ready in time for Sunday school but entered the sanctuary just before the worship service began. He intended to sit with Dare, but as he looked toward the area where she generally sat, he didn't see her. A minute later, he saw her sitting on a packed pew closer to the front. Singing had begun, so he hurried the girls into seats nearby.

He waited by the door after worship. Dare never appeared. He inquired of a friend passing by. "She sat down front this morning. I think she left by the side door. It's much easier when you're sitting in that section."

I told her we'd be there. Didn't she see us? Perhaps she looked after Sunday school and thought we just didn't make it.

He decided it best to return to the boarding house for a restful afternoon. It had already been a big weekend for the three of them.

Coming downstairs this morning thinking he could at least prepare coffee, Russell had been surprised to see Mary Nan Johnson scurrying from the kitchen into the dining room with coffee. "Good morning, Russell. I told Irma Rae I'd do my best to take care of her boarders today. It won't be up to her standards, naturally, but ya'll won't starve," she laughed.

"That's nice of you, Mary Nan."

Most boarders had gone home for the weekend, one gone only for the day. Other than Russell and the girls, only three remained. By tonight the house would be full again.

As he sat to eat, Mary Nan poured coffee as she apologized for the breakfast. "Hope ya'll can get by with toast and scrambled eggs this morning—that's all I could manage. I'll have lunch for you, too, but it'll be sandwiches or whatever leftovers I find in the icebox."

Russell was a bit surprised at seeing Mary Nan in this take-charge role. As Miss Bees' best friend, she was often at the boarding house, yet he'd heard little conversation from her. Actually, she was so shy she generally looked down or turned her head to avoid eye contact. He was seeing a different side of her, bubbly and happy.

She's rather pleasant looking—I hadn't truly looked at her in the past. Her skin is light and smooth, going well with her light brown hair, though there are signs of gray. She's tall, probably nearing six feet... taller than I am. She is too thin, though...

While she spoke, Russell heard dishes rattling in the kitchen. As he glanced toward the kitchen, he was surprised to see Dennis Sims exiting with another plate of toast. "Second order of toast coming up," he announced.

Russell remarked, "Why, Dennis, we didn't know you baked."

"Anything to help Mary Nan... and Miss Bee," he answered.

Mary Nan blushed. "He's been a lot of help," she giggled.

Another budding romance in the making? Two surprises in one morning. Russell hadn't noticed anything between these two. *Hmmm, they are close in age, Mary Nan possibly somewhat older... and at least an inch taller... but both are kind and quiet-spoken.*

"Dennis will help with lunch, too," she added with a grin.

Returning the grin, looking from Dennis to Mary Nan, Russell answered, "Then, thanks to you both."

Catching Dennis's eye, Russell winked. Dennis only widened his grin, obviously happy.

Russell explained to the girls that Miss Bee would be back later today and would be fine. "Just don't hug her too tightly. She'll be sore from her fall."

After lunch, Russell played Jacks with them for a while. Afterward, they contently played paper dolls while he read. By seven-thirty, Rose and Ella were asleep. He tiptoed out of the room and down the stairs to use the phone, which was in use. The boarder cut his conversation short soon after Russell appeared. Miss Bee had resisted having a pay phone installed but had a list of rules posted.

Thank God for Miss Bee's rules, the first being no long-distance calls unless you call collect. Anyone can talk for fifteen minutes unless someone is waiting. If someone is waiting to make a call, you must not tie it up for more than five minutes after they arrive. Well, here's hoping no one comes along while I'm talking with Dare.

Russell quickly dialed Dare's number. Her phone rang... four rings...six... ten. He knew he should hang up. She must be out... but at eight o'clock? He realized the irony of the thought as only a few months ago, he'd *worked* much later almost every night.

"Hello."

Finally.

"I was about to give up."

"I'm getting ready for bed."

"We waited by the front door of the church for you this morning."

"Oh? I didn't think you were there."

"It doesn't matter—they needed to get home and rest anyway. Were they too much for you last night?"

"No, I loved having them."

"You sound tired. Are you okay?

She didn't answer right away. "Yes... I'm okay."

"Dare, what's wrong? Did the girls misbehave?"

"No. They were as sweet as always. I don't want to talk tonight... I'm tired. But I do want to talk...*seriously*... as soon as you can."

"Tell me what's wrong."

His heart felt sick. Something was *very* wrong.

She didn't respond.

"Dare?"

"Russell..." Dare's words seemed to stick in her throat.

"Yes, honey?"

"They aren't yours... Rose and Ella... they aren't yours."

Now Russell couldn't speak.

"Russell, find a time to come to my house... *alone*... that is, if you have any explanation."

"Yes. I can explain... I'll arrange a time."

"Okay." *Click.*

She hung up without waiting for a reply

A wave of nausea came over him. Almost running for the bathroom, he closed and locked the door before vomiting violently. Then he put the seat down and sat to cry. How *could* he explain?

∼∼ 26 ∼∼

The Confession

After agreeing on a time, Russell approached Dare's front door. He was a nervous wreck.

He thought his life had fallen apart months ago—apparently, life wasn't through with the remaining pieces.

Dare opened the door and motioned him inside. She had remained in her work clothes. He knew she usually changed into more comfortable clothes immediately after work. She'd never looked more beautiful. The slim gray skirt, though not tight, hugged her hips perfectly. With it she wore a soft pink sweater, bringing out the flawlessness of her skin—which today was noticeably pale. Her only accessory was pearl earrings.

No turquoise. I've come to expect turquoise.

She'd even kept on her stockings and three-inch black heels. She was obviously determined to be formal. He stood just inside the door, yearning to embrace her, yet dared not even approach.

"Sit in the armchair, I'll sit across. I'll ask no more questions but I want *all* the truth of what happened in your life before you came to Beacon."

He sat.

She spoke calmly. "I heard the girls' prayers Saturday night. They are not your daughters. I said nothing to them, Russell. They never realized they'd shared news with me. When I realized you had them under false pretenses, I considered phoning the police."

"Dare!"

"I didn't. I did, however, phone Doreen and Bobby. They know you are here now and why. I told them no matter what story you concoct, I am positive you love them and they love you just as much. But, whatever the case, they aren't yours. I had to assure my sister I had no fear of being alone with you."

Russell's expression turned to complete dismay.

"If you don't give me answers, I will show you out of my home... *all* the answers. Either way, I'm not sure after that."

Feeling as if the blood had drained from him and thankful he was sitting, he didn't know where or how to begin. He took a deep breath.

"I'd hoped to explain..."

She glared at him.

"Dare, I'll explain everything, I *will*, but I must begin with my being hired and fired by the architectural firm. Every word I told you before was true. I did *nothing* dishonest. I made a stupid mistake in handing over the blueprints, but I did not knowingly do or say anything wrong. I told no untruths.

"There's something I haven't admitted. That young man I handed the blueprints to... I remember swelling up with pride that I was an up-and-coming architect, whereas, at the same age, he was *only* a courier. What's the saying, *Pride comes before the fall*? Whoever or whatever he was, he was responsible for cutting me down to size."

His mind went back to the day in June when he was fired— when he walked out of H. H. & J, Architects knowing his dream had been crushed, seeing the pieces of his life crumbling before him.

"Things actually got worse from there. It will take a while, but this time I will include every detail. Eventually, you will be able to fit the pieces together."

~~ 27 ~~

As it happened...

Being fired from the job he loved, knowing he stood little chance of ever again working in his field, he was deeply despondent. He left the office building feeling he'd lost everything. No job, no income. He would lose the expensive apartment and car, as well as his reputation. What does a man do when he leaves work in the middle of an afternoon with nothing left to do or for which to plan? Many stop at a bar for a drink—he didn't drink. What did other business acquaintances do? Some talked about a back room for gambling—not for him, either. Only one real friend came to mind with whom he could talk, Jason Harrison... and he was out of the country.

His girlfriend, Katherine? No, she'd dumped him months ago.

Girlfriend? Dare's face registered shock, not understanding, more confused than ever.

Katherine and Russell had dated for over a year when he had time, usually for special occasions, large corporate parties, and dinners. He'd met her at a corporate party, the date of an associate who had moved away the following month. She was striking in a tight, black, cocktail dress, and her hair elaborately accented with diamond combs. He thought they had a lot in common... he was climbing the corporate ladder and she wanted the life it promised. She was patient and understanding about not hearing from him if she knew he was working—he was getting ahead, for them. He didn't realize there was a significant difference—he actually dreamed about the buildings and his contribution to the world of architecture, though he knew money would follow. To Katherine, the status and money were all that mattered. In any case, he rather assumed she was the one with whom he would spend the remainder of his years. She would fit well into a corporate life.

She had ended the relationship by confessing she had fallen for her new boss at the modeling agency. He'd been in the picture only a few weeks. Russell vaguely remembered him as being much older and unattractive, though powerful, wealthy and prestigious—an old story. He was hurt and begged her to reconsider. He was accustomed to her, after all. Waking the day after the breakup, however, he realized he'd been upset but was perfectly alright. Not at all devastated about losing her. It seemed wrong to feel so little. He wondered when he became so callous. She had been in his life over a year and he'd seen her as part of his future. Yet, she was only a habit. Not an admirable trait, just letting go of someone without pain. But there it was—he didn't care. Katherine was forgotten. But he cared about his career—it was everything.

✳✳

Russell glanced at Dare from time to time. He wondered why he included details that would hurt. But it was time to tell her every single thing about himself and his past. Explaining it to her, hearing the words aloud, he realized how sordid it was. But he would omit nothing. Memories of the past months floated in and out of his mind.

"On the day I was fired, I had no idea what to do if not working. It was too early even to eat. By now, I'd arrived at my apartment building without realizing it. I stepped into the quiet elevator. In less than a minute, I walked down the silent hallway and into the apartment for which I would not be able to pay the rent. I looked at the space, large and empty. Leaving it wouldn't break my heart either. I hadn't spent much time there, and it never felt like home.

"But I *did* have a bright spot left... Brenda."

Dare's eyebrows rose, questioning, hoping.

He observed her as he prepared to give the first of many answers.

"Brenda was my sister."

She gasped.

Russell was desperate for Dare to understand. He knew he'd lost her love and was heartsick. But he didn't want her to hate him. His only hope... *prayer*, was for her to see him as a decent man who made bad, very bad, choices. But he would continue, leaving out nothing.

**

"Brenda was three when I was born. We had good parents..."

His thoughts wandered for a moment.

"Mother said Brenda seemed to think I was *her*s. She loved me unconditionally. According to Mother, she wanted to do everything for me until I was a year old, then began trying to *teach* me everything.

"After marrying, she lived in Evanston, Illinois, a small town barely outside of Chicago. I think the girls have mentioned it. I could drive to her home in less than thirty minutes, barring traffic snarls. I needed her that afternoon... after I was fired. She was the only person who would still believe in me. But I was so distraught and I knew I would only upset her, so I decided to wait until the next morning. Our parents had been dead for several years—Brenda's house felt like home, wher*ever* she lived. She was my only family. Well… not quite. She was a young widow with two little girls, Rose and Ella. I actually had *three* bright spots left in my life."

He looked up. Their eyes met, but he didn't see what he had only days before. She was intent on listening to every word, trying to understand.

The woman I believed to be his deceased wife was his sister. The girls… not daughters…his nieces.

He continued. "Brenda had married Gary Townsend, another family line, of course. There were many jokes about it, but that's why the girls' last names match mine.

"Anyway, those wonderful girls—my *nieces*—though I was desperate to talk with Brenda, I didn't want to upset the girls either. When I woke the morning after being fired, it was six o'clock, the time I woke every morning. I'd slept little. Coffee would fix a world of hurt at this time of morning, but it only served to remind me I needed to eat. I'd had nothing since early the day before. I waited until eight to phone Brenda.

"Good morning."

"Hi, Russ," she answered. "What's up?" She knew he was generally immersed in work about now.

"I have an unexpected day off. If you're going to be home, I'd like to come by." Brenda laughed. He could easily picture her on this bright Saturday morning. She would be in jeans and an old shirt, probably cleaning the kitchen to a chorus of children's voices. Her laughter was one of the things everyone loved.

"We looked nothing alike, both a mix of our parents' features, who were total opposites physically. Though my name came from my father's family, I favor our Italian mother. I inherited her dark skin and facial features, including a nose she called, 'classic.' I thought Mother was beautiful, but viewing my own reflection in the mirror, I'd think, *The nose looked better on Mother.* Our father was six-foot-three. Regretfully, I didn't attain that height, but I was thankful not to be as short as Mother. I was *not* thankful for inheriting my father's dark blue eyes, strange with my dark skin."

Even with the stress of the situation, Dare's thoughts wandered.

Everything about you fits together perfectly... there's nothing I'd change about the blue eyes and tanned skin... I can get lost in your eyes... but I'm trying to listen and understand who you are...

Quietly, she asked, "Why do they call you *Pop?*"

A hint of a smile appeared as he answered. "When I was young, I loved *Hopalong Cassidy*, a big cowboy movie star."

"I remember him."

"I pretended to be *Hopalong* so often, Brenda nicknamed me, *Hop*, which she called me through the years, even after she married and after Rose's birth. When Rose began saying a few words, she called me *Pop* one day, apparently trying to say *Hop*, like her mother. By then Ella was a baby and Brenda didn't want them to call me by her nickname. She resumed calling me Russ and repeatedly told them I was *Uncle Russ*. It didn't work. Rose had already decided I was *Pop*. After a while, we all grew accustomed to it. Their dad,

Gary, didn't mind, so that was that." His expression changed, the grin turning somber. "Must admit, their calling me Pop worked to my advantage.

"Back to Brenda... she was only five-foot-five, with small features and petite build, but Brenda favored our father. Her hair was dark, but a shade lighter, kept short and simple, the perfect frame for her pretty oval-shaped face. Her expressive eyes were light blue, lashes long and dark. Her skin was light. She had a small nose which could almost be called pug, which Ella inherited.

"My sister wouldn't have been called beautiful, but *so* cute, and her beauty oozed from inside. Her husband Gary once told me, *She's like a little doll, adorable, as if she could be nothing but perfect. Then you push the button and she becomes so animated you have a hard time keeping up. The laugh she shares with everyone absorbs and makes you happy. But most don't see her strength, her absolute insistence on doing right. You see it when you mess up... meaning me. Brenda will forgive and will be like a tiger if you need defending. But you better straighten up if you're on the wrong path.* Wistfully, he'd said, *She's almost unbreakable... but delicate in a way, vulnerable. How could I not have fallen in love with her?*

"Brenda and Gary had the kind of rare marriage everyone wants. They were solid. When he died, she mourned deeply, but wouldn't allow herself time to feel sorry for herself. She told me simply that she had his two girls to rear and she intended to do it happily.

"But, back to my phone call that morning..."

"Come on over, Russ. Whatever's wrong, we'll find the right glue."

"She knew there was a problem without my saying, without even seeing me. This was a problem she couldn't repair, but I needed her support to keep from crumbling... along with my career and the McGuire building.

"Opening the door at Brenda's, the girls ran to me as usual."

**

"Pop!"

Rose, barely seven, reached him a split second before six-year-old Ella, but he grabbed them both, easily lifting them as they put their arms around his neck. This was as close to heaven as a person could be, these precious children loving him, their pure, innocent little hearts untouched by the world.

He pretended to stagger as he made his way to the sofa. "Help!" he called out, "you're strangling me with hugs and kisses." He leaned over and dropped them onto the cushions as he began tickling them until they cried out for Brenda.

"Not helping you. You deserve what you get," she laughed.

"Okay, I quit," he said as he dropped down on the sofa with them. He motioned them to his lap and they were settled within seconds.

"You have no idea how much I love you two little mites."

Unwittingly, tears began forming in his eyes. He blinked and widened his grin, hoping they wouldn't notice. It worked with Rose and Ella, but Brenda noticed. He'd hidden very little from her over the years.

"Alright, girls, off Russ and upstairs to finish cleaning your rooms. Then finish the pictures you were doing for him before you come back down. It's my turn to talk *grown-up* with him for a while."

They groaned and complained but ran up the stairs.

"Come into the kitchen, Russ. I started a fresh pot of coffee when you called."

"After I told Brenda about being fired, she exclaimed, *I can't believe it. What I have the most trouble believing is that your superiors would think you could do such a thing, knowing it could destroy your career.*

"I told her I didn't know what to do. They were right about no one hiring me again. What would I do with my life?

"She answered, *I don't know. But I know you, and you will figure it out. And we'll both pray the truth, whatever it may be, is uncovered before long.*

They sat quietly for a few minutes.

**

Focusing on Brenda, he realized there was something more in his sister's face.

"Russ. I hate the timing of what I have to tell you, but I have news I can hide no longer. You thought you were coming over to unload on me, but I'd planned to call *you* today. First though—something I've been wanting to mention." She paused. "You've seemed to drift away from God in the last years. Am I wrong?"

"I've been busy building my career, working twenty-four-seven, Brenda. You know that."

"That wasn't the question. I know you haven't attended worship in years. I almost understand that with the way you've worked. But there's more to leading a life for God than attending worship—your attitude about life and other people, your prayer life... talking with Him... listening... and talking *about* Him."

His head low, he didn't answer.

"Honey, I don't intend to preach. You gave your life to God when you were fifteen. I remember the day of your baptism."

Weakly, he replied, "Yes."

"He's the one who can help you. With everything. I brought it up because I am about to add to your problems and you're going to need Him even more."

Giving him time to think and focus, she waited.

"I finally gave her my full attention. It had been a long time since I'd thought only of another person, but now my concern was for Brenda."

"What's wrong?" I asked.

"She dropped a bombshell I could never have anticipated."

~~ 28 ~~

Brenda

Brenda observed her brother closely. She needed assurance he wasn't daydreaming about architecture and would hear every word.

She knew her brother well. He was focused—not inwardly this time but on whatever she was about to reveal.

"Russ, I had my routine yearly physical last month. They called me in for more tests, then another and another. I saw my doctor a few days ago... he believes I have no more than three months to live. *Don't interrupt...* I have to say it all at once... the answer to your questions are yes, I'm sure, and no, there is absolutely nothing we can do. I have a cancer that spreads rapidly. It is already confirmed in several locations of my body, which means it is most likely in others.

"I want you to go to my lawyer's office with me this week to go over my will and property. One timing that *does* work well is that I want you to move in here with us. You won't have to be concerned about income. Thankfully, money will not be a problem, at least not for the foreseeable future.

"Now... the most important thing. When I'm gone, I want you to take Rose and Ella. I *know* you're single and don't know where your life is going. It's terrible timing, to say the least. But you are the one—the one with whom they will feel most comfortable and closer to my memory. They love and trust you completely. As do I." She ceased talking, sighed, and put her hands in her lap.

Tears streaming, he could barely utter her name. "*Bren.*" He reverted to his childhood name for her. What was there to say? His best friend in the world... gone? This precious woman who'd never done a bad thing in her life?

He tried again. "I'd do anything for you. You know how much I love you... and Rose and Ella... but..."

She was calm, replying quietly. "It has to be you, Russ. I can go in peace if I know they will be with you."

"Their grandparents, though, Gary's parents? Wouldn't they want them and offer a more stable home?"

"Their health isn't good and they're too old to rear children. Truthfully, Gary didn't have a happy childhood. They're not *bad* people, but they aren't *warm*... he would not want them to rear our children."

Russell's problems faded into oblivion as he absorbed the reality of his sister's impending death.

He paid the fee for breaking the lease on his apartment and moved to Brenda's. He would do what he could to help and would begin learning the girls' routine. Brenda's symptoms were already apparent.

"I want you to remain in this house with them, Russ. Not forever. I won't tie you to a location, but long enough to adjust somewhat. Then sell the house and move wherever your future seems to be."

She was bedridden six weeks after their initial conversation.

One afternoon as a nurse made her regular home visit, Brenda noticed her being chattier than usual.

"It's getting close, isn't it?" The nurse avoided her eyes.

"I want to *know*. There are things I need to do for the girls. *Please*."

"You need twenty-four-hour care, Mrs. Townsend. I'm not a doctor. But... dear, I think your time is near. You may have only a week or two in which you are alert enough to make decisions. If you quote me, I'll have to deny it. I'm not supposed to comment or make these kinds of observations."

"Thank you."

A week later, she insisted on being hospitalized. It had been a choice earlier, but she had preferred to remain at home.

"You don't have to go to the hospital, Bren. Dr. Edmondson agreed we could have twenty-four-hour nursing care, and you know I can handle anything the nurse can't do. Since your room is downstairs, I'll sleep on the sofa or get a folding bed to be close by at all times."

Her voice weak, she took his hand. "I wanted to be here as long as possible, to have time with my daughters. But I don't want to *die* in our home. I think it will be better for them if it happens in the hospital. I've talked to them and tried to be honest. They're young, so I know they don't completely understand, but I've told them that I will have to leave soon to go to heaven. And I won't be back."

Choked up, he agreed. He'd begun praying again these past weeks. His prayers were tentative, difficult—it had been too long. But he began to feel a strength he knew was not his alone.

Thank you, Lord, for helping me do what Brenda needed. I thank you for putting her in my life. But I don't understand why! Lord, why are you are allowing her to die, leaving her children orphans? Help me understand more... forgive my anger and weakness. Help me carry out her wishes and take care of her babies.

In less than two weeks, her medical team informed him she had only hours remaining. Her in-laws were at the hospital. They demanded to take their grandchildren away before Brenda's final breath.

"I understand your feelings, even why you think it best, Mr. and Mrs. Townsend. But I know Rose and Ella, and I know the amount of time Brenda spent preparing them for this day. They understand more than you think and are handling it better than anyone could have hoped. They want to hold Brenda's hand when she goes to heaven."

They were irate at Russell's refusal. They left alone.

Brenda looked exactly like an angel, the one she'd always been in Russell's life. The medications had taken away the pain. Her breathing was quiet. He'd asked the nurse to dress her in her favorite pink gown and comb her now-thin hair.

He brought the girls into the room. Rose held Ella's hand as they entered, neither saying a word.

Rose whispered, "Ella, you get on the bed by mama, but be easy." Ella obeyed, taking her mother's hand. Rose went to the other side of the bed to take her mother's other hand.

"I'm bigger, Pop, I can stand *beside* the bed."

Russell held himself rigid to keep from collapsing. "Your mother is proud of you both."

He stood beside Rose for a while, finally pulling a chair close to the bed. He sat, and lifted Rose onto his lap. She never released her mother's hand. He put his hand over theirs and sat quietly for about an hour. A nurse came in and out of the room periodically to check vital signs. When Brenda's breathing could barely be heard, he looked at the nurse—she nodded agreement and left them alone.

Brenda's breathing became more and more shallow, with longer periods between breaths. At the end, she took one last short breath, and her chest ceased movement.

It wasn't what he expected. He felt God's presence in the room and a peace like nothing he had ever experienced. As her body no longer moved, his relaxed. He'd cried so much the past weeks, he had no tears left as his precious sister departed their lives for good.

His hand remaining on Rose's, which was on Brenda's, he reached to put the other on top of Ella's. Such sweet softness. "Your Mama has gone to heaven. If you want, you may tell her goodbye." Speaking in a tiny voice, no longer sounding *bigger*, Rose asked, "Can we *kiss* her, Pop?"

"Yes." They each kissed a cheek.

"I love you, Mommy," Rose whispered. "We'll be good for Pop." Ella began to cry, difficult to watch as she tried so hard to be courageous. "Bye, Mommy. I wish you didn't have to go to heaven yet."

He bent to kiss his sister's cheek for the last time. He whispered, *I'll take care of them, Bren, go with God in peace.* He took her daughters into his arms and left his angel, the person he'd always turned to, lying peacefully in the bed.

He corrected himself—his angel was no longer there. She had gone to a better place.

～ 29 ～

Head down, tears streaming, Russell completed his story. He raised his head. Dare was sobbing.

"I've realized something," he said. "The day Brenda died, Rose acted the big sister. She withdrew after that and let Ella take the lead.

"Brenda left what was most precious to her in my care. I couldn't love them more."

Dare was absorbed in what Russell had endured in the months before she met him. "Brenda told you to take the girls and you've taken care of them. Why lie?"

"I never planned to lie, Dare. I wanted to get away from Chicago and go where no one knew us, but I hadn't planned to lie about our relationship. Not saying I wouldn't have done it if necessary, but I didn't plan it. And... in the beginning, I didn't lie. People assumed they were my daughters. It surprised me at first, but I simply didn't correct anyone. I don't think I ever actually lied. I just became evasive.

"Our last names were the same, but another thing that worked by accident was that Brenda's husband's middle initial was *R*... so the birth certificates read, *father, Gary R. Townsend*, and I suppose the school assumed the *R* stood for Russell."

Dare rose from her chair and moved to the end of the sofa near him. She took his hand. "What a terrible time you've lived through. Losing your career... and losing the only family you had... and loved." She leaned her head to his shoulder.

He felt as if his entire being was shaking furiously. He studied his hands, motionless in his lap—the turmoil was internal. She was close, holding his hand and speaking affectionately, what he'd longed for...

Abruptly, he stood. Dare was startled. "Russ...?"

"I haven't yet told you what I *did*. Why I *really* left the state."

**

The Worst of it.

"What do you mean, why you *really* left? You needed to get away from the city and the pain of losing your sister, who, I'm just realizing, did not die in any storm, but of cancer. Everyone was acceptant of the fact she'd died in that *seich*."

"I honestly don't know where that story came from. It wasn't mine."

Dare smiled weakly. "I believe *I* have the answer to that one. But it no longer matters."

He answered, "It was true I needed to get away from the city and the pain of losing Brenda. I miss her so much... I can't *tell* you how much."

His pain was almost tangible. Dare's heart hurt for him.

He continued. "She asked me to live in her house with the girls until things settled. But I couldn't... someone else had a different idea."

Dare leaned back against the sofa, drained.

It was tearing his heart out, reliving Brenda's death and all that happened, but he had to keep going. Dare had to know everything, even though he knew he'd lost her. Earlier, he told himself he could make her understand. And she did. Thus far. Maybe even the rest. But he wasn't the same in her eyes now and wouldn't be again. His special, wonderful Dare... his love. For him, he knew she was gone.

"The anger of Gary's parents at my insisting the girls stay at the hospital the day Brenda died... it never lessened. They were cordial during the planning of the funeral and never commented about my being at the house. They knew I'd moved in while Brenda was ill. They never visited during that time but had phoned a few times. The night before the funeral, after the visitation period at the funeral home, they told the girls goodnight and added, *After the funeral tomorrow, you're going home with us for a while.*"

"Rose looked at me, but Ella asked, *For a visit?*

"They replied, *We'll talk about it later.*

"While the girls talked with other people and prepared to leave, they called me aside. *You do understand they will live with us, don't you?*

"I said no, I was sure you were aware Brenda specifically asked me to care for them. I told them we would remain in the house, their home, and attempt to keep their lives as consistent as possible. I told them they would always be welcome.

"I've never seen such a smug, ugly, grin as I witnessed that day. Mrs. Townsend replied. *Russell, my dear. You may have the house, we care nothing about it. We are also aware you are unemployed and have need of it. You may even have most everything in it.*

"I stared at them... they were treating me like a child who didn't understand. But they planned to *take* the girls. They finally agreed to give them a week with me. Then I was to help them pack whatever they wanted to take to their grandparents. They made it clear they were willing to take legal action if I didn't comply, in spite of Brenda's stipulation in her will, and I knew they had the money to do it.

"The friend who stuck by me was Jason Harrison. I talked with him often that week. We weighed every fact. The one that weighed heaviest was that Brenda *wanted* them with me and I had promised I would take care of them. However, and though it hurt, I concluded they might truly be better off with their grandparents. They seemed in decent health, had full-time people to care for their house and whatever was needed, and a nice home and community. It was less than two hours away, and there would be two of them… a woman to understand them better than I would, and a father-figure. I was aware I had no idea how to be a father. I convinced myself that I *was* taking care of them by assuring they were actually in the best situation.

"The day before they were to pick them up, someone phoned me with news that caused me to take them and try to disappear. The person called by mistake and never seemed to realize what he'd done. He worked with a boarding school in New York. Do you hear what I'm saying, Dare? A *boarding school* in another state. They had no intention of raising them. They planned to send them away. I couldn't stand it, I wouldn't comply. But I had only a day. The girls hadn't been told they were going to *live* with their grandparents yet—I'd planned to do it that night. Instead, I told them we were going on an adventure.

"I phoned Jason with information about my bank account. I told him I was leaving for a while and would be in touch. I didn't have time to get any money, that's why we were almost broke when we arrived in Beacon. I still had my car… a small, older sports model… in good condition, gleaming black, and *sharp* for a bachelor, or so I thought. I couldn't possibly fit the three of us into it so I sold it quickly for less than it was worth. I couldn't take Brenda's car and add to the Townsends' anger, so I rented a car. In another name, but I won't go into that.

"I was on the run. I was sure they would soon be looking for us and likely press charges of kidnapping. I even had the girls dressed in jeans and wearing ball caps for a while, hoping that if anyone were asked, they might remember seeing a man with boys."

"Did you cut Rose's hair?"

He choked, not answering. His expression was one of deep remorse, more profound than ever. "Yes. I regret that more than anything. She cried—I shouldn't have done it."

"Oh, Russ, I'm sorry I brought it up."

"She forgave me, you know."

He was exhausted. But it was almost finished.

"I didn't have a real plan. I'd only reacted. After we stopped in Beacon, I turned in the rental car. After a few weeks here, I was tired and we seemed to be relaxing. I won't say I was thinking ahead. I took a day at a time, knew they needed to be in school... and... well, we became comfortable. Happy.

"I had Jason wire money to a general delivery post office box over the state line. I didn't want him to know where I was because I didn't want him to have to lie. I took a taxi to pick up the money, purchased the car there with cash, no questions asked, though I did assure I wasn't buying a stolen vehicle." He sat again, putting his head in his hands. Dare remained silent. It was too much to absorb.

"Russ, what *now*?"

He could barely speak. "I'll take them back. I guess I knew I'd have to sometime. I'm not sure why they haven't found us. I may go to jail, but I love them more than anybody *could*... except Brenda and Gary." He raised his head, looking transported as he stared into space. "I didn't know anything about being a father. I got so many things wrong. But now... I don't know how I'll live without them."

Dare moved to sit closer. The feel of her hand on his arm brought him back to the moment. He felt numb as he looked at her, questioning, having nothing more to say.

"Russ, I'll help you. I'll go with you to Illinois."

He couldn't believe what he was hearing. But he knew she loved Rose and Ella.

"For the girls…"

"No. Yes… the girls, *too*… but for *you*."

She was the best person he'd ever known. Even now, she would help.

"What will you do first, Russ? Will you phone the grandparents, your friend… or just return?"

"I'll call Jason. We haven't communicated since I left, other than his sending the money without knowing where I was. He'll know the situation and whether there is a search or a warrant for my arrest. I'm in a lot of trouble. I know I shouldn't have left. Looking back, I'm not sure I wouldn't do it again. At least I've had these months with them and they know I love them. We'll always have that."

She took his hands in hers. "Russell Townsend. You are a mess. You've made bad decisions and been dishonest. A lie is a lie whether put into sentence form or not—you lied to all of us."

Weakly, he uttered, "I'm sorry."

"Russ… look at me."

Trembling, he looked into her beautiful, kind eyes. She smiled as her eyes again filled with tears, spilling over onto her face… her lovely, perfect, face.

She whispered, "Russ… I'm in love with you."

He couldn't trust himself, what he thought he'd heard. His eyes questioned.

She leaned closer. "I *love* you, Russ."

Rinnnng, rinnnng, rinnnnng, rinnnnng.

She scrambled from the sofa, leaving him dazed. "If I don't answer, Doreen will have the police here to arrest you.

"Hello, Doreen—yes, I knew it would be you. I'm okay. I'm *sure*. It took a long time, and there are things that must be done, but I'm fine... no, not afraid of being alone with him. Listen, please... yes, he explained everything... it's going to be okay... *please* let me hang up now. *Promise* not to call the police and I'll tell you everything later this evening. Yes, I'm sure. I'll call you back. Bye. I love you."

As she returned the receiver to its base, she turned around. She smiled weakly. "Well? I said I love you." Taking only a step, her voice low, she continued, "You asked me to let you know when I was ready. *Now*... I want to hear you say you love *me*."

He rose from the sofa, moving quickly. He wrapped his arms around her, lifting her to bring her face to his as his mouth hungrily covered hers. Her lips and body responded eagerly, warm in his arms as she clung to him. The world and its trouble stopped for a moment.

Slowly he lowered her to the floor. He stood in wonder at this unbelievable, astonishing woman. After all he'd told her, she was still here... in his life, saying she loved him. His hands remained around her shoulders. "Dare, it seems I've loved you an eternity, though it's been only months. I waited... but I didn't want it to be this way. I love you with all my heart and soul. I'll do everything in my power to clean up my mess of a life. I love you *so* much."

She took his hand, leading him back to the sofa. She smiled through the tears continuing to spill. He put his hand to her face to gently wipe them away.

"Russ, I have faith you'll live to build again... not just buildings, but a good life as well."

"How can you forgive and still believe in me? You're too good for me. I don't even know if we can *have* anything."

"Russ, hold me. I want to feel your heart beating. I knew I loved you weeks ago. I was afraid... but I love you so much... and now nothing else seems to matter."

With tears intermingling, they embraced again, each wanting to console and heal. He kissed her tenderly, stroking her hair, feeling her heart beat as she trembled in his arms. She responded lovingly, her hands touching the back of his neck and moving down his back.

His mouth and arms relaxed. He moved slightly away.

Hoarsely, he spoke, "Dare?"

"Yes... I know."

"I want to do what's right. God is moving in my life because I'm holding to Him again. I believe He's with me and will give me strength. The outcome may not be what I want, though. There are consequences to my actions."

Standing, he added, "I'll hold your words and touch close to my heart. But I won't think of it as a commitment."

He put a finger to her lips as she began to interrupt. "I love you with all my heart and soul. I'll love you until the day I die. But, darling, I will not allow you to make promises until I know and face the consequences to come. You said the words and I know what they meant to you. I must return to Illinois and face whatever is required. You'll stay here until I have answers, until I know whether I can offer a firm foundation for a life together."

"When?"

"I'll go back day after tomorrow. There's no need to put it off. But I won't tell the girls until after school tomorrow."

"I want to go to Illinois with you."

He kissed her forehead. "I know. I love you for that, too. But, no."

She stood to walk him to the door, weak with all that had taken place in a single afternoon. After he left, she stood at the closed door. Sighing, she walked to the phone to call Doreen.

Lord, he's leaning on you. Please help him. I'm calling on you to help us to do what's right... for ourselves and Rose and Ella. I don't want to lose any of them. Oh, God, please help us.

~~ 30 ~~

It was after three o'clock when he left Dare's house. He returned to the hardware store to talk with Daniel. Inside his office, Daniel closed the door. He listened quietly as Russell talked and stopped occasionally to weep. Daniel placed an arm around him, saying nothing.

"That's the condensed version of who I am and what I've done. I'm *so* sorry I deceived everyone, you especially."

Daniel squeezed his shoulder and leaned back. "Russell, I believe you're an honorable man. You made spur-of-the-moment decisions during a time of turmoil. You hadn't had time to absorb the fact that you'd lost your career and reputation before dealing with losing your sister. You had two major blows, not to mention the responsibilities of two children. Your actions were taken out of love. That didn't make them right, son, but if I can do anything to help, I'm here for you."

Filled with gratitude, Russell answered, "Thank you. I respect you as much as anyone I've ever known and treasure your misguided friendship and confidence."

"Anything I can do?"

"I need to call my friend in Chicago. I have no privacy at the boarding house, as well as call times being limited. Could I use your phone?"

"Sure. Take all the time as you need."

"Hello."

"Jason? It's Russell."

"Russell! Man, am I glad to hear from you. I've been praying for you to call. I have a million questions, but I've got news, too. Why haven't you been in touch?"

"I was scared. I didn't want to be found. I've made a sort of oddly comfortable life in a Southern town in Alabama."

"Alabama? You're kidding. What about Brenda's daughters?"

"They're fine and happy. They began school and adjusted better than I could have expected. We've been living in a boarding house... don't say it... I know how crazy I sound... what you won't believe is that I've fallen in love, too. The people in this town have been wonderful to us. They thought I was Rose and Ella's father and I let them believe it. The truth came out yesterday and everything has fallen apart. So, I have to return to Evanston to try to straighten things out. I'll make arrangements in the next few days to return with the girls and see where things go from there. I'll most likely have to allow them to go with their grandparents. I'd hoped you would know whether they filed charges, and how you think I should return... without making things worse."

"That's why I've been praying for you to get in touch, Russell. At the outset, they did file kidnapping charges. I've never seen such angry, bitter people. My friend, Richard, who is a lawyer, let me know they were coming into Chicago to press charges. I arranged to be in the building and tried to talk with them, but they were explosive. I don't know what happened since, but Richard called to let me know they'd agreed to withdraw the charges if you returned with Rose and Ella within the month. As of today, that would be less than a week from now. Richard had the impression they were cowed down, not so angry as fearful."

"They were probably genuinely concerned about their grandchildren. They thought them in the hands of a madman. Thinking back, perhaps I was..."

Jason could hear the tremor in his friend's voice. "Jason, I love them as my own. I only wanted to carry out Brenda's wishes..."

"I know, man. Listen, let me know what day you'll be back and I'll get in touch with Richard—he'll know who to contact. I really think you're going to be okay."

"I doubt it. But I'll let you know. I'll call again tomorrow."

"Well?" Daniel asked, returning to his office.

"I didn't find out much. But I'll be heading back… probably day after tomorrow."

Daniel nodded as he walked to his side to embrace him. As Russell felt his friend's strong arms around him, he heard him begin to pray. Nothing could have touched him more. He sobbed as Daniel asked the Lord to travel with him and put His arm of protection around him.

**

Russell's nerves were on edge the next morning but the girls didn't seem to notice. They left for school chattering about the new swings on the playground. He used the day to organize most of their belongings, pick up laundry, and get the car ready for the trip.

After supper, he informed Rose and Ella they were returning to Evanston. "I'm afraid we won't be staying long, but you will have time to choose what you want to take with you from your house, everything in your room if you want." He was having difficulty breathing. "Your grandparents are going to meet us there, too."

"Pop?" Ella was always the thinker, putting things together quickly.

"Yes, honey."

"What will we to do after that? Are we going to live in your apartment in Chicago?"

He couldn't lie. Not to her. Not to anyone anymore. But he couldn't go into everything just now. "I'm not sure, honey. Really, I don't know. I'd like you to live with me but you may be going to live with your grandparents. They want you and love you very much."

He had no intention of explaining boarding school—the two responsible parties would have *that* to discuss.

"Mommy said *you* would take care of us when she was in heaven."

How could he have this conversation? He was holding himself together with a thread, thinking if he took a breath at this moment, he would collapse. But he had to convince them things would be all right. "I'll always make sure you are okay. And no matter where you are, you will see me often. I promise."

Unless I'm in jail.

"Honey, Brenda didn't know the law might tell us that it would be better if you were with your grandparents. I have to do what the law says. Do you understand?"

"No."

"You *do* understand how much I love you, don't you?"

Lips quivering, Ella answered, "Yes."

"Then let's just wait to see what happens when we get home." The small girl, so wise at six, hugged him tightly before beginning to gather the last of her belongings. Rose had been listening quietly, but as Ella began packing, she commented, "I'm glad we're going home."

Poor Rose. She's had the hardest time emotionally. At least one of us is happy. Lord, please protect them. I pray there will be no lasting damage to them because of my actions. You know my heart, my wants, and desires. I thank you for Dare, a beautiful soul in every way. I want what's good for her. If I'm honest with myself, I fear that may not include me—help me to accept your will.

~~ 31 ~~

Hoping to talk with Miss Bee alone, Russell walked downstairs while the girls finished packing that night. *I'm as upset about leaving this old boarding house as I would be about leaving a real home.*

"Evening Russell."

He'd been so absorbed with his thoughts, he almost collided with a boarder at the foot of the stairs. It was Dennis Sims, with whom he had gotten somewhat better acquainted. "Good evening, Dennis." He continued walking, but Dennis spoke again. "Russell, can I ask how you are?"

Not sure he was speaking to him, he turned. "Me?"

"Not meaning to butt in… just noticed at supper you seemed troubled. Wondered whether there was anything… you know, whether I could help." He appeared frustrated. "I'm sorry. We're all fond of those little girls of yours… and *you*… I'm hoping everything is all right."

Touched, Russell placed a hand on Dennis's shoulder. "Thank you. It means a lot to me that you all care. We're leaving tomorrow. We have… complications. But thanks for asking."

I have little in common with this group of people, and they know almost nothing about us. But they care. I could not have landed in a better place.

He dreaded the conversation with Miss Bee but determined to be as honest as possible without going into all the wretched details. At the kitchen door, he watched this woman who had, in her own way, given much of herself to them in their time here. As usual, she wore a long apron over her clothing, focusing on organizing breakfast for the following morning. Daniel had been right—she was rather satisfied with her life. She had her own home and independence.

She sensed his presence and turned. "Russell? Why so quiet? You needin' something?"

"If you have time, I need to talk a few minutes."

She stood quietly, studying him. "Always got time for you, you *oughta* know that." Sensing this to be a private matter, she closed the kitchen door. "Sit down at the table and tell me what's the problem."

He sat slowly. "We're moving out... leaving in the morning. I'll leave an extra week's rent as I didn't give notice."

"What! Oh, well, I guess I knew you'd get a place of your own sometime—that's good news for all of you."

"It's not good news, at least not for me. I can't even explain all of it to you. I wish I could. We're leaving Beacon to go back where we came from. I'm not sure what we'll do when we get there... not exactly, there are things that have to be sorted out. You'll be hearing gossip about me soon, so I wanted to thank you for what you've done for us... for your friendship..." He was emotionally spent, weary of explaining.

She leaned in to put an arm around him. "Whatever it is, my heart knows you're a good man. You're a great father with a kind heart that's seen hard times before you came here to us. I hate to see you leave."

"Miss Bee, this has been our home for a while... *home*. I haven't looked for another place because I didn't want to. We've been content here. And I know you won't spread anything bad about me because you've seen the good. I will tell you, though, I'm not altogether what I seem. I haven't been completely honest and I apologize. First thing you'll hear that you won't believe is that I'm not Rose and Ella's father."

"What? Nobody better say such to *me*!"

"Miss Bee, I'm their *uncle*."

She inhaled sharply, taking hold of the table to steady herself.

"I'm sorry. My only defense is that people, including you, assumed I was their father and I didn't correct anyone. Our last names are the same. Their mother, my *sister*, did die. She asked me to keep the girls. The problem came when others thought they should have them instead, and I didn't do the right thing. I... just took off with them."

Recovered, she soothed, "Bless your heart, you poor dear... is there anything I can do? I'd stand up in front of God or anybody and tell them what good care you take of those girls. And it's a for-sure thing they love you more'n anybody on this earth."

Russell gave in to the woman who, at this moment, felt like a mother. He laid his head on her shoulder like a forlorn child. But only for a moment. He raised his head and stood. "Thank you. I've never known a finer woman than you."

Her eyes filled with tears as they stood. Giving his arm a squeeze, she said kindly, "How about you call me Irma Rae? I'm sure hoping this is not goodbye."

"I hope not, but I'm not sure."

"Will you write or call to let me know you're okay? Call *collect*, I'll accept."

Russell began to see this good woman more clearly. As with a multitude of people and things in his life, his vision had been blurred. She had changed physically since the day they'd met—her eyes were brighter, hair styled, and she wore a pale pink blouse which brought color to her face. She even wore a touch of lipstick. But there was more. Irma Rae was a giver, giving of herself humbly, never expecting or desiring acknowledgement or anything in return. Under the sometimes-gruff exterior she presented, she was a godly woman. That part wasn't new, and neither was her giving nature. He realized just how much he was going to miss her.

"I will let you know how we are, Irma Rae, but probably not for a few weeks. How about you promise *me* something."

"What's that?"

"Let me know how you and *Frank* are doing... maybe invite me to a wedding?"

She began to laugh heartily as she swatted his arm with a dishtowel. "You just get on out of here, Russell Townsend!" He grinned as he kissed her forehead. "I'll be in touch. I'll send the girls in to tell you goodbye before we leave in the morning."

As he opened the kitchen door to leave, he turned around. "At supper tomorrow night, tell the others we were glad to get acquainted... and tell them what I've told you." She nodded.

He didn't see her again before they left.

Leaving before breakfast, Russell sent the girls in to see Miss Bee with instructions to make it quick. Leaving her kitchen, they carried a large basket. "She sent goodies to tide us over on the road." Russell smiled as he settled them into the back seat, noting the *goodies* might feed several people for days.

Honnnnk, honnnnk, honnnnk.

About to pull from the curb, a car horn blew behind him. He turned to see Doreen opening her car door and motioning to him.

What now? No doubt, it would be bad. He felt sure she'd never especially liked him. She hadn't trusted him—and her instinct had been right, what could he say? He knew Dare had filled her in on everything. Doreen would be one angry woman. Wearily, he turned off the ignition and opened his car door.

"It's Miss Dare's sister. She's come to tell us 'bye," exclaimed Ella.

Oh sure, come to bid us a safe trip, that's all.

At their car now, Doreen stared daggers at him. "I need to talk to you a minute, in my car." It wasn't a request. Had she not been Dare's sister, he would simply tell her he hadn't time. Instead, he answered, "All right. Girls, I'll be right back."

Before he could close the car door, Doreen grabbed it and put her head inside. "Hi, girls. Came to tell ya'll 'bye and have a good trip." The girls cheerily bid her goodbye and settled back in the seat. She closed the car door and returned her attention to Russell. "Won't take long, I don't want them to get cold." She walked quickly to her car, assuming he would follow. He did.

Inside her car, he began, "Look, Doreen, I know you're angry and I have no defense. But I did... do love your sister..."

"Never mind," she interrupted, "I didn't come for explanations or tall tales."

I have it coming, might as well take it like a man.

"Russell Townsend... at least your name is right. I always speak my mind. Dare told me everything, and I was the most shocked that those girls aren't your daughters, and it makes me mad as *spit* that you lied to us. But, I'd swear in court, even though I don't believe in swearing, that you *are* their daddy—maybe not in blood, but the way you love them and they love you. And I'm gonna be praying hard that you get to keep them and will be okay."

Russell had never been as surprised in his life. He was speechless.

"Now, about my sister. It's been plain to me for a while that she loves you even though I wish she didn't... I think you love her, too, but that doesn't mean it's the best thing. I'm just here to tell you not to hurt her anymore. She's bound and determined to go to Illinois with you, I tried to talk her out of it, but I didn't get far. She believes God wants her to go with you. She told me you've found God again..."

For a split second, Doreen appeared overcome with emotions. Tears filled her eyes as she took a deep breath and continued, her tone softened. "Russell, nothing is more joyful than a child of God coming home. I'm glad."

"Thank you, Doreen. I..."

"Let me finish. I said I'd pray for you to keep those girls, and I will. I'll also be praying for what's best for *Dare*. I hope the two don't conflict. I'm asking you to pray for the same... for what's best for Dare—if you love her, you can do that. How about it?" She'd looked directly at him the entire time. Now, she held his gaze, waiting for an answer.

"Doreen... I *have* prayed for what's good for Dare. I hope it is that she will remain in my life forever... but I will try my very best to put her welfare first."

"Okay, then. Remember that a *lot* of people are praying for you, Russell Townsend. And God will get it right. You can get on with your trip now—have a safe one."

This is one unbelievable woman. I thought she was going to eat me alive. Instead, she's praying for me.

He sat for a minute, catching his breath.

"Doreen, you are remarkable. Dare is lucky to have you."

He reached for the door handle, then turned back and leaned over to kiss her cheek. "Thank you for stopping by this morning."

Astonished, Doreen said no more.

He got out of her car, closed the car door and walked back to his waiting girls. As he pulled out, the girls waved to her out the back window.

Driving down the block, a scripture came to his mind... *'My cup runneth over.'*

Why would I think of a verse about bountiful blessings in the midst of despair?

Because people care and are praying for us. I've never felt more loved.

Doreen continued to sit in her car. *He loves her and she loves him. More than that, only the Lord knows.*

∼∼ 32 ∼∼

The Inevitable Return

Dare had been adamant about making the trip. He'd thought it unwise and gave her a definite no.

"Russ, listen. I've prayed about it. I firmly believe the Lord wants me to go to Illinois... for this step of your journey. After that, we'll take it a step at a time. When you're *through* it, whatever that means... at *that* time... then we'll see where we are, you and me. But I'm *going* with you."

He had no further argument.

He arrived at Dare's house at seven o'clock. She settled into the front seat, maneuvering around the bags and coats stuffed in every corner. He decided not to mention Doreen's visit earlier that morning.

"Seems we accumulated more during our stay here. I know we weren't so jam-packed when traveling South."

"It's all right. I'll get my little nest made and we can be on our way." Looking toward the back seat, the large teddy bear won at the fall festival was wedged between Ella and Rose.

Dare giggled as Russell glanced around. "Yes," he commented, "their friend, Ted, could *not* travel in the trunk."

The November day was bitter cold, even in Alabama. The further north they drove, the colder the air. "Nearer Chicago, there will likely be snow on the ground."

The image of snow caused Dare to shiver, though cheers came from the back seat. "You like snow?" she asked.

"Yes!" came the cry in unison.

Rose added, "Sledding down the hill, building snowmen... it's *so* fun."

"And snowball fights," added Ella.

"I don't like those," Rose frowned.

"And," Dare teased, "what about school being cancelled for snow days?"

"We never get to stay home from school when it snows," complained Rose.

"When it snows in Alabama, you usually do. We don't have snowplows and chains for our cars as you do in Illinois, so they have to close the schools."

"Yay!" they shouted.

"Know what? You girls have traveled further than I have. You may not know everything about Alabama, but I know *nothing* about Illinois. You'll have to point things out to me as we travel."

Rose asked, "What else about Alabama? We've been here a long time and talk about it at school, too."

"Maybe, but you haven't seen a cotton field when the cotton bolls crack open and the fields are so white with cotton, they look like snow. And you haven't seen the white-sand beach and the beautiful water of the Gulf of Mexico in Gulf Shores. And in early spring, there are so many tulip and dogwood trees blooming, and jonquils and buttercups, and honeysuckle, the air is sweeter than perfume…" She stopped mid-sentence. Russell was smiling.

"I'm sorry. I got carried away a bit."

"It's okay. You love your home state."

Ella said excitedly, "I'd like to see cotton in a field, but I thought cotton was all colors. Mommy said my dresses are cotton and they're lots of colors."

"It starts out white, honey. When they process it into cotton for clothing, they dye it. But, I want you to tell *me* about Evanston, and Illinois."

"We have tulips when the snow melts, but in the ground, not on trees. I don't know the other flowers, but Mommy liked tulips. And the houses on our street are old. Daddy said they are 'spensive 'cause they need work all the time. There are new ones in other neighborhoods and in Chicago, though."

Rose interrupted, "Did you know *Tinker Toys* were invented in our town?"

Dare's eyebrows raised.

Russell answered, "She's right... the first ones were manufactured in Evanston. The inventor got the idea from watching children play with pencils, sticks, and spools of thread. And, the container, the *can*, was originated for less expensive mailing."

"That *is* interesting."

Excited, Rose added, "And we got a beach called *Mitchigan*—it's real big 'cause it's in our town *and* Chicago."

Russell added, "It's *Lake* Michigan, honey, but you're right about it being big. It's pretty special."

"I can't wait to see it," Dare commented.

Russell took his hand from the steering wheel for a moment to reach for Dare's hand, giving it a squeeze.

Two hours into their trip, they stopped for breakfast. "By now, we should all be very hungry. And, remember, we probably won't stop for another meal until tonight."

"We got Miss Bee's basket."

"That's true. We definitely will not starve."

After ordering breakfast, the girls scurried to the bathroom. Dare asked, "How do you think they'll react when they're actually *in* their house again? I think it will be more traumatic than they realize... for you, too."

"I think you're right. I'll just have to deal with it." He reached across the table for her hand. "Thankfully, we'll also have you."

"When will their grandparents arrive?"

"A few days after we arrive. I… hedged, a bit about when we'd get in town."

"Hedged?"

He looked sheepish. "Couldn't help myself. We needed time before dealing with them."

"I agree."

Dare also realized there were things *she* hadn't considered. *The reality is that I'm traveling with them to their home. To the area where Russell and the girls spent their lives. Alabama was only a brief stop, a vague memory in a few years.*

A sense of dread overtook her. She glanced at Russell, the man she'd known only months. She'd fallen in love with him. Blindly, she couldn't deny. The man she knew worked at a hardware store, lived in one room and drove an older car. He'd been a widower with two children. *In another day, he will be home. He will be the architect with failed dreams, the bachelor who lived in a big-city apartment and drove a sports car… an uncle with two nieces. That paints a different picture. Will I see a different man? I will be the same, though… a small-town Southern girl. Will he view me differently?*

Even with the prospect of driving in bad weather, Russell saw it as an *almost* happy day, making a trip with the three people he loved most in the world. He glanced at Dare, once more amazed at the resilience and goodness packaged so beautifully.

After a while, Dare began the game of counting cows with Rose and Ella.

"Ten black ones on my side," shouted Ella. "Not fair," complained Rose. "You got the right side of the road; there's more over there."

"You never know, honey, just keep a close eye out," soothed Russell.

He prayed that someday Rose would outgrow or overcome her tendency toward being negative and growing despondent so easily. She had improved, but the problem remained.

"I'll swap sides with you, Rose."

So typical of Ella, agreeable, happy, wanting to please. He had to keep on guard against letting Rose take advantage too often, especially as Ella didn't seem to mind.

As expected, snow flurries were swirling as they stopped for the night. Russell had mapped out the trip from Beacon to Evanston. With stops, he'd figured twelve or thirteen hours, barring unforeseen delays.

He'd phoned ahead for reservations for the night. "Can't always be sure to find motels where you want them," he'd explained.

"I hate the expense of two rooms, Russ. I could sleep with the girls and you could rent just one room."

He grinned. "My bed would have more space."

"Nuh-uh," she laughed in answer as they unloaded the car. "But I didn't have to have a room to myself... really. Would you like for the girls to stay with me so you could have time alone for a change?"

He hugged her to him. "You think I'd let you have another chance alone with them so they could spill more beans?"

"Russell Townsend, if there are ever any more *beans*, I'm out."

They both laughed. "No more secrets."

She stood on tiptoe to kiss his cheek. "Good."

On the road early the next morning, Rose and Ella became more excited with every mile.

"Wait till you see our room, Miss Dare. It's all pink, with flowers on the bedspreads and curtains," Rose described.

"I'm sure I'll love it. What about your room, Ella?"

"We have the *same* room—with twin beds, but sometimes we sneak and sleep in just one," she giggled. "We *like* to sleep together, like at Miss Bee's."

"Our room in our house is prettier, though," quipped Rose.

After maneuvering the heavy Chicago traffic, they approached the city limits of Evanston. The girls' energetic movements in the back seat could be felt in the front as well. Those in vehicles around them could most likely see the car rocking as Russell pulled into a service station.

"Russ, you filled the tank an hour ago."

"I'm going to the pay phone inside. I need to call Jason." In a lower voice to Dare, he explained, "I need to ask whether anything has changed. I don't want to be unpleasantly surprised at the house. Of course, he can't know everything, but he has a better handle on it than I."

"Of course."

Rose and Ella were protesting loudly at stopping so close to their house. Dare smoothed the situation. "Pop will bring back Cokes. If he doesn't, I'll just send him right back inside."

"We like Double Cola!"

At that, they resumed their giggles and making plans as to what they would do first when they arrived home.

As Russell approached the car, Dare rolled the window down. "No entry without Double Colas."

Appearing happy as she laughed with Rose and Ella, Dare was anything but joyful at this moment. Her stomach churned. *What might he have learned from Jason? And how will they handle the next step... when Brenda's house comes into view? Should I be here after all?*

~~ **33** ~~

Driving into Evanston, Russell explained, "We'll be there in a few minutes but, girls, let's show Dare part of *your* town on the way, okay?"

"Okay," they agreed reluctantly, "not *too* long, though."

To Dare, he said, "There are a few things I want you to see."

After pointing out a few landmarks, he turned onto a beautiful street near the lake. Almost immediately, a towering lighthouse came into view.

"Russ," Dare exclaimed, "the small beacons at home look like replicas of this."

Smiling, he answered, "Exactly what I thought. It's *Grosse Point Lighthouse*. It honestly did not occur to me at first. Rose mentioned it one day after we'd been to Beacon's Far Away Park."

Contemplating seriously, he added, "I wondered whether seeing the replica at the welcome sign that first night subconsciously caused me to feel I'd arrived *home*."

Dare reached to touch his arm. "Perhaps God was leading you to us."

He nodded, again reflecting on all that had happened in the last months, certain God's plan *was* at work. *God, don't let me mess up your plan any further.*

"The lighthouse isn't in use now, is it?" Dare asked.

"No. If I remember correctly, it was first operated in eighteen-seventy-four, but it hasn't been used since the early thirties."

"It's beautiful," she commented wistfully. "Evanston and Beacon... connected... in more ways than we knew."

Reaching to touch Russell's arm, she thought, *But our God knew.*

As Russell finally turned onto Brenda's street, he felt sick, as if his stomach had turned inside out. He'd lived for months without her, believing he was past mourning. He missed her anew. Though devastated at her death, he had been cried out when she died. He thought he'd accepted it. He'd whisked Rose and Ella away and had been too busy caring for them, and burdened with what he had done, to mourn further.

But it was hitting him again. *She isn't waiting at the window... oh, Bren, I've made a muddle of everything.*

He pulled into the driveway, cautioning the girls against opening the door until he had parked and turned off the motor. As soon as the motor stopped, they were out of the car, up the sidewalk and on the porch.

"Hurry, Pop!"

With effort, he smiled as he walked up the sidewalk holding Dare's hand.

"It's lovely," she observed.

"Yes," he answered, "and a good neighborhood. Gary and Brenda planned well." *Except for dying... Will life ever truly feel good again? Can I make up for the mistakes? I have three to love again, Dare, Rose and Ella. But is it possible to fill the gaping holes punched in our lives?*

While the girls squealed and ran through the house, Dare quietly looked around. Russell walked from the living room to the downstairs bedroom that had been Brenda's, then back again, not seeing or feeling anything.

"Russ?"

"I hadn't had a chance to tell you... I did get Jason. He thinks the grandparents have dropped the charges and that they simply want to pick the children up when they get here... tomorrow. I'd hoped for another day. I didn't do a very good job of keeping our actual arrival time from them."

Dare began talking in an attempt to reassure him, but finally realized he was hearing nothing. He'd walked into the kitchen and sat on a kitchen stool staring into space. She decided to go upstairs to check on the girls.

Forty-five minutes later, she returned to the kitchen. He remained on the stool where she'd left him, still staring blankly ahead.

"Russ? Are you okay?"

He turned his head. "What?"

"The girls are getting hungry. So am I, but I don't think any of you want to leave to eat. How about I go pick something up?"

"Yes… good. Did you see their room?"

"I've seen every inch of the house, and the back-yard swing as well. You've been sitting here almost an hour."

"I should never have taken them away."

"You can't dwell on that. We will deal with *now* the best we can."

"Brenda's plant is dead."

Dare finally realized where his focus had been.

"Do you think water might revive it?"

"Don't worry about the plant, okay?"

"The utilities are on… I hadn't considered anything about the house… I guess Gary's parents took care of it…so many things I didn't consider…"

He finally focused to look at her. She would leave soon, he was sure of it. This was the reality of what he'd done, what he was. She would tell him tomorrow. He would understand and attempt to accept it. He touched her cheek. "Yes, go get something to eat, if you don't mind. There's a chicken place a few blocks from here."

"I remember. I have your keys from the table. I'll be back in a jiffy."

He slid off the stool, walking aimlessly through the house. *I've hurt them so badly. I took them away from everything they knew, hoping to make a new life. But their grandparents were going to take them away. What should I have done? Will they ever forgive me?*

He'd told them earlier the house might be sold and they would need to decide what they wanted to keep. He slowly climbed the steps. He heard them laughing as they talked about the things in the room they'd missed.

"What about our dolls, Rose? Can we take them all?"

"Pop said to decide what we wanted. We can take everything. I wanted to stay *here*, in our house. But we'll be *closer* to Evanston—maybe they'll bring us back to see lake *Mitchigan* sometimes."

"I guess," Ella agreed.

They will be fine without me. They have each other, after all. They will be with their grandparents, a stable life, and I'll visit… if they let me.

When Dare returned with chicken plates, the girls were downstairs, full of giggles, showing Russell various toys they'd missed or rediscovered. He'd pulled himself out of his slump, trying to savor the moments. Dare was thrilled to see them on the sofa laughing together.

"Who wants supper?"

"Can we watch television in the living room while we eat… like we did at your house… please?"

"Tell you what… you girls go find an old blanket, or at least not one of the best ones. We'll spread it out on the floor like a picnic. It may be the night for *I Love Lucy* if we can find the channel. Okay, Russ?"

"Great plan. I'm starving. And I noticed there's wood in the fireplace. I'll start a fire."

As the girls left the room, he put his arms around her. "Thank you for being here." Tears filled her eyes. He reached to wipe them away and kissed her wet cheek. "No tears. Tonight is for indoor picnics and fun... a good old-fashioned family night... no worries about tomorrow or what might come. We'll wait for the Lord to figure out our tomorrows."

"Perfect." She looked around their lovely surroundings. "Russ... I truly love this house. It's been well cared for over the years."

She walked to the mantle and picked up a framed picture of Brenda with her daughters. Touching it brought new, unexpected emotions. Brenda was real to her now—Rose and Ella's mother who would not see them grow up. She could see a bit of her in each of her daughters, and even a slight resemblance to Russ, despite the distinct difference in their coloring. "Brenda was so pretty... I can see the love in her eyes in this picture. I'm so sorry you all lost her."

"Not *lost*," he corrected, smiling sadly. She remembered his telling her of the girls' exasperation with that word. "She's here," he said, "she will be with Rose and Ella wherever they are... and with me, too. Her sweet memory will never die."

"I can see why she thought it would be good for the girls to stay here... until you knew what your future held career-wise."

He touched the beautiful ornate wood of the bookcase. It had been cleaned recently. By whom? The grandparents knew they would be here, so taking care of the utilities and stocking the refrigerator made sense—they were taking care of their grandchildren. But they weren't hands-on people, they were rather formal. *Someone took care of these details, things I hadn't even considered... but no one watered the plant.*

Once again, he pulled himself back to the present. This moment in time was a blessing and he would not waste it. "Hey, what's taking so long to get a blanket? I'm hungry!"

The television program ended and Dare began clearing plates, cups, and paper napkins from the floor. Russell picked up the blanket and took it to the kitchen to shake the crumbs into the trash can. Returning to the living room, he said, "Girls, you need to get your baths and get ready for bed. It's been a long day. Ella, return the blanket to its place. I'll be up in a minute."

Dare interrupted, "I'll help with their baths tonight. I packed bubble bath just for tonight, and girls, we need to wash your hair so you can look and smell extra-nice for your grandparents tomorrow. After your bath, I'm going to give you a manicure before bed."

"Yay," they shouted.

"Russ, you are not allowed upstairs—It's a *girl zone* for a while. Girls, let's go."

He watched in amusement as his *three* girls clambered up the stairs.

An hour later, Dare shouted down the stairs, "You can come upstairs, Russ. It's an open zone." He took the stairs two at a time. Entering the girls' room, they were seated on one bed, grinning happily. Satisfied, Dare stood to one side.

"Look, our nails are *man-cured,*" declared Rose. "Like Mommy used to do. They're pink. Smell our hair, we smell good all over 'cause the bubbles smelled like flowers."

"Smell my hair, too," echoed Ella.

He smiled. *Orange blossoms.* He would have guessed.

After kissing them goodnight, he and Dare walked slowly downstairs.

At the foot of the stairs, he turned to her. "You're so good with them."

"My pleasure. I'm in love with *them*, too."

He took her hand as they walked to the living room. They sat close in front of the crackling fire with hands clasped and her head resting on his shoulder. The sounds of distant sirens, infrequent passing cars, and occasional bits of charred wood dropping were all lost in the relaxed feeling of shared warmth.

Dong, Dong, Dong, Dong, Dong, Dong, Dong...

The clock was striking midnight. They had fallen asleep in front of the warm fire. Dare raised her head from Russell's shoulder. With a sleepy smile, she said, "It's past time for bed."

He kissed her forehead. "Sleeping with you was as lovely as I expected."

"I'm glad. Hope you aren't one to *nod off and tell*."

"It will be our secret." He raised his hand to her cheek, touching her gently before beginning to stroke her hair. "You're incredible. You travel hundreds of miles knowing little of what will take place at the end of the road. You care for my children, feed us... and love us. You forgive me and keep me balanced. Among all our troubles, you bring joy."

Each were lost in the other's eyes for another moment, the silence of the night surrounding them. Their world was beautiful again, holding faith and hope.

She pulled herself up slightly to kiss his cheek, then moved to his waiting lips, lingering for a moment before pulling herself away to stand. She whispered, "For you... anything..." Tears filled her eyes again. *I can't form the words to explain what I feel for him... for all three.*

"Goodnight, Russ. I'll see you in the morning."

He watched as she walked upstairs before he stretched out on the sofa. He would sleep well tonight. Tomorrow was another day.

God can get me through this if I hold on. If I lose my grip... I don't know. God, please help me. Help us all.

**

The girls ran downstairs at eight that morning. Russell was drinking coffee while Dare fried eggs. Thanks again to... someone... there were fresh groceries in the refrigerator.

"Hey, sleepyheads. Did you like sleeping in your own beds again?"

They giggled. "We slept in Rose's bed together, like we did at Miss Bee's. We like it. Did you and Miss Dare sleep in Mommy's bed?"

It was Dare's turn to giggle.

"No. Miss Dare slept in the guest room. I slept downstairs on the sofa."

"Why? Weren't you lonesome?"

"Well, yes, I was a little lonesome, but... I was comfortable on the sofa."

They didn't appear satisfied.

"Girls, men and women... don't sleep together unless they are married. Didn't you know that?"

Dare mouthed the words, "They're *children.*"

"No..." answered Rose. "I didn't know. But you kiss her sometimes. Is *kissing* okay?"

Rinnnnng, rinnnnng, rinnnnng.

"Oh, gotta answer the phone."

They turned to Dare.

"He kisses me because we like each other a lot. Kissing is okay... just not... well, eat your eggs."

Russell Townsend, I'm gonna get you good for running out on this conversation.

There was no time. The *other* Townsends were on their way.

~~ 34 ~~

Grandparents' Arrival

Rose looked like a porcelain doll in a blue ruffled dress. She wore a matching bow in her shining blond hair, which had almost grown back to its original length.

Preferring a simpler style, Ella chose a yellow dress with petite bows on the bodice and a large sash tied into a bow at the back. Her hair shone, too, and she'd been convinced to add a small white barrette.

Ding-dong, ding-dong.

Dare chose to remain in the kitchen.

As Russell walked to the door, the girls stood at the bottom of the stairs. He took one more look. Once the door opened, they were no longer his. He'd thought he was prepared, but his heart raced, hands sweated and eyes blurred. How could he do this?

Did you forget so soon, my child? I'm with you. Trust me.

He calmed slightly and opened the door. "Mr. and Mrs. Townsend. Please come in." The two were dressed as if attending a funeral, both in black suits. Their expressions matched their clothing, somber and formal.

"Good morning, Russell."

As he closed the door, Rose and Ella squealed as they ran to their grandparents. Though miserable himself, Russell was pleased at their reactions. The grandparents leaned to hug them. "We're *so* glad to see that you are safe." They held their hands as they walked to the living room and sat with them on the sofa.

Rose spoke first. "I was glad to come home. Did you miss us a whole, whole, bunch?"

"Indeed, we did," Mrs. Townsend replied in a grating voice. "We didn't know where you were and we were worried. Your Uncle Russell took you away and we didn't know what he planned."

Russell could hear the ice in her voice. Was this to be her approach with her granddaughters? Sitting in an armchair, he remained quiet.

Cecil Townsend quietly appraised his granddaughters. He generally condescended to his wife in personal matters but wasn't in complete agreement in this matter. *I don't look forward to taking on the responsibility of two young charges, grandchildren or not. It seems there are not many choices and Lillian is determined. The uncle has been unreliable, perhaps unstable... but they appear to be unharmed and relatively happy.*

"They look well, Lillian."

"Yes. Physically."

Dare entered the room with a tray of coffee.

Russell stood and walked to her side as she placed the tray on the table in front of the Townsends.

He touched her arm lightly. "Mr. and Mrs. Townsend, this is Dare Perry, a friend from Alabama—she's been of great help. Dare, these are the girls' grandparents, Cecil and Lillian Townsend."

"It's nice to meet you. Rose and Ella have been eager to see you."

They glared. Finally, Mrs. Townsend asked, "Where do you live, Miss Perry?"

"I'm from Beacon, Alabama, thank you. I've made fresh coffee, and have sugar and cream on the tray."

"Did you *travel* here with our grandchildren... all together?" Cecil inquired.

Russell answered, "Of course. It was a long trip." His last statement was apparently a mistake. There would be no civility today from either grandparent.

Cecil Townsend's back straightened, his eyebrows rose, and his face contorted into an ugly frown. "We are well aware of the distance. You had no right to take our grandchildren out of town, certainly not across the state line, hundreds of miles away to what we understand is a backward country town in *Alabama*. We were worried sick about our girls and what kind of care they were receiving."

Dare took a step back, incredulous at the behavior of these people. *He spoke the word, Alabama, as if it were the scum of the earth, and sounds as if he believed Russ capable of mistreating his granddaughters. I can't believe what I'm hearing. I'm glad I'm here... to know the situation. It is much worse than I imagined.*

Russell observed these two angry adults. Jason thought their anger had subsided, but it had certainly raised its ugly head today. He observed Rose and Ella... they were confused. Taking a deep breath, he replied, "I apologize for causing you concern. I shouldn't have acted so rashly. I know you love them and want what's best for them. Their welfare was always my top concern. They've been in school since the new term began and have been well-cared for—it's been an *adventure*."

This unpleasantness wasn't good for the children. They'd been happy this morning, adjusting well and looking forward to seeing their grandparents, even accepting the fact that they would most likely leave with them. But everything was being torn apart and he hadn't the least idea of how to handle the situation.

Ella's small voice interrupted his thoughts. "We had fun with Pop… on our adventure. He took good care of us, Grandfather."

The Townsends stared at her as if she hadn't any part in this, but she continued. "Alabama is nice and we liked the school, and Miss Bee, and going to Miss Dare's house. We went to a festival, too, and a *parade*." She looked up at her grandmother. "We saw President *Eisenhower*."

The small girl, struggling to make things right, waited for a reply, some reassurance. None came.

"Really, we had a good time."

Rose was doing her best to shrink into the sofa, but Ella would not allow her to be invisible. "Rose, tell Grandmother how *good* Pop took care of us."

Weakly, Rose replied, "He tucked us in bed every night and listened to our prayers and reminded us to keep the door locked when he was gone. And Miss Bee checked on us."

"*Who* is Miss Bee?" Lillian Townsend demanded.

"The boarding-house lady," Rose answered.

Disbelieving, Lillian glared at Russell and raised her voice. "You kept them in a *boarding* house?"

Poor Ella, again attempting to set things right, answered. "We had a *nice* room, Grandmother. It had two beds, and a big window with chairs by it, and Miss Bee cooked good."

"One room? You had only two beds and lived in *one room*?"

"Mrs. Townsend, please," Russell interjected, "it was different from the norm, but I can assure you, things were alright and *temporary*. I love my nieces more than anything on this earth. Please believe I cared for them. I never meant any harm."

She replied coldly, "Would you leave us alone, please, with the girls? We'd like to talk with them without being interrupted… before we take them home."

"Of course."

Russell walked to the sofa and leaned to kiss each girl on the forehead. "I'll be back in a few minutes. Be good for your grandparents and answer their questions about our adventure so they will know you were okay."

Lillian continued to glare. Cecil remained silent, seeming to have separated himself from the situation entirely. Russell took Dare's hand as they walked to the kitchen.

Closing the door, Dare said solemnly, "I really believe Mrs. Townsend's look could freeze well water in Alabama on an August afternoon."

She looked at Russell and began giggling, breaking the tension. "Sit down. I'll pour coffee for the two of *us*."

Thirty minutes later, they heard movement from the living room.

Cecil Townsend opened the kitchen door and joined them at the table. "Russell, we've talked with the girls and are satisfied you took care of them to the best of your ability. We do not approve of their travel and living conditions, but they appear unharmed. We've agreed to drop all charges against you, provided you cooperate. Now, let's get things straight. You *do* have a legal case for keeping the girls. However, we are next-of-kin and have the finances to fight you, which we would be willing to do. Your reputation has been tainted of late, beginning with your being fired from your position. Your fleeing with the children over state lines, leaving us to suffer with worry, would not look good in court. We would win."

"Sir…"

"I haven't finished. It also appears you have been in an inappropriate relationship with this woman… in the *children's presence.*"

Dare retorted, "There has been nothing *inappropriate* in our relationship! I love Rose and Ella."

Russell stated adamantly, "Dare has an *exemplary* reputation. She's cared about us and has been a great help—they love her."

"Nevertheless... Russell, you have no job, no income, no apparent future. We have agreed not to cause a problem with Brenda's leaving you her house, though our son paid for it. You may live in it or sell, as you wish. You may have all the contents, with the exception of the crystal punch bowl and cups in the dining room. Lillian purchased the set, along with the silver, and will take it with her today—our chauffeur is packing it now. We will take the girls and whatever they've decided upon to take with them."

Russell was trembling. His girls were actually going. He wasn't ready, but it was to happen in only a few minutes.

"I think they would like to have their bedroom furniture later, as well as the spreads, curtains, and other decorations. It would make them feel more at home."

Cecil's expression didn't change. "They'll have no need of any of it in our home. Lillian has instructed them what they may bring."

"I told them they could take all their dolls and toys..."

Cecil was shaking his head. "They have selected a few of their favorites."

Approaching the subject which hurt him the deepest, Russell asked, "Do you intend to send them to boarding school?"

"None of your concern."

"It is my concern. They won't be happy. They haven't recovered from losing their mother. I can accept your rearing them in your home, having a relationship with them. But if you intend only to send them away, why take them from their home... *here*, where I could continue to care for them?"

"Russell, they are not to stay with you in any case. We have yet to finalize all our decisions, but they will always be in the very *best* of situations."

"May I visit?"

"Lillian will speak to you regarding visits before we leave. I hear them coming downstairs now."

As Russell and Dare followed Cecil into the living room, Ella came running. She grabbed Russell around the waist, hugging him tightly. "Pop, I don't *wanna* leave you, can't you go too?"

"No, honey, you will be fine with your grandparents. I'll come to see you soon, I promise."

He realized Mrs. Townsend's eyes were on him. He returned the gaze, raising his eyebrows.

"Tell your uncle goodbye and go to the car, Ella. Our driver has your things in the trunk."

Russell picked Ella up and hugged her to him, covering her face with smacking kisses. Finally, she began to giggle. He put her down, saying, "I love you bushels, Ella-Pella. Be good for your grandparents."

Not objecting to the nickname, she replied weakly, "Okay."

Rose stood silently beside her grandmother. When Ella began walking toward the front door, Rose approached Russell. He was unsure of this one's reaction and feelings. In truth, he was especially worried about her—her emotions were fragile. She stood in front of him, looking up. He stooped to her level and kissed her cheek. "I'll miss you, sweetheart, but I know you'll like living with your grandparents."

Unseen by her grandmother, tears flooded Rose's eyes and spilled over her beautiful little cheeks. Quietly, she sniffled, "Pop... I love *you*."

He wrapped his arms around her, wanting to hold her forever. Her arms had gone around his neck and he could feel her little fingers on his hair.

"Rose," Mrs. Townsend spoke authoritatively, "It is time to go."

Russell let go of her and she let her arms fall to her side. "Bye, Pop."

"Bye, honey. Remember how much I love you."

"I will."

"Remember, Rose," Mrs. Townsend interjected, "we are having a big Thanksgiving meal in a few days. Cook is preparing the menu today."

Rose brightened slightly and walked slowly with Ella to the chauffeur-driven limousine.

Mrs. Townsend stepped out onto the porch.

"Russell, you may not visit for a month. They will be settling into their new lives. Understood?"

He stared.

"After a month, you may phone and speak with me about arrangements for a visit." She handed him a card with her address and phone number.

A business card? Russell pulled himself together and stood straight. "Mrs. Townsend, I will honor your *request* for the month of adjustments. When I phone, I will expect an immediate visit. It will be close to Christmas and I'll expect to work out a schedule for the girls to spend time with me in *my* home. If you have a problem with that, I assure you I have lawyers available to me and will not negotiate further. In fact, if there are problems or questions, I may decide to sue for complete custody."

"You would lose. I will accept your call in a month. Good day."

Appearing smug, she walked down the steps and climbed into the limo, the driver in front, and the foursome in the two seats behind. Russell caught a glimpse of Cecil before the door closed. He didn't appear satisfied at all. Lillian seemed to be the only happy one of the four... he corrected himself—he saw *no* happiness in the group. Lillian was the only one *satisfied*.

~~ 35 ~~

As the limousine pulled away, Rose and Ella waved as long as they could see Russell. As he turned to enter the house, Dare stood waiting.

"What *am* I going to do?" he asked, about to break entirely.

She took his hand as they returned into the house. "You will sit on the sofa while I make sandwiches. After we eat, you will take a long nap upstairs *on a bed*. After your nap, you will shower and dress in a suit and take me out to eat at a very expensive Chicago restaurant."

He looked into her face, basking in the love and comfort. "Good. I know what to do now." He smiled wearily and slumped onto the sofa as she walked toward the kitchen.

"One more thing about our dinner tonight at an expensive restaurant—the dress code cannot require anything more than what I wear to church."

Slightly cheered, he replied, "No problem. There are numerous places in Chicago *out* of our price range where you could be seated wearing jeans, though I would still be required to wear a tie. I know several great restaurants you'd love… and you'll be the most beautiful woman there, no matter what you wear."

"Sounds good. Tomorrow, we'll discuss what comes next."

"A few days from now is *Thanksgiving*. I hadn't even remembered it, had you?"

She nodded. *I've never been away from Doreen for Thanksgiving.*

"They've taken my girls. I've realized how self-centered my life was before… before I was fired. I thought of nothing but myself, my career, getting ahead. I loved Brenda and the girls, but I gave them little of myself. Then... Brenda was gone, and Rose and Ella *became* my life... I don't know how to live without them." His gaze wandered. "A day of thanks?"

"I know, Russ. But there is always much for which we should give thanks." She walked back to him, leaning in to kiss his cheek. "Tomorrow we will discuss what comes next in your life. For now, ask God for understanding and patience, and for clearer vision. Though I'm heartbroken over the girls' leaving, I'm still thankful for them... and for you." She straightened and turned back toward the kitchen.

"Dare?"

"Yes?"

"Thank you."

The evening in the city was exactly what they needed. Dare wore her favorite dress of midnight gray, with a high neckline and slim skirt. The detailing at the neckline and sleeves set it apart, and the slim silver belt at her waist drew attention to her perfect figure. She wore three-inch black heels and, again, turquoise jewelry.

Russell was ready and waiting as she walked down the long staircase. She stopped midway. "Am I acceptable for the big city, Mr. Townsend?"

He'd expected a beauty but seeing her looking down at him from the stairs, he was overwhelmed. She looked like a perfect doll, but it wasn't only her beauty that took his breath, it was the sweet, appealing voice, and the kindness he knew completed the package.

"My dear, you would be more than acceptable at the *White House*... or anywhere. And I'm only taking you to a fine restaurant. I hope everyone I ever knew is there to see you."

As she reached the bottom of the steps, she spoke just above a whisper. "Thank you. You are very handsome, Russell Townsend."

He assisted with her coat and leaned in to kiss her.

Standing close, he said, "I've changed my mind."

"Aren't you taking me out?"

"Yes. But I want you to myself. I hope to see *no* one I know."

He reached to gently touch her turquoise brooch. "You wear turquoise well… and often. Is there a special meaning?"

"Yes," she replied. She placed her hand over his. "It reminds me of my daddy. My birthstone is aquamarine, for March, but he mistakenly gave me a turquoise ring when I was twelve. I told him I liked his choice better, so it became our thing."

He kissed her cheek. "Sweet. I wish I'd known him."

Dare was enthralled by the city and his expertise at maneuvering in the traffic. She loved *the train above the city*, which he explained was known as the *El,* short for elevated. "It's one of the things for which Chicago is known."

The restaurant was on the top floor of a prominent skyscraper, a view of the city from every side.

"Russ, it's so beautiful at night, the city and lights reflecting off Lake Michigan. No wonder you loved it."

He enjoyed watching her, but followed her gaze, seeing it anew. "It is beautiful. During the day, it's noisy with traffic, horns blowing, sirens, and people rushing everywhere. But it's also exciting to have hundreds of restaurants from which to choose, going from place to place on the *El*, or walking through town instead of driving. There are numerous theaters, and at Christmas it's breathtaking. The holiday lights will be on soon."

She turned to watch him. His excitement was evident. He had realized it possible to become excited about life again… at least for the moment.

"You're *home*, Russ, and it's pretty special."

"Yes, though I don't remember stopping long enough to appreciate it before. It's not the same for me now. Without a job, for one…"

She placed her hand on his. "We discussed taking one day at a time. No complaining or looking back. Tonight, we will enjoy a great, overpriced steak and good company. And I'm already thinking about dessert. Think they have hot fudge sundaes?"

"Doubtful, though another of Evanston's *claims* to fame is their insistence the ice cream sundae was founded there. They have a lot of competition to the claim. Anyway, if this restaurant had such a thing on the menu, they'd have a different, more exotic name for it in order to charge more. I'm thinking you'd enjoy cherries jubilee—it begins with an exquisite vanilla ice cream. As they bring it to the table, it bursts into flames."

Driving home, he pointed out interesting areas and places he'd frequented over the years—a coffee shop, newsstand, bakery, and several restaurants. "On the right, you'll see my apartment building."

She gasped. "The building is enormous… and *beautiful*. This is the high-rent district, isn't it?"

"Yes. I lived high. Thing is, I was always working, so what difference did it make?"

The remainder of the drive was quiet. She was taking everything in, wanting to know as much as she could about his life before Beacon.

I knew he had a different life. I hadn't realized how completely different from everything I've known until now. Can we bridge the gap?

Entering the house, Russ helped her out of her coat, removed his own topcoat, and hung them in the closet.

"It was a wonderful evening, Russ. I loved Chicago at night and having you tell me about it. The steak was the best *ever*... and dessert on fire," she laughed. "Wait till I tell Doreen about *that*."

He loved watching her when she was so animated and delighted. *I've caused her more unhappiness than good moments, though.*

"It's two a.m., Russ..."

He wrapped his arms around her, pulling her close as they lingered in an intimate goodnight kiss before she walked slowly up the stairway to the guest bedroom. *I love him completely, with all his problems, none of which appear to be improving or going away. But can he ever let go enough to build a new life?*

Russell watched her, his heart in a turmoil. *I love her so much, with all my heart. But what do I have to offer? A beautiful house hundreds of miles from her family and everything she knows. I have money enough for a while, but no job and no prospects. Can I let go of my career as an architect to pursue work of another type? Can I let go of my guilt about the girls? Will the weight of my problems ultimately destroy her love for me?*

~~ 36 ~~

Russell slept in the girls' room on a twin bed. He spent the night there, but it mattered little as sleep continued to elude him. At seven, he sat at the kitchen table with coffee. When Dare came through the door, he greeted, "'Morning, sunshine. About time you joined the living."

"What do you mean? It's seven o'clock and I've showered, dressed, and applied makeup."

As she poured coffee, he came to stand behind her, putting his arms around her waist and nuzzling her neck.

"I've missed you. I've been up since five, awake earlier."

She turned to face him. "I'm sorry. I'd hoped you might sleep well in a real bed after such a nice evening. But, for your information, I need coffee before I get in the mood for *neckin.*"

"No one's called it *necking* for quite a while."

She laughed. "Whatever you call it, coffee comes first."

She sat at the table with her coffee mug as he opened the refrigerator door. "We still have eggs. How about I scramble a few?"

"Sounds good."

Ka-thud.

"Russ, what was that noise?"

"Probably the newspaper. I phoned yesterday afternoon to have it delivered. I need to know what's going on in the city. And I'm praying not to see my name connected to the McGuire Building scandal."

"Didn't Jason say he hadn't heard anything?"

"Yes, but it's been in the paper. It couldn't fail to be. And I need to know when there are updates. I'll scan want ads, too, though I don't expect much from that source."

"I'll get the paper while you finish the eggs."

As she returned to the kitchen, he asked, "Was it the paper?"

"Yes. You had a stack of mail in the box, too. You checked it when we arrived, didn't you?"

"No, didn't think of it."

She laid a thick stack on the table. "Well, quite an accumulation."

"Probably junk. Could be things forwarded from my city address, though, and possibly bills for the house. There are so many things I dismissed from my mind when I left… I'll go through it. Oh, I forgot to ask yesterday if everything was okay with Doreen and home. I know you talked with her."

"They're fine. She's worried about me, though. I assured her I'm fine, here with you in a fabulous house. I told her about the girls, and she wanted you to know how sorry she was… I explained there were things to be done before I could come home."

He set the plates on the table and sat beside her.

"*What* needs to be done? And why are you talking about going home?"

Was he serious?

"Russ…"

"I know I need to find a job…"

"Nothing has been done in the house since Brenda died. You have to deal with it."

"What?"

She put her hand on his arm. "Russ, honey, her room. Nothing has been touched. The bed hasn't been changed. Her clothes are still there. Everything. I'm rather surprised the in-laws didn't go through it, but apparently, they didn't.

"I'd be glad to do most of it for you, but you have to go through her personal things. She most likely has papers or notes, perhaps legal documents. I'm sure there's jewelry you need to decide about keeping for Rose and Ella."

She could see him processing the reality of the moment. "Thank you... again. It will be hard, but it will help to have you with me."

"The other thing is, the bedroom will be yours eventually. After we finish cleaning and sorting, we should take the drapes down and have it painted. You need new drapes, everything different."

"You're right."

"I need to check in with Doreen. Then I'm yours for the day."

"You just talked with her *yesterday*... I'm sorry... of course, she needs to hear from you every day." He'd begun sorting the mail, already placing several in the discard stack.

"Russ... I'm going back to Beacon in a couple of days."

"No, please don't leave."

She sat again. "I can help you go through Brenda's things. Afterward, you need to begin rebuilding your life, looking for a job, setting up a schedule to see the girls, possibly have them visit. Since the grandparents didn't want their furniture moved to their home, the girls will like knowing their room is waiting as it was when Brenda was alive."

"How'd you get so smart?"

She smiled. "Probably when I met you." Standing again, she continued, "I'm going to call Doreen. *Then* we'll begin in Brenda's room."

"I'm on board. Really. But I couldn't have handled anything without you. Can't you stay longer?"

"No. I have a job, home, and family in Beacon. And, I believe it's best for *both* of us. You have many decisions to make… on your own."

He answered sadly, "Okay… your life has been on hold long enough. Tell her I said hello."

As she left the kitchen, he called out, "Oh, and tell her I've decided not to hold it against her for wanting to have me put in jail." He laughed aloud.

"I'll tell her, but I'm not sure she doesn't still have it in mind." *He laughed. He's getting better.*

Surprisingly, Dare and Doreen were finally able to keep their conversation to three minutes, satisfying both there would be no long-distance charges today. As Dare replaced the receiver on the base, a wave of homesickness came over her. She'd never been away from Doreen before. She missed her. But leaving Russell would tear her heart out. She realized it had to happen sooner or later, and it wouldn't make it easier to delay the inevitable. Her job would not be held forever—she'd taken vacation time, but Mr. Matthews wasn't happy with her taking time off without notice. She could smooth it over, but not if she were gone much longer.

Walking into Brenda's room, she began stripping the bed as she glanced around the lovely room, family pictures scattered about, hand-stitched throw pillows in the chair, her Bible and other reading material on the nightstands. *I didn't know her, but I feel her presence. Her influence is seen in both her daughters. I'm sure she was a loving, wonderful mother… I would have liked her.* Tears came to her eyes thinking of the woman she hadn't known, the life she had and left behind.

She piled the dirty sheets in the corner and opened the closet door. Where was Russell? Was he avoiding it after all, after assuring her he was ready?

"Dare," Russell shouted. "Where are you?"

"In Brenda's room, where *you* are supposed to be."

He rushed through the bedroom door, grabbing her up to swing her around. "You won't believe it! Honey, the impossible has happened," he shouted through his laughter.

"Put me down so you can tell me."

He lowered her to the bare mattress and sat beside her. He handed her a large envelope and several pages of correspondence. "The mail... it was in the mailbox all this time... just sitting there waiting. No one knew..."

"Russ, what is this?" She turned her attention from the papers back to him.

"You are looking at an architect."

"I *knew* you were an architect."

He picked up the papers she'd laid on the mattress. "Read it. I hope you read fast ... I'm about to burst."

It helped to know she was about to read good news, but as she unfolded the three pages, she couldn't fathom what was coming. The first appeared to be from the firm where Russ had been employed and fired...

H. H. & J. Architects
Chicago, Illinois
September 4, 1954

Mr. Russell Townsend
12490 Crownstone Ave., Apt. 61
Chicago, Illinois

Dear Mr. Townsend,

This is to inform you of the most recent updates on the legal findings in the case of H. H. & J. Architectural Firm,

Chicago, Illinois, vs Kelly Architects, St. Louis, Missouri, reference ownership of original Blueprints HHJMCG A-Z-0.01-0.294, known as the McGuire Office Building. The following facts have been discovered and attested to:

~~Blueprints for the building hereafter referred to as the McGuire Project were originated by H. H. & J. Architects associate William Trinney in October of nineteen fifty-three, ownership being established and proven to be H. H. & J. Architects.

~~Referenced blueprints were illegally removed from H. H. & J. Architects property by a person misrepresenting himself to H. H. & J. Architects associate, Russell Townsend. It has been attested to by a representative of Kelly Architects, St. Louis, Missouri, that Mr. Townsend had no knowledge of the illegal action taken, or plans for illegally reproducing the aforementioned McGuire Project blueprints, or any tangible interest in the St. Louis Project.

In light of the facts above, you, Mr. Russell Townsend, have been proven innocent of any intentional wrongdoing, barring any new discoveries.

Brenton Worthington, Dir.,
Legal Department
H. H. & J. Architectural Firm

"Russ, how *wonderful*!"

He motioned to the other pages. "Read the other two."

The second page had obviously been dictated by Mr. Hurt, Russ's former employer.

Altered Plans

From the Office of Julian Hurt
September 4, 1954

Russell,

I trust this finds you recovering from the experiences of June and the abrupt dismissal from your position with our company. I do not apologize for my action. You are reminded it was your bad judgement which caused irreversible damage to our firm.

However, I was pleased to find you were blameless of intentional wrongdoing leading to damage to the firm to which you had vowed loyalty. We are currently in discussion with associates of the Memphis group and believe we may be able to reach an out-of-court settlement agreement in months to come.

Though you were innocent of intentional wrong, this does not change the fact of your remaining unsuitable for employment by H. H. & J. Architects. This should not, however, prevent your employment at other architectural firms. I have personally channeled information regarding your excellent qualifications and experience to the Illinois Architectural Association. This clears your record and your road to reemployment with other prestigious firms.

In the event a reference is required, I am attaching a suitable letter. I sincerely wish you a bright future,

Julian

～～ 37 ～～

"**R**uss, you can *work* again, doing what you love—I'm so happy for you." He beamed as she looked up at him. Grinning, she added, "You look like a child on Christmas morning and I love seeing it."

She turned her attention to the third page. Russell, however, was impatient. "You don't need to read that one now. Read it later. Honey, Julian wrote a remarkable recommendation—with it, I can take my career anywhere or as far as I want."

She moved closer to him as they embraced. The man holding her and the warm lips covering hers were those of the man she'd fallen in love with months ago—warm, inviting, giving. She responded with the depth of love she felt, pressing her hands into his back, willing him closer.

After a few minutes, she laid her head on his chest.

"Dare?"

"Yes?"

"Now that my reputation has been cleared, I can build a *life* again. Every avenue is open to me once more. I'll be able to be bolder in dealing with the grandparents... after I actually have a job, of course. We can plan for the future. I love you so much and can shout it to the top of the highest skyscraper in Chicago. You can stay here, get a job if you want. We'll have this great house..."

"Russ, stop."

"But..."

"You're moving too fast. This is great news and I'm thrilled, almost as much as you are. To put it in your terms, this is a *foundation* for your future. You have a lot of building yet to do."

He clasped her shoulders. "You want to be *part* of the building, don't you? I know I'm thinking ahead, but we love each other. Surely you won't return to Beacon *now*, will you?"

"I have to. Your news opens things up for you. But you still have decisions to make on your own. I'm leaving day after tomorrow—I've reserved a bus ticket. You need to get your life in order again, your life *here*. My life is in Alabama. It's an old, boring story, but it's *our* story. *For now*, Russ. Then we'll see what comes next. I love you more than I can put into words." She touched his cheek. "Surely you know that..."

He was devastated.

"Russ, you wouldn't allow me to make a commitment before we left Beacon... no promises. It was wise. I don't take lightly the things we've said to each other, the things we've shared..."

He interrupted, "I don't take it lightly either, *never* took it lightly with you."

His sincerity was so sweet. She replied softly, "Russ, you must rebuild and feel grounded within. And, darling, I have much to consider as well."

Her hand moved from his cheek to his temple, touching his hair, then moving back to his face and down to his neck... she gently moved her hand across his strong shoulder and down his arm... she didn't want to break this physical connection...

He sat still, cherishing her touch, feeling the warmth as his heart beat faster. His arm moved slightly—he would take her into his arms, cover her mouth with his, stop this talking, and all would be well. Nothing else would matter.

She dropped her hand as their eyes met. *The tenderness, the eyes that took me in at first... his look, his touch, melts*

*me. If I wait another second, I'll be back in his arms...
because it's what I want.*

She averted his eyes as she hurriedly moved to stand.

The silence was heavy around them. She knew what she
wanted but reminded herself of her own words—the time
wasn't right. They must wait. Slowly, she began, "Let's clear
Brenda's room... I've only begun."

He moved from the bed to face her, his eyes hurt and
pleading.

"Russ... start on the nightstand drawers, then the dresser,
where I'd think you might find more personal things. I'll
begin in the closet. Do you want to keep any of her clothes?"

He answered slowly. "No... we can take them to the
church or they would come for them." He began sorting
through Brenda's nightstand, his mind attempting to process
that she would be leaving in two days. *How can I tell her
goodbye? She will be hundreds of miles away.*

~~ **38** ~~

Russell's gaze followed until the Greyhound bus was out of sight. Dare had promised to phone when she arrived home, and he'd promised to keep in touch regularly about his job progress and news of the girls.

How can we simply say we'll keep in touch? When she returns home, will she find she doesn't need me and my complications?

He walked slowly to his car, the trip home a blur. He didn't know how to take the next step alone.

You're not alone. Lean on Me.

His renewed faith had strengthened him somewhat, but he knew he was weak. He needed Dare so much it hurt. The entire year had been about loss… his career, sister, Rose and Ella… Dare. He didn't know whether he could hold on… *Lord, I know you tell me to hold to you, but I'm flesh and blood—I need the people I love!*

Entering the empty house, words came to him almost as a faint voice in the distance, perhaps a memory of scriptures learned long ago… *No eye has seen, nor ear heard the things God has prepared for those who love him.*

He would try. After all, he'd believed his career gone and had been given another chance. He would begin there. Julian Hurt, the man who fired him, had given him this second chance. One of the last things Dare said to him before leaving was to remind him of this gift. "Russ, do you fully realize what Mr. Hurt has done? He's *forgiven* you for damaging his company—that's no small thing. Thank God for it. And someday perhaps you can thank Mr. Hurt."

**

On the bus, Dare clung to the window as long as Russell remained in sight. He appeared so forlorn, she'd briefly considered asking the driver to stop, say she'd made a mistake. But her inner-self told her it was time to depart. *It's the right thing. Both our lives have changed too quickly. We have to have time to be sure of our feelings and where we might fit in the other's life.*

She began to weep, already missing him, wanting his touch, his love. An older lady sat beside her. She glanced as the woman settled into the seat. She had lovely white hair, otherwise rather nondescript except for a bright crimson scarf.

The woman reached to pat her knee. "Dear, if you want to talk, I'm a good listener."

Kind. Dare shook her head. A great deal of conversation would be required when she returned home. She didn't want to talk to anyone in the meantime. It would be almost twenty-four hours before she arrived in Beacon and she needed the time to think and compose herself.

Sympathetically, the woman nodded. "I understand. May I pray for you?"

A wave of emotion poured through her, bringing a new torrent of tears. She nodded and turned back to the window to let the tears flow into her jacket. Before long, however, she felt enveloped in peace and drifted off to sleep.

When she woke an hour later, a quiet young man sat beside her.

**

Russell called every day the week she left. Painters began in the master bedroom and the drapes would be hung next week. He was enthusiastic about composing a resume to mail to architectural firms in Chicago. No, nothing new about the girls.

The second week, he phoned twice. *But I told him it wasn't necessary to phone so often. Long distance is expensive.*

She'd turned her work calendar to December. Russell phoned, his mood uplifted. "I have resumes ready to mail out tomorrow. I've made a few unofficial contacts and feel confident I'll have at least one offer by January. The painters completed the bedroom, the new drapes are up, and I've moved into the master bedroom. It looks great, thanks to you. Things are going so much better, honey, but I miss you."

"What about the girls? Have you heard anything?"

"I'm honoring Lillian's request to wait a month before contacting them."

"You haven't talked with either of the grandparents?"

"No."

"Russ, don't you want to know how they're adjusting, whether they're with their grandparents or in the boarding school?" She was incredulous he'd not even made an attempt.

"Of course, but I'm honoring the agreement."

This is not the man who cared for those girls twenty-four hours a day.

"If you think I should, I'll try to phone tomorrow."

He sounded good, she told herself. She'd worried about his being depressed but he was coping well. Why didn't this make her happy? *Because he sounds like a stranger. Happy with a job search which would allow him to resume his old life... and seemingly unconcerned about Rose and Ella.*

She didn't hear from him for several days and decided to phone. *I can share a portion of the expense of long distance calls.*

"Hi, Dare. I'm glad you called. You should see the snow—we've had the first big snowfall, at least two feet. It's beautiful."

"I'd love to see it... with *you*. Russ, did you call the Townsends?"

"Yes. They weren't even cordial, nothing new. I asked how the girls were adjusting. They told me nothing but did give me a time to visit."

"It's already Christmas break in many private schools. Beacon schools don't let out until the week before, but others have different schedules."

"Hadn't thought of that."

"Let me know as soon as you see them. I've been worried... and I miss them."

"And me?" he asked.

"I miss you most of all."

She was miserable without him. There was little on her mind other than how he and the girls were adjusting. But she held back when talking with him. She felt a subtle difference in him... the distance between them had grown, not only in miles...

Lord, Your will be done. Help me to accept it.

~~ 39 ~~

Russell felt more himself. He was excited with the prospect of returning to the work he loved, he'd see the girls soon, and life was leveling out. Dare was right, he'd needed time to determine his direction in life… for himself. He missed her, but his vision of the future remained muddled.

He sat at the dining room table with the telephone book, his portable typewriter, stacks of typing paper, envelopes, and newspapers scattered about. *Anywhere I want to go with my career.* With a quick scan of his surroundings, he felt a wave of satisfaction. *It's a great house, completely paid for, thanks to Brenda and Gary. It's beginning to feel like home— a bit empty, but I was accustomed to that before. I can commute to work and have the girls visit from time to time. I do miss Dare… but I can't see the whole picture yet.*

It had been over two weeks since Dare left. He'd been consumed with composing resumes and making contacts. The word was out he had returned to the area and was available for employment and society. He'd received a few phone calls with mundane comments about missing him and vague invitations. He understood. Acquaintances were testing the waters before making commitments.

Jason remained a loyal friend. He'd been the one who checked on the house and stocked the refrigerator before they arrived. They were in contact often, going out to eat and discussing possible positions. He had stopped by the day before Dare left and asked about her each time they talked. "Man, she's an original. Don't let her get away."

"I know and agree. Life is just so complicated, and I can't do anything until my career is anchored again."

Besides, the Christmas season is upon us and there is no better time for making contacts. At this point, getting invitations to the best gatherings is important to my career.

Ding-dong, ding-dong, ding-dong, ding-dong.

At his typewriter, Russell was concentrating on another letter. He glanced at the clock. *Already noon. But the workmen have finished—I'm not expecting anyone else.*

Opening the door, he stood speechless. Katherine stood before him dressed to the nines, diamonds dangling from her ears, wrapped in a mink coat, and wearing four-inch heels. She held a basket of fresh out-of-season fruits, smiling her sweetest smile. He could not deny her beauty. She might yet become a famous model. She had the height, perfect figure, dark hair to her waist, and a face that went perfectly with all of the above.

"Hello, Russell." Her voice was even melodic, but his eyes were drawn to her full, moist, dark red lips.

She stepped closer. "Aren't you going to invite me inside?"

"Katherine. I never expected to see you again, certainly not at my home."

"I brought a Christmas basket. You might consider it a peace offering." She held the basket in her outstretched arms. As he took it, he stepped back to push the door further open.

"Would you *like* to come inside?"

She stepped over the threshold, her gaze taking in the large foyer and furnishings, the living room to the left, dining room to the right. Removing her coat, she held it out to him. "Will you hang it up? It's not a coat to be draped across a chair."

A short red dress, suitable for a dinner party, cut low… why is she here?

He closed the door and set the basket on the hall table before taking her coat. "Would you like to come into the living room?"

He felt like a robot, seeming to have lost control. He hadn't even missed her. Nonetheless, her presence was unsettling.

She stepped closer, hugging him warmly. "I've missed you, Russell. Could we talk?"

"Yes, of course," he answered weakly. *Why did I allow her inside?*

She sat on the sofa. "Sit by me, Russell."

"Katherine, we're finished—*your* decision, remember? I've coped quite well."

She patted the seat beside her. "Please?"

He sat as she smiled confidently, openly looking him over. He suddenly felt inadequate in his jeans and old shirt.

"Katherine, what about the old guy who replaced me... Leon?"

She turned to him, placing her hand on his knee. Smiling, she moved her legs slightly, her dress slipping up another inch. The house was too warm...

"Leon?" she answered, dismissively, "I grew weary of him and he slithered back to his wife... oh, Russell, I made a horrible mistake. I realized it the week after we broke up, but I was too full of pride to phone. I heard about you losing your job and wanted to rush to you, to comfort you... but I didn't think you would talk with me."

"I've been cleared of any wrong-doing. I expect to be working again by the first of the year."

"Oh, darling, I'm so *glad*. My heart was broken for you." Her eyes darted, scanning the room. "The house is gorgeous. Is it yours now... since your sister died?"

"You knew about Brenda's death?"

"Yes, I'm so sorry, I know you were close."

"I didn't see you at the funeral service. Were you there?"

"I *wanted* to be there, but friends convinced me I'd only upset you."

He was regaining his senses and courage. After Katherine broke off their relationship, he'd realized she'd never cared for anyone besides herself. He doubted she'd changed. He sat straighter. "I asked before, why are you here?"

"Russell, I'll swallow my pride. Breaking up with you was the worst decision I ever made. You're all I ever wanted. I've been so lonely, missing you more every day. You must be lonely, too, in this big house."

She didn't miss a beat as she moved quickly onto his lap, putting her arms around him and pushing his back against the sofa. Her voice just above a whisper, she said, "Please, darling, say you've missed me."

She was beautiful. She'd missed him and was available.

∼∼ 40 ∼∼

The days of December drifted by slowly. Dare decorated her house for Christmas, but without the joy of the season. She'd baked the required cookies, attended the work parties and had Doreen and Bobby to supper. She would go to their house on Christmas Eve to spend the night.

Russell was phoning less often. *He always says he loves me, but he sounds distracted. Was our relationship so weak it couldn't survive a brief separation?*

Christmas Eve

Dare made fudge and wrapped the plates in tin foil. She was expected at Doreen's by five o'clock. "Earlier if you can," her sister had pleaded. "You know Christmas Eve is the *best.* I love the anticipation. Try to come by four."

It was four o'clock. Russell hadn't phoned. *It's Christmas Eve, a time for people to be with those they love. We're apart and I haven't heard from him in days. Is it over?*

She had tried to phone him the day before but got no answer. She was afraid he hadn't kept Doreen's phone number and willed the phone to ring before she left. The hands on the small kitchen clock seemed to stand still. She walked to the bedroom—her bedside clock read the same. She sat on the bed. Tears sprang to her eyes and spilled over. She straightened her back and wiped her face.

No. I will not do this. I knew we needed time. If it's over, God has saved me from a worse mistake. I asked God's guidance.

Lord, now I'm asking for strength… I love him more than ever… I don't know how to let go.

At four-thirty, she slipped into her coat.

Rinnnnng, rinnnnng, rinnnnng, rinnnng.

She dropped a plate of fudge onto the floor, shattering the plate into bits as she ran to the phone.

"Russ?"

"It's Bobby, hon. Doreen wants to know if you'll be here soon."

Stifling sobs, she answered, "I'm on my way. Bobby, don't tell Doreen I thought it was Russ... please?"

Bobby hesitated. She knew they kept nothing from each other. "Bobby, please. She'll just worry and it's not good for her pregnancy."

"All right."

She could hear Doreen calling out to him, "Why isn't she here?"

"Tell her I had a food disaster and will be there as soon as I clean it up." She forced a laugh. "It's true. Good thing I had two plates of fudge or she wouldn't be able to satisfy her chocolate craving."

The evening she always enjoyed so much was only exhausting. Attempts to appear happy and excited throughout the evening totally drained her. She didn't fall asleep until after midnight.

They'd decided to sleep late Christmas morning. "Not long until our late mornings end. When a baby arrives, I don't think it's allowed," Doreen laughed.

Watching Doreen and Bobby together was the exception in her stressful evening—it was always a delight to see them together. They were as much in love as on their wedding day, each devoted to the other in their own unique way. Doreen was bossy by nature, and an outsider would think she told Bobby every move to make. It was partially true, but the other part was Bobby did as she wanted if it suited him. If not, he just did it his own way, the outcome often hilarious. She loved them dearly.

Waking at seven was not her idea of sleeping in, but she could sleep no longer. *I'll put the coffee on and try again to phone Russ.* A thought occurred. *Maybe he has Rose and Ella! If that were the case, he would have time for little else.* The possibility soothed slightly.

Noting Doreen had prepared the percolator the night before, she plugged it in and closed the kitchen door to make her call, hopefully without being heard.

I wonder if he received my package. She'd been excited to find a beautiful hand-crafted knife made of steel forged in Alabama. She'd had his initials carved into the handle made from native Alabama woods. She dialed the number and waited as his number rang again and again… and again. It was early, but… she'd been sure he would answer on Christmas morning. She sat numbly, holding the receiver until she lost count of the rings. He wasn't home. *Could he be with the girls at the grandparents' home?* She replaced the receiver and sat staring out the window. He could have called, though, from anywhere.

Hearing movement from Doreen and Bobby's room, she rose from the table and began setting out coffee mugs, cream, and sugar. She saw a dim reflection of herself in the window and forced a smile, hoping to hold it for her sister's sake.

"Ho, ho, ho," laughed Bobby as he entered the kitchen.

"Merry Christmas, Bobby. I have coffee ready and the oven heating for Doreen's cinnamon loaf."

He hugged her tightly and kissed her on the cheek. "You're a good woman, no matter what your sister said about you last night," he laughed.

"Bobby, do you know how much I love my sister's husband?" she grinned.

"I think I do, but don't get any ideas. I'm too afraid of Doreen to play around."

"What *about* playing around?" Doreen asked from the doorway.

Dare laughed. "Me and Bobby. But I think he just ended it. His heart belongs to a woman with an enormous belly. Go figure."

Doreen sat. "Well, I'm beginning to feel like a big ol' elephant and still have months to go, so I'm glad he likes fat women. Bobby, will you take the tin foil off the white dish and put it in the oven? I see Dare has it preheated. Oh, but I need a cup of coffee first."

Bobby obediently brought a mug of coffee to Doreen, leaning down to kiss her. "I love you, bossy woman."

He put the dish into the oven and turned the radio on for Christmas music. Content for the moment, Dare smiled at the happiness reigning in her sister's home.

Doreen studied her. "You okay?"

"Yes. I was thinking what a happy home you have and how lucky your child will be." She laughed, "More importantly, when do we open presents?"

"After breakfast. This child I'm carrying is hungry."

Doreen was well aware Dare wasn't hearing from Russell regularly, but, for once, she wasn't asking questions or commenting. *She's hurting and there is nothing I can do until it's final. If it's over, I'll be there to help her pick up the pieces. I still believe God will get it right, but I remain unsure what that might be.*

By nine-thirty, they had opened gifts and emptied stockings, and were stretched out in the living room with another cup of coffee.

Rinnng, rinnnng, rinnnng.

"Who in the name of Santa Claus calls on Christmas morning?" Doreen asked as Bobby went to the kitchen.

Dare's heart leaped. Maybe…

"Wrong number," Bobby explained when he returned.

"You were gone a while for a wrong number."

"Yeah, a mixed-up elderly woman wanted to argue with me. I tried to help her."

Doreen looked at Dare. "He *is* a sweetheart, isn't he?"

After they removed the torn wrapping papers from the floor, Doreen went to check the turkey she'd put into the oven earlier, their Christmas feast planned for late afternoon.

Dare walked to the guest room to dress, returning in less than thirty minutes to help Doreen.

When Doreen came from her bedroom, not yet dressed, she had an expression Dare couldn't read.

"Doreen, are you okay?"

"Yes, I'm fine."

"If you want to lie back down, just tell me what to do."

"I'm fine," Doreen snapped.

Something wasn't quite right, but her sister was, after all, pregnant—mood changes were to be expected. "Okay. What can I do to help?"

"Empty the ice trays into the plastic bowl in the freezer and refill them. I'm basting the turkey."

Rinnnng, rinnnng, rinnnng.

"And answer the phone. I've got my hands full."

"Hello."

Dare slumped into a kitchen chair. "Russ. I tried to phone you this morning."

"You did?"

Dare looked at Doreen, confident hearing Russ's name would make her unhappy. Her sister smiled weakly and left the kitchen mouthing the words, *Going to get dressed.*

"Russ... yes, I tried to phone—it's Christmas and..."

"Dare, I love you, I miss you... only you... do you hear me?"

"Yes."

"I haven't shown it enough since you left Chicago. I called to wish you the best Christmas *ever*."

She was trembling, happy to finally hear his voice. "Thank you." She didn't know what more to say.

"Honey? The knife is wonderful—I hope you don't mind that I opened it early. I couldn't wait. It's perfect."

"I'm glad you liked it... have you seen the girls?"

"Yes. And they're fine. I didn't forget your gift. I'm sure you thought I did...."

"I haven't received anything in the mail, but it's okay."

"It's a surprise. Something special for Christmas Day. Could you take a few minutes to go home? You'll find it outside."

"There are no deliveries on Christmas Day."

"There are exceptions to everything. I promise. Your surprise has an extra-large red bow on it. Will you go *now*?"

"*Now*?"

"Yes, I can't wait for you to see it. Just watch for the big bow... you'll see the bow way before you get there."

"Well... okay," she replied weakly. "Will you call again later?"

"I'm anxious to know your reaction to my surprise... Dare... I've missed you so much. Please know I love you with all my heart and soul. Hold that thought."

Confused, she couldn't seem to speak. He was saying he loved her, emphasizing it, yet she hadn't heard from him... he wasn't *here*.

"*Dare?* Will you go *now*... please? I love you."

"Yes, okay."

"Alright. I'll see you soon. Bye."

Click.

She sat holding the receiver, dazed. What did he say? He wanted her to go out in the cold *now*, to drive to her house.

Her surprise would have a big red bow—it didn't make sense. No gift could explain his absence, not hearing from him... her stomach was in knots.

He kept saying he loved me...

Turning her head, she realized Bobby held her coat out to her.

"Bobby?"

"I heard enough to know you're going back to your house to find Russell's Christmas gift... right?"

"Yes... will Doreen be upset?"

Doreen answered from the doorway. "It's okay. I understand nothing he does. But it *better* be wonderful."

Flabbergasted that Doreen wasn't angry and demanding she *not* leave the house, Dare took her coat from Bobby and walked out to her car.

~~ 41 ~~

Russell anxiously awaited Dare's discovery of his Christmas surprise.

Invading his happiness and thoughts, a dark cloud overtook him briefly as he recalled the visit from Katherine…

In one quick move, she was in his lap, pressing her body against him as she opened her mouth and hungrily covered his. "*Russy*, I love you." she moaned.

He pushed her from his lap. "Katherine…"

Ignoring him, her hand went swiftly to the neck of his shirt. Her lips brushed the tip of his ear as she whispered, "Let me unbutton your shirt; I want to show you how much I love you."

Roughly, he pushed her hand away and scrambled from the sofa to a standing position. "No! This is a mistake."

Her words were ringing in his head. *Love. She said she loved me.*

This… *is* not *love.*

She stared at him, eyebrows raised, eyes wide and body still slumped. The woman before him was most *un*attractive in her rumpled red dress, mussed hair and smeared lipstick. His heart still pounding, he saw her and the situation for what it was.

Suddenly… strangely… a calmness came over him as he realized how close he'd come to throwing away everything important. His head cleared. *I had the same thought months ago, thinking I'd lost everything important in my life. My priorities have changed—my career was of no importance at all.*

Katherine's beauty was skin deep. Her disguise had fallen away and there was nothing lovely inside.

A vision of Dare came to mind, physical beauty enhanced by beauty within, goodness and caring shining through.

He became angry, the anger rising up inside him, ready to explode, largely at himself. Katherine, though, had been about to destroy him.

"Katherine, everything about this is wrong. You need to leave—I'll get your coat."

He left the living room, retrieving the luxurious mink from the closet. He turned. She sat straight on the sofa, her dress and hair smoothed. Walking back into the living room, he held the coat out.

"Sit beside me." She patted the sofa beside her, smiling. "You've been through a lot. We can take our time."

She was not giving up easily.

"Katherine, listen. I'm sorry. I am. You are a gorgeous woman and any man would be tempted. We were a couple for quite a while and maybe we believed we had love—it *wasn't,* not then and certainly not now. We were merely convenient for each other."

"Russell," she continued, "don't you see how much you need me? You'll be back in society soon, and the right wife can help a man in ways you could never guess. I can help you get to the top of the ladder and make this big house a place for entertaining business prospects... and I'd be *here* with you... every night."

"I see. You heard my career was back on track and I'd inherited a big house. You want to be the wife of an architect who lives in an impressive house in Evanston, socializing in the city, and..." He shook his head, hoping to clear it completely of this entire scene. "You need to leave."

"I only wanted..."

He stopped her, saying more forcefully, "*No*, Katherine, I know what love *is*. It's a woman in Alabama who is giving and kind, whose greatest beauty comes from her soul. She's the one I want and need. You not only pale in comparison, you don't even appear on the scale."

She stared for a minute before a sly smile returned. Openly goading, she held her hand out to him. "Russy... come back to the sofa... I'll show you *all* about giving..."

He tossed the coat to her and walked to the front door, opening it wide.

Finally recognizing defeat, she became angry. Her expression turned to hate as she moved to slip quickly into her coat and shoes. Storming to the door, she turned to him. "Now I know why I dumped you the first time. When I found out you had been cleared of the charges and could resume your career, I decided to give you another chance. You have brains, but you are *stupid* about life. I hope I never see you again, and I feel *sure* I will never see you in any of the best circles of Chicago society."

She swung around, lifted her chin into the air and walked out. Walking briskly, she heard the door close behind her and a lock turning.

Russell leaned heavily against the closed door. *God, I almost lost it all. No, I almost threw everything away. She disgusts me. Lord, I'm so weak. Forgive me. I see the way again. Give me the strength and wisdom to walk in Your ways.*

A long-forgotten proverb came to mind. *The wise see danger and take refuge...*

He'd regained his foothold. He now had that firm foundation on which to rebuild his life. He could envision it coming to reality.

As he walked to the living room, he wondered, *What has been wrong with me? I convinced myself there was nothing I could do about the Townsends taking my girls! I was taking the cowards way out and about to settle for living without the three loves of my life. Thank you, Lord, for not forsaking me—You've cleared my vision. It is now crystal clear—I know exactly what to do—the immediate first step is to see Rose and Ella.*

The house remained empty and quiet, but Russell smiled, He was at peace and felt the warmth of sunshine returning. He could almost envision a rainbow above.

"For I know the plans I have for you, declares the LORD, plans to prosper you... to give you hope and a future."

~~ 42 ~~

Dare turned the key in the car ignition, shivering with cold as she brushed strands of hair from her face. The wind had picked up, forcing its way through the trees and moving dry leaves across lawns. Perhaps they'd have snow soon. It would be nice this time of the year.

What am I doing? Russ is hundreds of miles away, hasn't even been in touch, and I'm leaving the comfort of my sister's home to drive back to my house just because he phoned out of the blue. On Christmas Day.

Driving through the familiar neighborhood, she observed jubilant children on new bicycles and happy parents at doors. Knowing almost everyone between her house and Doreen's, she waved and forced a smile. Several driveways were filled with extra vehicles, suggesting family gatherings and joyous afternoons. Festive decorations at every turn, her drive should have been filled with joy. Instead, she felt doubt and dread. *Why didn't I simply tell him I wasn't going out in the cold without an explanation? Because... I've almost always turned a blind eye where Russ is concerned. And, in spite of everything, I still love him.*

Still a few blocks from her house, she caught a glimpse of Sister Benson standing on her porch. She returned her wave, wondering why she was standing in the cold. Perhaps she'd just returned from Christmas Mass. Turning her attention back to the street, she slammed on the brakes. There, stuck into the narrow patch of grass between the street and sidewalk, was a large handmade wooden sign, topped with a massive red bow.

Had she not been observing the neighbors' activities, she would have seen it a block earlier.

DARE
Merry Christmas

After a moment, she realized she'd stopped in the middle of the street. Thankfully, there was no other traffic. She pulled slowly to the curb. Continuing to stare at the sign, the car motor running, she caught a slight movement out of the corner of her eye.

Russ! He stood on the porch of the old Pennington house watching her. Realizing she'd finally seen him, he grinned and held out his arms.

She was frozen, not from cold, but shock. She continued to watch him but didn't move. He let his arms fall to his side as he began to walk slowly toward her. She turned the key to shut the motor off and opened the car door. Russ stopped halfway. She got out of the car, closed the door and walked slowly toward him. Their eyes met as he stood unmoving, but again held his arms out to her.

A few steps away, she stopped. Her voice unsure, almost inaudible, she spoke. "Russ? … you're here."

"I hope this is where you want me to be… here with you."

She felt rooted to the spot as her tears began to flow. "I hadn't heard from you. I thought…"

With long, quick strides, he moved to her, taking her in his arms, feeling her warmth against him as she sobbed and buried her head in his coat. He held her, a hand on her back, the other holding her head close as she sobbed. He could smell orange blossoms even on this freezing Christmas day. "Dare, I'll never let you go again."

She lifted her head. He put his hand under her chin. "*I'm* not your Christmas surprise, though… not entirely."

"What do you mean?"

He took her hand. "I'll show you." He guided her down the sidewalk, onto to the porch of the old house, taking a key from his pocket to unlock the front door. "This house is your surprise."

She entered, looking around at the beautiful, old, neglected house. Turning back to him, her breath caught.

He was kneeling. "Dare, I've prayed your love hadn't faded." He raised a hand, revealing a diamond ring. "I've made an offer on this house. Will you marry me… and endure living with me as we remodel the house and our lives together? I love you from the depths of my soul. *Please…* will you marry me?"

~~ **43** ~~

Dare's legs gave way. Almost collapsing, Russell caught her as they fell slowly to the floor. Sitting amid a thick layer of dust, they embraced, pulling each other closer. Their lips met as the rest of the world faded away.

She was in the arms of the man she loved.

"Dare, darling," he whispered.

She opened her eyes, their faces inches apart as she attempted to absorb the moment. She wasn't dreaming. He was here.

"You haven't answered my question. I waited so long for you to be ready to hear the words *I love you...* now I'm waiting to hear only one word. Will you marry me so I may spend the rest of my life showing you the depth of my love?"

"Oh, Russ, *yes. Now*, today, as soon as possible."

He kissed her again, softly. "I'm a very happy man." Grinning, he added, "But I do need to get up from this floor, and I'm praying I can do so without assistance."

They struggled to stand before she asked, "Will you explain again, about the house? You're truly going to buy it?"

"I made the offer contingent on your agreeing to marry me. The family was delighted it might be restored. I'll phone Monday and arrange to finalize the deal. It's cold in here, though. Do you want to take a quick tour before we leave?"

"Yes. Now that you're not holding me, I'm freezing." She paused to look at him in wonder. "You remembered this old place and how I loved it."

"I remember *everything* about you, your words, what you like, how you smell... your funny laugh, your sweetness... your touch..."

"Oh, Russ, you know I'm thrilled about the possibility of living here… but I don't have to have this house to marry you. I'll go back to Evanston with you and you can resume your career there."

"I know the house isn't the reason. But I've so much more to tell you. First, I have a good job offer in Birmingham."

"Birmingham? I didn't know you were interested in working there."

"When I came to my senses, I realized it would be perfect. I've talked with the president of the firm. It's not as large as the one in Chicago but is one of the top firms in the South. They're more family oriented, too. I told him I would never again work fourteen hours a day on a regular basis, and he agreed. I can easily commute and could work from home a number of days. This old house has numerous possibilities for a home office."

"You'll be too far away from Rose and Ella, Russ—think about it… I'll go back to Evanston with you. It's a lovely town, the house is great, and the girls will feel at home when they visit. I can be *happy* there with you. I don't want you to change everything because of me. Things are different than when I left Evanston—you are back in reality. I'll live and make a home wherever *you* are."

He placed his hands on her shoulders. "I *told* you there's a lot to catch up on. I want to live *here*, and it's going to work out perfectly. Now let's take a quick tour of the house and get back to Doreen's where it's warm. She's getting Christmas dinner ready for us."

Nothing but her love for Russ seemed clear at the moment. "She knows you're here?"

"Yes. We'll explain everything later, but she arranged with Sister Benson, next door, for me to call you from her house, in order for me to be able to get here quickly enough to wait for you."

"The reason she stood on her porch when I drove up… she was watching for me, too?"

"Yes. Now, honey, the tour… then to Doreen's, okay?"

She'd been in the house only twice as a child but it was everything she remembered. She was overwhelmed with the thought of all her dreams coming true. She would live here… with Russ.

I can see it in my mind, the house restored, furnished, glowing with love. The largest bedroom upstairs will be ours. The one with double windows and the lovely built-in shelves will be painted pale pink and decorated for the girls' visits, the room at the end of the hall will be perfect for an office, and we'll still have a guest room and… nursery. Lord, thank you.

"It's perfect."

Having also envisioned their lives here, Russell beamed. "Yes. And soon the old house will no longer be *sad*."

As they began the walk downstairs, he laughed. "We'd better brush all this dust from our clothes before we leave, else your sister might have me arrested before I can explain."

After a final check for dust, she turned to him. "Thank you… for thinking of the house…for everything. Before we leave, though… would you hold me close once more?"

"My pleasure."

~~ 44 ~~

When Dare pulled into Doreen's driveway, Doreen and Bobby were at the window. When Russell drove in behind her, they disappeared.

Holding hands, they walked toward the front door. Doreen rushed out before they reached the porch, shouting, "Congratulations! I'm so happy, I could burst... have you decided on a date... did you love the house? Did you see the red bow right away...?"

As Dare stepped onto the porch, Doreen hugged her close and Dare felt her sister's tears against her face.

"Doreen, you're okay with this... you knew?"

Delighted, Doreen laughed heartily, "And you thought I couldn't keep a secret. Honey, this was the ultimate. 'Course I didn't have to keep it long... just since this morning."

Doreen turned to Russell. "Come here and hug your fat, future sister-in-law."

He laughed as he walked to embrace her. "I'm still afraid you'll have me arrested."

"And well you should be. Let's get inside."

Dare asked, "Where's Bobby? I saw you two at the window when I drove in."

Helping them remove coats, she answered. "We were waiting at the window to find out whether you said *yes*—our answer came when he drove in behind you."

"You've answered one question."

"Bobby had to make a phone call. Have a seat. Our feast is cooking, so there's nothing to do but have coffee and a Christmas cookie or two until it's ready. A couple of hours, probably."

Dare and Russell settled on the sofa, sitting close as Doreen returned to the kitchen to fill coffee mugs.

Ding-dong, ding-dong.

Bobby appeared from the kitchen. "I'll get the door."

"Who would be out on Christmas morning?" Dare wondered aloud.

Voices echoed from the door, "Merry Christmas!"

Rose and Ella ran into the living room, grabbing Dare around the neck, Ella covering her face with kisses, and Rose crying out, "Let *me* kiss her, too."

She was speechless... again. Catching her breath, she realized Miss Bee was standing in the doorway smiling happily. "My darlings, what a wonderful surprise. I didn't know you were in town."

Ella giggled. "We were part of your secret surprise. Know where we spent the night?"

"Where?"

"At Miss Bee's. A new boarder was living in *our* room, but she had another one. Pop had to sleep on the living room sofa, though. Santa Claus came to see us early at our house in Evanston because Pop told him we were coming here... we came on an airplane... the *stew-ess* lady gave us sodas... they didn't have *Double Cola*, but they had sandwiches and peanuts... are we a good surprise?"

Dare had begun to weep tears of happiness again. "You two are the best surprise *ever*." She glanced at Russell. "A second *part* of the happiest surprise ever." Concerned, she asked, "How long can they stay?"

"Dare, my beautiful bride-to-be, I confess to holding out on you again."

She looked around the room. Bobby, Doreen and Miss Bee appeared thrilled as they looked on.

"What?"

"When you marry me, you get two children in the bargain. I was afraid to mention it before sealing the deal."

She had countless questions, not knowing where to begin.

He took her hands in his. "If you're willing to take all three of us, we'll be the happiest family in the world. Their grandparents have agreed to give me full custody."

Dare nearly broke down as a roller coaster of emotions overtook her. "My darling girls." No further words were needed as they laughed and cried together.

After sharing coffee, Miss Bee bade them all a Merry Christmas and began to get into her coat and hat.

"Please stay. We'd love for you to have Christmas dinner with us," Doreen pleaded.

"Thank you. I have plans, but I'll see you all at church tomorrow."

At four o'clock, the happy, combined family sat to enjoy a Christmas feast.

Lord, Bobby prayed, *we thank you for the bounty of blessings you have poured into our lives. We are thankful for the way You are increasing our family... for Russell, Rose and Ella, and our baby to come. Help us to be mindful of the source of all good things. Thank you for Your grace and for the food we are about to enjoy. Forgive us our sins. In Jesus' name, Amen.*

The happy family enjoyed a feast of turkey and dressing, corn, green beans, sliced cranberry sauce, sweet potatoes *cooked the way they are supposed to be, with little marshmallows on top,* Doreen declared, and a few other side dishes. Afterward came fruit cake, dutifully made ahead of time and kept with a wine-soaked cloth in the middle.

Looking at Rose and Ella, Bobby inquired of Doreen, "We have fudge, too, where is it, honey?"

"There isn't any left."

Dare began to snicker as Doreen hurried around to get cookies from the Christmas tin.

"But there was a big plate. Oh…" Finally realizing where the fudge had gone, he explained, "Sorry, girls, we seem to have someone in our midst with a chocolate craving that cannot be controlled."

After dessert, they discussed plans for the next weeks and months. Russell and the girls would live at the boarding house temporarily. Rose and Ella were excited about seeing their friends again when school resumed. Russell would put Brenda's house up for sale when the time was right, and much of the furniture would be shipped to Beacon, including all furnishings in the girls' room.

After a while, the girls tired of adult conversation and bundled up to go outside.

Doreen turned to Russell. "So, the Pennington house sounds great, but it's going to cost a fortune to get it livable. I hope you got a good deal."

"Doreen…" Bobby began.

She didn't miss a beat. "We're family. I can ask."

Dare grinned at Russell, knowing he'd just have to adjust to Doreen's forthrightness.

He winked at her before turning back to Doreen.

"It's okay. I made what I considered just *above* a fair offer so we wouldn't waste time. It will be well worth it in the long run."

"Well, so long as it wasn't over nine thousand—it needs a lot of work."

Amused at his future sister-in-law, he rose, walked to her, and kissed her forehead. "You *are* family," he answered, "and I love you. I offered ten and they agreed. And it's just between *us*, right?"

Bobby was shaking his head, thankful his future brother-in-law was understanding. *He's a good guy. He'll love Dare as she deserves. They'll make a good life.*

After watching a Christmas movie together, the happy group began to disperse.

Dare left for her house as Russell left to drop the girls at the boarding house. Irma Rae had assured him she would be happy to have them *after seven.*

"Miss Bee will tuck you into bed, but I'll be back by ten," he assured them. "I love you two little bugs. Did you know you have made this my best Christmas ever?"

"Yes," they shouted.

~~ **45** ~~

Dare opened the door as he hurried up the steps. "I've missed you so much. Never, ever, leave me again."

Closing the door, he took her in his arms and kissed her passionately.

"Dare, our wedding day cannot get here quick enough."

She tilted her head back and reached to touch his lips. "I know." They stood close, savoring their love and the blessings in their future. Finally, Dare said, "Sit on the sofa with me. I want to hear everything about how you managed to get custody of the girls."

As they settled on the sofa, Dare pulled her feet under her to sit cross-legged. "I want to hear everything," she said eagerly.

"There is something else I need to tell you first, honey."

"Yes?"

"You remember my telling you about Katherine?"

"Yes. What about her?"

"She came to the house unexpectedly with a basket of fruit as a peace offering. I made the mistake of letting her inside."

Apprehensive, Dare asked, "What happened?"

He told her everything.

"Please forgive me—I should never have let her in the house."

"She kissed you?"

"She kissed me. I was shocked and pushed her away, as I explained. I was so foolish—I hate the thought of her." He began talking more excitedly, saying, "*Yet...* darling, her visit seemed to clear my head! I realized I was standing still, taking no action about what was important to me—the future—you. I could never live contentedly without *you* and I'd made no steps toward getting the girls. Strength and resolve seemed to well up in me, from the Lord, I know, and I could not wait to begin putting things back together."

He looked into her eyes. "Dare?"

"I can't stand the thought of her so near to you, touching you in that way…"

"And neither can I, honey. I will never again put myself in that situation with anyone."

Dare remained silent… intent on his every word.

"Honey, I love only you. I've heard the words, love, honor, and cherish many times. I now know what they *mean*—I want nothing more than to cherish and protect you the rest of our lives."

She moved her legs back to the floor as she slid closer to him. He leaned to kiss her gently before looking at her questioningly.

"Russ, yes, I forgive you. And I'm glad you told me about it—I realize you didn't have to do that. I would likely have never known."

He wrapped his arms around her and held her quietly.

"Russ, you've shared so much… everything… I feel I need to share other things with you about me."

"What things?"

She sat straighter as she began. "Well, I told you about Edward, the guilt I carried for so long, and you not only understood but helped me put it in the past. Other than that, you think I'm an open book, that you know everything about me."

Smiling softly, Russell answered, "What I don't know, I look forward to finding out. We have a lifetime ahead of us."

"No, Russ. That's not what I mean. What I do mean is that I'm afraid you think I'm perfect."

"You *are…*"

"Let me finish, Russ. Seriously, because I had to learn about you little by little, you thought you had the whole picture of me. I just want you to know how imperfect I am— otherwise, you will be greatly disillusioned someday soon."

"Okay."

"Honey, I sometimes have bad thoughts, am judgmental, have moments of jealousy, and lose my temper… just like most people. I have to pray repeatedly asking forgiveness for things I've said carelessly, and for things I know I should have done, but neglected. I am overly organized, it's true, and sometimes I fail to do things that are much more important because it would interfere with my schedule of the day."

"Honey… is that all?"

"Russ, I am *not* perfect. You've asked me to forgive you so many times…" She smiled adding, "*As* you should have… but I don't want you to feel the scales are uneven… I need forgiveness every single day."

Russell grinned. "Okay. Perhaps I *have* put you on a pedestal. I'm aware you are not perfect. If you feel you have cleared that up, I can only say, you are perfect for *me*. May I just leave you on the pedestal for a while longer?"

She leaned back, smiling. "The air has been cleared. Everything is good. *Now*, tell me about our girls." She became giddy. "Oh, Russ, they are *ours*! Tell me everything."

He grinned as he began to talk, excitedly. "I wasn't sure the Townsends would tell the girls I was to visit that day, but when I arrived they ran out the front door. They clung to me as if they would never let go again. Of course, I felt the same. The Townsends finally *dismissed* them—*Go to your room*

*while we talk with your Uncle Russell. You will have all the
time you want with him later.*

"They exhibited a complete change of attitude. Rose and
Ella had been so miserable at the boarding school, the
administrators asked them not to return after the holidays.
They decided to bring them home and hire a nanny. After
only a week they decided it was too much for them. They
realized travel, social activities, their entire lives, had become
too complicated, even with a live-in nanny, cook, and other
servants in the house. Moreover, the girls' desolation was
unabated. They actually *admitted* the girls cried all the time.
Later, the girls told me they'd told them they missed Pop,
their school in Alabama, Miss Dare, Miss Bee, and the park
with the different places... and that they wanted to go back to
Birmingham to see the man with no pants, have boiled
peanuts, and go to the town festival again next year.

"I'd gone to demand their return, but it wasn't necessary.
Not accustomed to admitting defeat, Mrs. Townsend
remained cold. She believes we will be living below her
standards but maintained the attitude that she was *willing to
make the sacrifice.*

"She questioned the man in Birmingham *whose bottom
the girls had seen*, somewhat soothed when I explained it
was a statue, but mumbled words to the effect of having no
desire to visit Birmingham or anywhere in Alabama."

Dare laughed aloud. "Hysterical!"

Russ continued seriously, "Cecil Townsend's behavior
was strange. He let his wife do all the talking. He was cordial
to the children, but nothing like a grandparent. He was
relieved to see them go. Actually, they were both relieved,
but Lillian didn't want to admit it."

"It's sad, Russ. It shouldn't be, '*they lost and you won.*' It
should have been about doing what was best for Rose and
Ella. And those little girls should be able to love and enjoy

their grandparents. The Townsends don't seem to cherish the blessings their son left—they saw them only as a battle. I feel so sorry for them. They lost more than they will ever understand."

He watched and listened to this incredible woman as she spoke sympathetically of two people who had shown her only disdain.

"They asked only for a yearly visit."

"Maybe they'll change over time, Russ. I'll pray for them." She looked at him, understandingly. "I know they've hurt you deeply, as well as the girls. Can you forgive them?"

"I believe I will eventually—but I'm not there yet; I'll try. Seeing them through your eyes, I *do* feel sorry for them. They don't seem to know the real meaning of love."

She squeezed his hand.

"Dare, I didn't know the meaning of love myself until I found it in two little girls and you."

Considering his own statement, he continued, "No, that's not true. Brenda and I had a good, stable home. Our parents taught us love and lived it. Brenda continued their legacy. She was *always* loving, and so was Gary—they taught it to their children. It was *me*... I turned my back on it when I became so goal-oriented and ambitious that I threw everything else aside. I lost my way."

Knowing he needed to talk this through, Dare remained quiet. He seemed far away for a few minutes but turned his attention back to her. "I can't bear to think of the person I would have become if I'd reached all the goals I set for myself. It took losing my job and my sister to bring me to my senses... eventually... I didn't get it right until I messed up again and again."

"Russ, you never lost your core values, not entirely. You were never dishonest at work and it sounds as if you were forthright with your coworkers. You never lost touch with Brenda nor the love you shared with her family."

He was quiet, reprocessing painful memories. "Dare… do you think Brenda had to die to bring me back to God?"

"*No!* Oh, Russ, no. I believe God used her disease and death to bring good out of bad, but *please* don't think that way."

"I guess I don't… God is love… it's just something that crossed my mind. I'll always miss her."

He smiled. "No more sad talk. I haven't finished telling you about the girls, the *best* parts."

"More?"

"Much more. First of all, you need to know that they were first to bring up returning to Beacon. I had, of course, thought through a number of ways to suggest it, but they asked about it after we left the grandparents, even before we reached Evanston. That confirmed my belief that they were happy here."

"I'm so glad to hear that. I was concerned about their feeling uprooted from Evanston again."

He beamed. "Dare, everything is working out *so* well—the other thing I wanted was an idea of how they would feel about our marrying. The day after we returned to Evanston, I mentioned it as a *someday* possibility, thinking I was being casual. They picked up on it and became excited about your living with us all the time. They began discussing the things we'd do, one being bubble baths all the time."

Dare was delighted.

"They embraced the idea completely. They thought Miss Bee would very much like your living with us at the boarding house but wondered about not having enough beds in our room."

"Live at the boarding house? Why not *my* house?"

"I don't know, except the boarding house was home to them while in Beacon. I thought it was cute, especially when Rose remembered you could sleep in *my* bed if we were married, so the two beds in the room would be enough."

Imagining the scene, they began to laugh, picturing themselves making their home in one room at the boarding house for the rest of their lives.

As their laughter subsided, Russell wrapped his arms around her. "Do you have any idea how I treasure having you to love and laugh with?" Lost in the moment and the love reflected in her eyes, he spoke tenderly, "We've been through a great deal—secrets, pain, fears, and tears, with days and hours of happiness in the mix. But we loved in spite of everything. Merry Christmas, darling."

Joy comes to those who wait.

~~ 46 ~~

On Sunday, the day after Christmas, Samuel Allen, minister of the Community Church, appeared pleased as he spotted Russell, Rose, Ella, Dare, Doreen, and Bobby file into the church building together. They filled a pew near the front.

I somehow felt those families needed to be together. Thank you, Lord.

Just before the service began, Irma Rae and Frank came in to sit behind them. Irma Rae was aware of raised eyebrows and whispers—she stood straight as they stood for the first song and proudly reached to hold Frank's hand.

Monday afternoon, Russell phoned Dare. "The Pennington House is *ours*. I met with the owners this morning to finalize the sale."

"I'm so excited. I can't believe how wonderful life is right now."

"While signing papers, one of the owners mentioned knowing you."

"I don't remember knowing any of the family except the older Mr. Pennington who died years ago."

"She asked if you had recently returned to Beacon on the bus. She described you perfectly."

Dare was puzzled. "Can you describe her?".

"An older woman, nothing distinctive. About all I remember is white hair and a bright crimson scarf—it stood out as there was no other color about her and one of the younger men teased her about her *trademark color*. Anyway, she expressed great pleasure in hearing about our upcoming wedding plans. She commented, *I knew something good was to come for that sweet young lady on the bus. I just felt it.*"

"I do remember her—I'll tell you about it later."

A bright crimson scarf. The stranger on the bus who prayed for me. Lord, thank you for sending people into our lives when we most need them, even when we don't recognize the blessing at the moment.

~~ 47 ~~

Nineteen Fifty-Five

Dare and Russell married on Saturday, January twelfth, in the living room of the Pennington House.

The house had been cleaned and heated, but little else.

Doreen advised determinedly, "You *know* a bride and groom can't see each other on the wedding day until the moment the ceremony begins."

Ignoring her, Russell and Dare drove to the house together late that morning. Arriving, they found an oversized white bow on the door with an attached note. *Congratulations on your wedding. We're glad you have a new home—and thanks for ours, Jim and Hiram.*

Touched, tears sprang to Russell's eyes. "These are the men I helped with the small building by the railroad tracks."

Dare happily walked upstairs to change as Russell welcomed those who were to set up tables and chairs and members of the wedding party. Jenny arrived and joined Dare upstairs. Other than the flower girls, Jenny would be Dare's only attendant. Doreen had insisted she had enough to do *organizing everything*, and added, "I fear I might *fall* down the stairs rather than glide."

At two o'clock, Sister Benson, who considered herself partially responsible for the proposal going smoothly, turned the record player on to begin the wedding march. Jenny descended the stairs wearing her best Sunday dress, a flattering aqua, and holding a single red rose.

Rose and Ella appeared at the top of the stairs holding small baskets of rose petals, looking like angels in their matching dresses of white. As instructed, they walked slowly as each dropped one petal per step.

The glowing bride appeared, watching the girls she loved descend the stairs. She wore her mother's white satin floor-length dress. As there was no veil, she wore a circle of small white roses in her hair. An extra glow seemed to fill the entire staircase and room below. As she descended the stairs on the arm of her brother-in-law, Bobby, she saw only Russell.

The groom wore a gray suit, white shirt, and dark gray tie. He awaited his bride with his best man, Jason Harrison.

Minister Samuel Allen performed the ceremony. "It is with the greatest of pleasure I finalize the joining of two people who clearly belong together. I've known Dare since her years as a teenager. Russell is a newer acquaintance, but I witnessed the stars in his eyes early on when Dare came into view, and Dare's view of life changing after she met him."

A few minutes later, he spoke the words for which they'd waited, "I pronounce you man and wife. What God has joined together, let no man put asunder. Russell, you may kiss your bride."

She whispered, "I love you." He put one arm around her, his other hand under her chin. "I will never tire of hearing it. I love *you*." He kissed her, knowing they were now one before God.

After a minute, the minister smiled and held up a hand to signal the audience to begin applauding.

The newlyweds reluctantly separated and turned to their guests.

"Ladies and gentlemen, I present to you Mr. and Mrs. Russell Townsend, and Misses Rose and Ella Townsend."

Invited guests were Irma Rae Broadnax and Frank Weathers, Mary Nan Johnson, Dennis Sims, several friends of Dare's from work, her supervisor, Mr. Matthews, mailman Billy Carl Hicks and Mrs. Hicks, Daniel and Mabel Connor, and their granddaughter, Holly Jo Conner.

The reception was in the dining room. The beautifully-decorated wedding cake was compliments of Mabel Connor, who had owned a bakery in years past.

Dare had chosen *boiled custard* to be served rather than punch. "It's a Christmas custom in our family, but perfect for January, too. It's made with milk, eggs, sugar, vanilla, and a touch of nutmeg.

"Another name for eggnog?" Russell asked.

"Much better."

Doreen had made *party* sandwiches, meaning she'd trimmed off the bread crusts. In addition, she furnished the *fancy-kind* of mixed nuts in her best glass dish, which *looked exactly like real crystal.*

At three-thirty, Doreen helped Dare change into a blue silk suit considered appropriate traveling attire for a new bride.

Returning downstairs to waiting friends and family, Doreen placed Dare's hand in Russell's. "I leave my sister in your hands, *Mr.* Townsend, well aware she is now your wife." Grinning, she added, "Just never forget she has a very protective older sister. And now, for better or worse, so do *you.*"

Everyone laughed and applauded.

Russell kissed Doreen's forehead. "I love you, Doreen… but I'll always be a little afraid."

"Good!" she laughed.

Amid laughter, a few tears, and shouts of well wishes, Mr. and Mr. Russell Townsend left the house in a shower of rice.

As they began their honeymoon, they made one detour, stopping briefly to see Jim and Hiram to deliver generous amounts of sandwiches and cake. They promised to see them again soon.

They were only a few hours from their honeymoon destination of Gulf Shores, Alabama. They cared not in the least that it would be too cold to walk in the gulf.

FINALE

After the wedding…

Jason and Jenny continued in conversation, reportedly leaving together.

Rose and Ella stayed with Aunt Doreen and Uncle Bobby, who encouraged a more appropriate name for *Miss Dare.* After their initial choice, *Little Pop,* they finally agreed on *Mimi.*

Though Mr. and Mrs. Cecil Townsend declined the wedding invitation, they sent a small sterling silver bud vase, and a book titled, *Etiquette and Social Graces for Newlyweds.*

After the wedding announcement appeared in the newspaper, Ginger Lee sent a genuine crystal candy dish to the newlyweds. She was dating Thomas Gray.

Frank Weathers had proposed to Irma Rae Broadnax on New Year's Eve. A large church wedding was planned for March. Russell would give Irma Rae away.

Dennis Sims whispered to Russell that he was shopping for a diamond ring and planned to propose to Mary Nan Johnson on Valentine's Day.

~~~

The friendship between the Townsends and Connors would last a lifetime.

Doreen and Bobby's twin boys were born in late February.

The Pennington House soon became known as the *Townsend Home*. The complete renovation took over a year.

As years passed…

Having been employed by *Covenant Architects of Alabama*, Russell became a renowned architect throughout the South and beyond.

Bobby was soon hired by the firm as Public Relations Representative, significantly increasing his salary.

Doreen became the second female principal of Beacon Elementary School.

Dare founded the *Beacon Historical Preservation Commission.*

~~~~~~~

Residents of Beacon would recall and retell stories of the Townsends and their home for years to come.

The stories varied but always began the same. "Russell Townsend was an out-of-towner. He came in and won the heart of a local girl, Dare Perry.

"The Townsends continued to live in the historic home with their five children… four lovely daughters, Rose, Ella, Laura, and Debra, and son, Russell Townsend, Jr., known as Rusty."

The story always ended the same. "A nicer family would be difficult to find."

THE END

Authors' Notes...

Non-fictional places of interest, in order of appearance, in
Altered Plans...

~~Mammoth Cave, located in central Kentucky near
Brownsville, with portions in Edmonson, Hart, and Barren
counties.

~~Ave Maria Grotto, Cullman, Alabama.

~~Woolworth's, generally known as the 'Five and Dime
Store,' 1878-1997

~~Anniston Ordnance Depot, Bynum, Alabama, adjacent to
Anniston, Alabama, was renamed Anniston Army Depot in
1962.

~~Vulcan statue, Birmingham, Alabama.

~~Shinbone, Alabama.

~~Munford, Alabama

~~Grosse Pointe Lighthouse, Evanston, Illinois.

~~~~

I sincerely hope you enjoyed getting acquainted with my
characters in *Altered Plans* and traveling in your imagination
from Illinois to Alabama. I must admit that by the time my
novel is published, many of my characters begin to feel like
neighbors and friends.

I would love to hear from you about your favorite
characters or any comments or questions about *Altered Plans*
or *Only a Breeze.* You may contact me at
oabgm8@gmail.com.

If you have enjoyed reading either novel, a brief review on
Amazon.com would be appreciated.

Barbara

Read more about the author and updated news at:
https://www.amazon.com/author/bwhill

~~~~~~

Also, by Barbara Wesley Hill

Only a Breeze

"Yes, honey, you are in America. It's just that the South is a distinctive difference."

A story of intrigue, romance,
history, faith,
and generous doses of humor.

Only a Breeze is the story of small-town people touched by events across the world in the 1940's. We are reminded storms, which come to every life, begin as only a breeze.

Aleksander Nordin is a young father in Russia who will do whatever necessary to make a better life for his son, even to sending him to another country.

The lovable five-year-old Mikhail, wins hearts and friends as he adapts to small-town life in the American South. After Aleksander reunites with his son, friendships, a promising career, a complicated romance, and a new faith develop.

More unexpected are accusations of dishonest deeds and malicious acts. As we follow Aleksander's struggles, we also find laughter again and again in the young boy who is the reason he will never give up.

Only a Breeze has earned consistent
Five Star Reviews on Amazon.

Available in print or Kindle,
http://www.amazon.com/dp/1546930248

Barbara Wesley Hill